The Long Beat of the Metronome

The Long Beat of the Metronome

Stories

Volume 3

Bruce Adam

 Ara Pacis

The Long Beat of the Metronome. Stories, Volume 3

Copyright © 2008 by Bruce Ormsby Adam.

All rights reserved. Printed in the United States of America. No part of this book may be used or reproduced in any manner whatsoever without written permission except in the case of brief quotations embodied in critical articles and reviews.

Title page drawing, cover and book design by the author.

First Paperback Edition, 2008

Ara Pacis Publishers
P.O. Box 1202
Des Plaines, IL 60017-1202
www.arapacispublishers.com

ISBN 0-9661318-7-8
ISBN13: 978-0-9661318-7-1
Library of Congress Control Number: 2008922552
Manufactured in the United States of America

Contents

The Long Beat of the Metronome 3
The Shrinking 8
Dreams of Murder 32
Police Blotter 37
The Old Sun 40
A New Moon 50
Legion of Ghosts 55
The Power of Hate 59
The Old Bullfrog 62
The Shadow State 66
The Cry Room 77
Waiting for Voyager 85
Losing Face 89
A Spider Pays its Respects to the Dead 93
Orpheus, Looking Back 96
The Choir Master 103
Bad Time Stories 105
The Minister's Garden 111
Momentary Loves 115
Henry Collins 118
Susie Inchon 140
A Seagull in the Snow 143
Life in the Palms 147
Making the Turn 152
Fresh Start 163
Some Kind of Song 171
Dudot
   Ol' Man River 179
   Vain Empires 183
   Dudot Dreaming 187
   The Last Days of Pompeii 189
   The Catch-Phrase Memoirs 193
   The Intruders 195
   Central Intelligence 197
   The Ride of Your Life 199
   The Sense Creeping In 202
   A Rare Occasion of Happiness 207
   Selfty Struction 213
   Genetic Lynx 218
   Preparing for Voyage 221
   On the Brink 228
   A Drop in the Ocean 233
   Mary and the Fish 238

The Long Beat of the Metronome

To Donna

The Long Beat of the Metronome

The Long Beat, as it is commonly called, is an empowering secret of life for a few who have managed somehow to pin down exactly what it is and how it works. In *Plato's Dialogues*, Socrates seems content to have examined his subjects in flight. We don't get an exact definition of what things like courage, knowledge, temperance and love are, but we know that the discussions have placed them clearly in our view in a roundabout way. These are non-terminating subjects. You can talk about love for volumes and never quite define it, but Socrates manages to teach us how to think about these things without sticking a pin in them for our collection.

The long beat is another thing entirely, and it is required that it be understood completely in order for advantage to be gained from knowing it, but alas, I have failed in my attempts to conquer it, and have been utterly mystified over the years, which hasn't done much for my self esteem. Because I cannot own it, the best I can do is be a teacher and put others in its vicinity in the hope that it might facilitate grasping it completely at some point.

The idea I want to convey is that all the things I thought I could do have been blown off by the ever-so-slow blasting impact of day-to-day living, and whereas I once had so many aspirations and plans, now I can only do what I can, which is hardly what it used to be in a day. I feel all I have left in my heart is a single thread, and such a thick rope it was, all due to slowly being eroded, as if my capsule had entered the atmosphere with both a heat shield and a parachute in perfect working order, but it took thirty years to land, rusted and obsolete by the time it made it down. Maybe you can last eons if you're a heavenly body in space. Here you're lucky if you can make it past thirty. I know on any given day I sit here that it may seem calm, but it's just a split second taken out of a hurricane. By itself, it is nothing to brace against, but tied to every other bit of itself, it will eventually wear you down to your bones as you stand against it.

The first aspect of the long beat is the most obvious. Consider literally what the long beat of the metronome is. Take a metronome, wind it up, pull the weight to the very top of the wand and set it in motion. If you are musically inclined, you will realize that this beat is too slow to actually allow you to play anything because the mind will fail to "connect the dots" if you will. Even with excellent concentration, trying to wave a finger at the exact point that each beat sounds proves to be very difficult.

Now, try to apply this concept to life. It seems easy enough to do. Life is a slow process, too slow to be made easy. It takes many years to detect the long beat of its rhythm, much of which is reasoned in hindsight, as in how a decade evolved. You could look back at the history of bad language as it emerged in film and television. If you lived through those years, you would recall the "pioneers" like Lenny Bruce and his various arrests for the language he used on stage in his comedy routines. At some point, foul language made its way into a film or two, then into television by degrees, and now it is so prevalent that some might believe it has always been allowed. No, it got here by the long beat of the metronome, but that still does not do justice to the concept. Let me try to put it another way.

Each day is a beat of a sort. I suppose each hour is a beat if you want to look at it that way. Every second counts. OK. There's so many divisions of time that the concept of time gets in the way because we're so quick to consider time as the key factor. If you want to win at the stock market, you have to consider the long term. You have to be able to ride the ups and downs, ignore the here and now, and consider the long term. Does this help elucidate the concept here?

Not really, because the rhythms are not on the outside but the inside. The long beat is a spiritual connection first and foremost, and once that is understood, then of course, yes, it ties into time because we are all prisoners of time, but only when one clearly understands the slow rhythm within does one conquer time, get past it, beyond it and succeed in completely understanding and being empowered by the long beat of the metronome.

I haven't done a very good job of explaining this, but I knew that I wouldn't. I only completely understand it in moments, in occasional glimpses, which in themselves are revelations that create a strong desire to live in the momentarily perceived meaning of the rhythms. The problem is that I fail to truly see the actual rhythm of my own spirit. I'm too caught up in the history of the world, in the rhythms of time, in the evolution of society, in the conflict between one system or another as they battle for ascendancy. I have far too much interest in the world to actually conquer the secret of myself.

But the history of the world is a diagram for what it would be like to understand myself. My own rhythm would start out in some kind of rudimentary spiritual beginning. It would proceed to some kind of early self awareness and embattlement with authority, and might enter into an age of enlightenment, and perhaps there would be an industrious age along with a few revolutions, a few breakthroughs and additions of technology, some economic fluctuations with a tendency toward prosperity, some attention to developments in the areas of application of the best health care available, and an eventual enlightenment of what it all meant before it all finally ends.

I suppose that's where the rub is, that one can really only detect the current of the long process in a kind of awakened hindsight, while living by the long beat of the metronome requires some kind of inward grasp of what next step to take based on the last beat of the metronome, and the beat before that, all pointing the right way, a way that the spirit itself is leading, which becomes a chicken/egg problem, for if you must be led by the spirit to achieve the spirit that will lead you, what comes first?

You see, in the end, the best I can do is make general observations and provide examples that will start to define it, a little like putting out the dots that you must connect, where it's like a face in the dark. There is the silhouette, then the impression of features, then finally a face, and if you recognize it, you must have known it all along. If

The Long Beat of the Metronome

it is a strange face, then it will always be a stranger to you. You may come to know it better as I have done over many years, but you are not one of its family.

If you're still lost on this, it may be due to my being a bad teacher. I do not wish to leave it like that, so let me provide one last example. How does a composer put forth a long symphony except one note at a time? But that is not at all how it happens. There is a vision of the music, and that somehow is brought forth out of the conscious mind or soul, and brought out whole, much as it was seen inside. And so it was maintained as a whole while it was being chopped out into notes, one at a time, on paper, such that when performed, the whole is once again established. We all have something to blurt out, but unless it takes on a cogent form that we can translate using words, sounds or colors, we cannot speak in spiritual form, only indirectly about such things as spirit and art and truth and music.

In the end, we cannot keep time with a real metronome's longest beat. It just won't work, and there are no songs, at least none that I know of, that would require this tempo. It's just there on the scale like the maximum speed on a car's speedometer. In much the same way, most of us cannot discern the long beat of our inner rhythm, but in this case it is not analogous to the literal metronome, for the spiritual long beat is the only timing on which one can truly be synchronized, the single rhythm that one must recognize and fall into step with in order to march to the beat of the metronome, which of course, again brings us back to time as the main unit. I cannot seem to escape it no matter how I try, but I insist the secret lies in getting beyond that. Still, perhaps I might lay a better foundation for the understanding of time, and when you stand on that firmer ground, you might reach an understanding as well as grasp what I cannot convey. I'll give it one last try, and I'll take my time.

The metronome is the measure of our lives, and its beat can be set so we can hear the constant clicking. But its real beat is too slow to know except in hindsight's fast-play mode. Once we understand its operation, we can use the metronome to our advantage by stepping into a section of days yet to be lived with a sense of how the metronome will play it out before us. This way, we can undertake

The Long Beat of the Metronome

great tasks and spread them out, much as we can look back over many small tasks spread out over smaller portions of days and see a trend. If we understand the metronome well enough, we can even manipulate situations so as to structure experiences (into what can later be inferred as foresight) into living a plan. We must sense the absolute stillness, however, and know the motion, almost as if we join a parade and have to march one step an hour, waving our hand at the same pace, in order to be seen by the crowd.

All of our actions are no more than a fly beating its wings while stuck on sticky paper. All these words I am writing are really only one letter of a word in a much longer sentence, and hearing this letter, one cannot possibly know what letter came before or what will come afterwards, at least not anyone else but myself, but it can tune anyone to isolating what letter this happens to reveal in their own lives. In that sense, this is just a bubble of air spaced between pages. There is no sound. It is the crowd cheering for you, stuck on the street for what seems like forever in only the briefest span of time before they're all that's left on an old piece of film taken on that day.

I dream of a sub-dial on a new, luxury watch that measures creation itself, not just the rotations of galaxies, star systems and far-off nebulas, but everything since it all began. One hand on this particular dial is calibrated to advance once every million years. Once around the dial is 100 million. In a neighboring aperture, an animation will show the creation of stars much as the phases of the moon are visible on some more popular models. I trust the accuracy of this timepiece to remind me that everything is moving, even though it seems to stand still, and to number my days or become a snowman in a dark forest of eternal winter. Tonight there is s a small crystal of ice outside on the window. If it is me, I must wait for the rising sun to enable me to run down the window, where though I might collect myself and pool my resources, I could do nothing to forestall my slow evaporation. If I do turn to mist, I will pray for dew point somewhere in the night. And by the measure of this new watch, the dial will be spinning when it comes, for the long beat in me, elusive as it is, and seen only in flashes, comprises countless eternities and shines like a tiny crystal, tuned and ready to be divided into a symphony.

The Shrinking

Truth be told, I'd always been curious about what made me tick, but I've never been much of a fan of psychiatry. I've seen people who had undergone analysis were afterwards less able to understand themselves and sometimes more screwed up than when they started. I'm not trying to disparage the industry. I've just always believed that there are other paths to understanding, and the science of the mind is not only late in the game but still in its infancy.

But something came up that changed my mind. It seemed like a marriage of the best of both worlds, that of mythology and psychology, and as soon as I heard about it, I decided it was just the thing for me. I read about it on the internet news one morning, and that same day I was on the phone with this fledgling company hoping they would use me as a guinea pig for all that I might learn about myself. I've always thought a "snails/puppy dog tails" approach bears more fruit somehow than an "ego/libido," but that's just me. Still, when they put the cap full of wires on my head, I wondered what I was in for. It didn't seem like a "non-scientific" methodology.

But the technology as it was explained to me would generate images that would be meaningful more in terms of personal mythology and explain me to myself in ways a psychologist would never be able to, so I was intrigued and felt like I was on track when the procedure began. Basically they were going to monitor me in a variety of situations and not just record the results but feed them through an image processor that would generate the results. The cost seemed prohibitive until they explained it was significantly less than months of office visits. Also, I would learn to analyze myself in the process such that the results would be more meaningful, so I figured it was probably worth it. They would record me while awake and while sleeping, while I was lost in thought and while I was having conversations. They would give me specific things to do, watch specific programs on a television monitor, for example, and later they would hook me up with a wireless device and record me in my normal life. When I asked if I should tell anyone what was happening, they said I should just keep it all under my hat, and literally that's what I did. The wireless connection was installed in a baseball cap that I had to wear whatever I was doing. There were times I could not wear it, but they said that they should get enough information for about fifty separate mind recordings while I was connected.

 I don't know how they built the database over which they poured the images collected from my brain or how the software was able to render a new set of cogent images that might go far in explaining myself to me. I know there are some who will say that there will always be outside influences that corrupt the system, but I was more curious than in need of intervention, and I was not looking at the process as something like voodoo compared to medicine. Perhaps it will be seen more like reading one's horoscope than a true perception of what goes on inside a person, but the most interesting thing about it was when it was finished and generated, they asked me to comment as I watched the results, the idea being that my interpretations or reactions would enhance the meaning, and while they made comments, they said that how I received them was significant and that I would know if they were off the mark, just as one whose dream it is, knows when the interpretations are on the mark. But the paradox for me was looking at these recordings and wondering if they explained the way I look at things.

 So after all the data was collected and processed, I was called in for a screening of the finished result to be conducted with a psychiatrist and his team. I was surprised to see that many of the images were dark, and I saw little of myself or people I knew. There were plenty of strangers, but many times I knew the man in the images was probably me, or while watching, something would trigger a recollection of someone I knew, and this was supposed to be important.

The Long Beat of the Metronome

All of the images were related somehow to my inner life, but not all of them were deep and meaningful. Some were generated out of simple reactions to visual stimulation, or they might go to explain how my mind might turn something into a joke. So they indicated before starting the session that I should expect to have more questions when it was all over than have all my questions answered. With that, they started showing me the images.

In the opening scene, it becomes obvious that a man is having an extramarital affair and is a passenger in a car his mistress is driving. I was not married, but somehow the images make me feel uncomfortable. It occurs to me I have not been entirely faithful to my girlfriend. I watch with interest. The man gives his mistress directions to drive by his house so he can point it out to her. He feels only a slight degree of fear that he will be seen by his wife, but he is shocked when they approach the house to see his wife crossing the street. His mistress was nervous about getting this close to the house and is driving too fast. She puts on the brakes and stops just in front of the man's wife. As she looks into the car, he shrinks beneath her view on the passenger side to avoid her. In fact, he finds that he actually shrinks to a smaller size. He becomes just a tiny thing and runs in a panic off the seat and across the floorboards to hide. He doesn't know where to turn. Should he go behind the gas pedal or under the seat? He can't decide. He peeks up. His wife is still looking in the window. Then he realizes that he let his mistress drive *his* car. Surely his wife must have recognized it. In a blind panic, fear begins to choke him. He feels all the gears, heat and noise of the car closing in. Has he somehow wound up in the engine? There's such a conglomeration of sounds, smells and moving parts that he can't find his way. It is too much for him, and he loses consciousness. At this point, the view switches to a view of the street with his wife looking in the window at him and his mistress. He is sitting in the passenger seat, unconscious after fainting when his mistress nearly ran over his wife. I am not sure how to react to this. Am I the kind of person who is already known to be deceiving another, dreaming that I am not?

In the next depiction, there is just an apple. A worm goes into it, then another, still another, until the apple is teeming with worms.

The view rotates. It turns out the apple is actually inside the head of a man, as the rotation reveals there are two eye slots, and we can see the outside world and light streaming in. The view switches to the outside and the man's face. It is contorted and upset. Then a doctor steps into the frame and opens the head and takes the wormy apple out. But one worm drops back in. The doctor puts a new apple in and closes it up. The last frame shows the worm that dropped in going for the new apple. I do not find this particularly disturbing as it reminds me of a poem by William Blake.

In the next image, there are many people entreating a young man to get ahead and to prove himself. There is a fence, and everyone is trapped together. Everyone seems to point to the boy as being the best hope to escape, that he has the most ability and is the chosen one, but he cannot succeed without their combined help. They need to make some kind of pyramid with their bodies and allow him to climb up, but as soon as he steps on the back of anyone, the individual turns to a kind of protoplasmic mush, and he cannot get off the ground. Once he stops, the piles of mush he tried to stand on turn back into people, who once again encourage him to be the one to make it to the top. I don't know why, but this one does make me angry at some people I know.

The next image is a young boy who wants to be an artist. He declares that someday he will be a great one. He stands before two houses. One of them is in disrepair. It hasn't been lived in for many years. The fence is broken as are all the windows. The lawn is full of nothing but weeds and deep crab grass. The other house is well kept, nicely painted, with a quaint gazebo and garden. Feeling a sense of beauty, the artist prays, *Oh God, if you make me an artist, I'll try to paint things beautifully.* The scene fades out, then fades back in, and we see that he is grown up and is an artist. His work is quite beautiful, but his life is without success. There is failure, personal tragedy, anger and depression. He has gone into seclusion to work. Nothing has been heard from him for years. The one or two family in touch with him are estranged and say he is brilliant and crazed. We see him in his studio working feverishly on a large canvas, but we do not see the painting. When he has finished, he picks up a gun and shoots himself in the head. His works are brought out, and the critics hail him as great. His estranged family becomes rich. In the last scene, there's an auction for his paining of his old, broken-down house. The bidding is already in the millions of dollars and continues as the scene fades out. This one seems to me to have come from some movies I've seen, but not especially from anything I witnessed in preparation for the experience, but I remembered that images I would see here could come from anywhere in my life in such a way that I would not necessarily recognize them.

    The next scene showed a man who attaches a hook with a long line to himself for each one of his bad habits. For smoking, there is a line. There are also lines for drinking and cavorting with women. Each one is a long-term threat to his life, but he accepts that. Since the threats are deadly only in the long term, there is plenty of slack, so he sets each hook fearlessly and goes about his business. Then there are scenes that show him at different ages, 30, 40, 50, with the slack tightening progressively. Finally, death comes to collect him, and the man doesn't go quietly, but seems to explode as he is pulled asunder from all sides. I see that and put out my cigarette.

    Next came something on the surrealistic side: balloon heads leaving real, human bodies and rising into the upper atmosphere. Some explode. Others blow downwind. As they float back down, there are bodies running around trying to grab them, bumping into one another. Meanwhile, men in an office are looking out the window. They keep their balloon heads on with a string tied to a vest pocket button. The balloon head rises above the shoulders a few inches. You can see the strings. There are no necks, just strings. The curtains are pulled aside. They are peeking out at the scenes below of headless bodies running around and people on the streets losing their balloon heads. I wasn't sure what to make of this one, and I asked about it. The response was that I might have some latent anger against people, thinking they are empty headed, and perhaps I harbored some ill will against corporations. I said that sounded like a psychological analysis and that it was dead wrong as an interpretation of my true feelings, never admitting there was some truth in the suggestion. The shrink, (I know I should say *psychiatrist*), looked at me and said, "We'll ask the questions."

The session resumed with a depiction of the death of a man. His family cries and goes into a deep depression. Even his friends and their families react the same way. The neighbors are also deeply affected. There is such a tremendous impact that the story is covered on television. The whole nation weeps. It goes across the Atlantic, and around the planet, until the whole world feels deeply saddened. The earth is shown at a great distance, whimpering. Then the focus shifts to one who has watched all of this on television. He is laughing. It has caught on next door, across the nation and around the world. Soon the whole world is laughing so hard that the view shifts to space where its laughter rises to a crescendo, and then the planet explodes with a bang. Now, the focus shifts to one who's watched this entire sequence on TV, who doesn't think it's even the slightest bit interesting and turns the channel. I suggested that if it were not so obvious, this might be considered a mystery wrapped in an enigma hidden in a conundrum. When asked if I thought it revealed anything obvious about me, I said it didn't.

At about this point, though it was still early in the presentation, I merely began to watch the scenes unfold. I reacted to them, but I don't remember each thought that I had. I do recall giving blood at the office and having trouble with a man repairing my car at a service station recently, but on the whole, it was almost as if I hit a zone and watched these sequences just as if they were coming to mind. It was all very comfortable, and they told me that this was exactly what is supposed to happen.

In the next sequence, it appears that a celestial being, perhaps God, is helping a man. When the man leaves work, there's an empty elevator open to take him down immediately. An empty taxi pulls up just as he arrives. The streetlights turn green as soon as he gets to them. All of this happens in such a way that just as he arrives at his house, an out-of-control vehicle kills him. He does not see it coming. He is at the right place at the right time, which is to set up something going terribly wrong. From this I realize I have an underlying expectation that bad things will happen when everything seems to be going well.

Then there was a sequence that showed people walking around with boulders on their backs. Everyone is weighed down by the great burdens that they carry around. They grimace, and they groan. But when they pass, they ask each other, "How's it going?" And without fail, each one of them answers, "Fine! Everything's just fine, thanks! How's it going with you?" At this point I just happened to turn and see the psychiatrist not just watching the screen but nodding his head and smiling. I wondered what he was thinking.

The following scene was very intimate, showing a man and woman who are just finishing making love. She asks him to snuggle very close when he's finished. From the look on his face, he seems to be annoyed at having to do this. Then, as he is pressed against her, her fingernails grow into branches, and she envelopes him. The scene switches to the street, where there are many women carrying men in cages that are made of branches extending from the fingernails. Then the scene switches to his nervous face. It was all in his imagination, but he gets up abruptly and gets dressed.

At this point I asked for a break. The shrink said, "Take fifteen," then got up and left without looking at me. We'd already seen about a quarter of the scenes, and I wondered if he thought I was abnormal. The last scene of men in cages, what was that all about? While I find the scenes interesting, I'm not sure what to make of them, and I wouldn't say I recognized them as having come from me.

When we resumed, the first images were of a man sitting in his chair brooding while forces hover around him. These are cloud-like, mean things. He smokes, has a cup of coffee, and continues to brood. Suddenly, he gets an idea. Waves circle out of his head, pushing the forces away from him. There's a close-up of the forces that are fighting to get close. Now he works feverishly (not brooding) until a project is complete. He succeeds and rejoices. With the passage of some time, the circles of protection that surround him break. Then the mean forces wend their way in, hovering over him, and he goes from intermittent smiles to coffee, smokes, and brooding.

Next we have a short history of mankind. First, man is depicted as living in small families, isolated from others. Parents are guiding their children back to the family dwelling. There are many dangers

The Shrinking

about, not enough communication and certainly no trust. Each family lives in a cave. The next depiction shows that man has moved out of the caves into small but close-knit communities. There is sharing, farming and the domestication of animals. There are also fences. In the next scene, man has moved to towns surrounded by walls. In the center of the town, there is a castle surrounded by a moat. People are polite, passing each other in the street and bowing, but far above in one of the castle windows, there is a lookout posted to keep watch on a similar village on a hill far away. The next scene shows modern cities and millions of homes. Some have been ravaged by war. It shows people on the streets paying little or no attention to one another, and newspapers revealing the crime and collapse of society. It also shows people frustrated in cramped offices. The final scenes show parents watching carefully over their children with the specters of drugs and disease hovering near. They manage to return safely to their small house and lock the door.

Next there's a scene of a man sitting listlessly in his chair. He seems to remember something, gets up, passes a table, sees a letter on the floor, picks it up, goes back to his chair, drops the letter and becomes listless. Then he seems to remember something, gets up, turns on the fan, sits down, and becomes listless. The fan blows the letter back to where it was on the floor. In time, he remembers there was something he wanted to do. He gets up, sees the letter on the floor, and does the same thing over and over. The letter is addressed to him with words on the envelope that say, *Welcome to Hell.*

The next scene shows a man who has an idea that he thinks will change the world. He writes a book delineating the idea and publishes it, but nothing happens in his lifetime. The book sits around for years before he dies, and for years after he dies. It has very few readers, and each one has a similar response. One reader says, "This doesn't do anything for me." Another falls asleep. Another can't get finished with the first page and puts it back on the shelf. Then one day, someone reads it and becomes incensed with its power. It becomes something like a Bible for him as he follows its precepts religiously. He works hard and becomes a politician. He gets elected and rises to power. From this perch, he commands commanders of his armies, and wielding this power, changes the face of the world. Later on, when he's retiring, a reporter asks him in an interview what the changing point was in his life. He mentions the book. When that news goes out, the book is an instant sensation. It rises quickly to the top of the best-seller list and is sold everywhere. But as before, one buyer says it didn't do anything for him. Another can't get finished with the first page and puts it back on the shelf.

The next scene is rather strange, almost like an animation. Whether it is based on something in my mind or reveals something about me is debatable, but I am still amazed that they were able to render it from a technological viewpoint. It seemed to be all from a camera's point of view pointed at a mirror, such that the camera can be seen looking at the mirror, but there is a character made of clay on the shelf below the mirror. He is looking at the camera. He begins to climb the mirror with his sticky grip of clay, leaving a smudge trail. When he reaches the middle of the mirror, he turns and leaps for the camera. The view has always been from the camera, and now the character is seen flying closer to the lens. It quickly gets closer and soon blocks the light. When this happens, the view suddenly switches to the mirror looking at the camera. The last moments of the character's jump are seen. It lands smack on the lens and grasps and totally covers it. The character climbs on top of the lens, and the view switches momentarily back to the camera. The scene shows only a camera in the mirror, but there is a figure on top of the camera. Now the figure bends over and looks into the lens. The large, upside-down face of the character is visible in the immediate foreground. Now the scene switches back to the mirror's perspective. The character is still looking in the lens, but all we see is his back. Now he climbs back up to the top of the lens and looks back at the mirror. He jumps. He gets closer and larger until he blocks all the light. The view switches back to the camera's perspective looking at the mirror. The clay figure has hit the mirror. At first it is stuck, but now it slowly slides flattened and lifeless to the shelf below, leaving a trail of smudge as it goes.

In the next sequence, earth has been destroyed in a nuclear holocaust, and a contingent of angels from heaven have been sent to clean up the place for archival storage. In organizing everything on the planet, they make huge stacks and piles of things. For example, all of the gold in the world is in one pile. They place all of the diamonds in the world in another. When everything has been completely categorized, they survey the results. One of the angels makes the following observation, *Pointing to the diamonds, gold, money and the like*: "These are the things that mankind wanted so badly. Look at how much of it there really is, and how much it corrupted him. In these things were the seeds of man's destruction." *Then pointing to the art, literature, philosophy and the like*: "These things couldn't buy mankind what the other things could and weren't held highly enough. He didn't want them very badly, but these things enhanced individuals and held the keys that would have saved him."

After that fades out, there is a scene where everyone is depicted as having invisible elves strung to them. These elves walk along with people, some even a distance ahead of them, helping them along if they work well and keep their virtue. They are just as busy to help out in one's daily schedules and plans. But if the soul sours and turns in life, so do these elves. They begin to impede progress by pulling against people. Life feels heavier to them because they're dragging so many elves pulling against them. Everyone after a while tires out and wears down, kept from achieving their real goals. In the final sequence, the person is being carried in a casket by the elves that destroyed him, while passing the funeral from the other direction is a group of elves literally carrying someone aloft on their shoulders, helping to make life easier for him because he kept his virtue.

The next scene is of man who is in bed, trying to fall asleep. Inside his head, consciousness, personified into a little character with a nightcap, is seen going down a flight of stairs. He reaches a platform. In the middle of the platform there is a hole which is *sleep*. It is a dark abyss. He puts one foot in, then the other, and sits down, but this isn't sleep. It's insomnia. The view switches to the man in bed. He's wide awake. Back inside his head, the little man tries to jump in the abyss, but he catches himself at the elbows. Then he tries to dive in, but the toes of his feet catch him. No matter how hard he tries, he just can't seem to be surrounded by the darkness of the hole. The man in bed continues to get close to dozing, but something holds him back at the last second. Finally, the little character gets through, becoming so tired himself as he hangs on effortlessly over the pit. He falls. Suddenly surrounded by phantoms and clouds. Suddenly something like a hand flicks him back up through the hole. The man sits up in bed. He'd dozed, but woke suddenly. He lays back down and the little man, who was floating over the hole like a ball held up by a stream of air slowly descends into the abyss. This time, as he enters the ever-darkening zone, he becomes one of the phantoms and flies off. The final scene shows the sleeper in bed, dreaming peacefully.

The next thing I see is a ladder that stretches from the bottom to the top. At the bottom lies mediocrity. At the top is genius. The scene depicts a man who has reached the top of the ladder for him. He is just above average, and the ladder stops. There is a gap that his reach cannot span. He is standing precariously on the last rung, flailing in the gap. The next segments, continuing on to excellence and brilliance, are beyond him.

I said I needed another break, and this time the shrink sat in the same room, but he said he didn't want to answer any questions. I'd been trying to keep track of the sequences, and by my count we were at about twenty. These last ones seemed more normal, but my palms were sweaty, and my throat was dry. For days I'd been anxious to learn more about myself, and though I didn't have a clear idea of the meaning of any of the images, I still found myself dreading the next sequences. Paradoxically, much as I was blind to the meaning, I was uncomfortable with so much of myself being revealed.

In the first scene after the break, I watched what appeared to be an effort to depict God's view of the globe. Earth is at the center of a spherical lens in a heavenly laboratory. Around this lens, a heavenly device records everything that takes place on the planet, both action and spirit. As God looks on, cells from his skin, if one can call it that, fall and become new souls that wend their way down to earth through an opening in the lens. This too is recorded. There is also a repository for souls departing from the planet. Some into a fire that provides light to the earth, while others reconnect to God.

The Shrinking

Abruptly the scene switches to the middle of the city. There is a man selling books on the street. He is dressed in a military uniform. He wrote the book. He has many followers, his military subordinates, working with him to sell the books. They are trying to round up more followers. These subordinates are organized in troops. The book contains all the rules and regulations of the author's vision of the perfectly organized society that he will rule. For the author and the troops, selling is simply a matter of shouting orders from the book and gathering those who are willing to obey. A few stand and gape, while hundreds of people walk by without interest.

Fade out and in to a scene of a man as he passes an art gallery and sees a painting through a window. Above his head, we see two frames. In the first, he is younger, trying to paint. In the second, he is older and disgusted, tearing up the work. He passes a museum with sculptures. Above his head, we see two frames. In the first, he is younger, chipping a statue. In the second, he is older and disgusted, using a sledge hammer to pound his work into rubble. He then passes a musician on the street. Above his head, we see two frames. In the first, he is younger, trying to play the saxophone. In the second, he is older and angry, bending it. He then passes a bookstore. Above his head, we see two frames. In the first, he is younger, trying to write. In the second, he is older and frustrated, wadding up another page and throwing it into an already full can of wads. He arrives at his job. He is a stock clerk in a grocery store. A woman barks at him. Above his head, we see two frames. In the first, he is younger, frustrated, working in the store with various dreams above his head. In the second, he is older, with an insane look of happiness on his face as he stands in front of the store. He is pushing down a plunger to blow up the supermarket. A younger version of him with all his dreams stands in the window, watching.

The next sequence shows a man down hard on his luck because he's too weak to change his habits. He drinks and smokes too much. He's always overdoing it. When he tries to quit, he fails. He seeks guidance. The counselor advises him to fill his mind with some kind of hobby or work. He's told, for example, to clean up his house from top to bottom and see how it goes from there. Now we see him sweeping the living room. A pile of dust has accumulated. He sweeps it to the door and opens it to sweep the pile outside. He takes one huge swipe at it with the broom, only for a blast of wind to blow it all back in a cloud that fills the room and begins to slowly settle.

After that, the scene changes to show a boy who is out waling and stumbles on what turns out to be a magic hoop. It is just large enough for him to crawl through, whereupon he discovers it is actually a gateway into another world. The exit remains clearly visible, but he can stay and play in this fantasy world as long as he wants. Then the family moves and the hoop is misplaced. He misses the adventures. As he grows up, the world of school and business bore him. He turns into a somewhat successful but unhappy adult. Then one day while visiting his parents' house, he finds the hoop in a crawlspace beneath the house. He is overjoyed. It brings back such memories. It has been a stressful time, and he wants to use it again, but he finds it doesn't fit over his shoulders. It still has magical properties as he can put his arm through it and watch it disappear, but there's no way he can go into it fully. Still, he can at least put it over his head and look around in the wonderful fantasy world he enjoyed as a child. He takes it with him and begins to use it in that way, wearing it more and more often, losing contact with the world around him. Even in the rain, his head is filled with a vision of a beautiful sunny day. The last we see of him is during this thunderstorm. He is a soaking wet, headless body wandering aimlessly in the streets. A hoop can be seen on the shoulders, just where the neck should be seen.

In the next sequence, a man is at his job, inching slowing toward the woman of his dreams. He hovers over her. It is obvious that she is uncomfortable. She tells him to leave her alone. She makes a scene, driving him into a corner. As she moves in for the kill, the entire work force stands behind her. He is squeezed against the wall. There's no room to breathe. He chokes. And then he wakes up. He is stifling in bed against the wall. His wife has snuggled up so close that he can't breathe.

The scene changes, and there is a man holding a woman at the point of a knife. She is out of her mind with fear. He's scraggly. She's beautiful. He says, "Now let me tell you something," but fear shuts her ears. He becomes uglier and more threatening. Then he says, "Look honey, after I've finished these last two months as an intern, I'll be able to set up my own practice." A slow metamorphosis begins to take place. He begins to become handsome. The knife turns into a ring. It is then shown that they're in a car in front of her house. He walks her to the door. They kiss. She says she had a lovely time.

The next scene shows a man who has many things to do, but in trying to get up to do them, is tied down by many creatures. Their job is to keep him from doing anything at all. As soon as he tries to move, they work to hold him there. Their technique is first to literally hold him down, then to tell him how difficult each task will be to accomplish. They explain that there are just too many things. To even try doing one thing is useless. They tire him just by making him think such thoughts, and the last scene shows this man surrounded by creatures just relaxing next to him, with him weighed down by all kinds of fears and doubts.

In the next scene, a man is talking to a woman on a train platform. He does not respect her. She is a balloon figure, entirely empty and inflated, and he is talking to her like she is an air head. You are so stupid, he shouts. At that, his arm juts up, suddenly filled with air. Your leaving me is perfect timing, he shouts. *You're just an air head. I never loved you.* Another part of him turns into a balloon. He continues to insult her and turns more and more into a lifeless bubble. Meanwhile, the woman, in tears, turns into a whole person who watches him float away above the platform as she boards the train.

In the darkness between scenes, I glanced over at the shrink, and when the lights came up, I saw he'd taken his eyes off the screen and was watching my face, at least until he realized I saw him. I figured he must have concluded that I have some major issues with relationships, and that he would probably ask me why I thought such a thing, and whether I thought I had problems. I wondered what scenes would come from his mind. I felt healthy enough, but I also realized I was defensive and that if asked, I would lie.

Next, there is a scene of a man who has had a very good life by learning not to dwell on the negative things. He has many fond memories and wishes to relive many of the ones he has exaggerated in his mind. The negative aspects that he has learned to ignore surround him at this moment in the form of fears of what will happen in the future. He doesn't want to die. These fears are the reason why he is concentrating on the joys of the past. He was safe there, and he cannot shake the reality of so many negative things that may happen in the future bothering him all at once. They have even gone so far as to permeate his character. They have changed him into one who looks backward and forward, not at where he is. This is exactly the opposite of what he used to be: a contented man whose focus was the present. In order to fulfill his dream of reliving some of the best parts of his life, he goes to a scientist who has a device that can send him back and forth between the past and present. On going back, he carries with him, unawares, the effects of this fear of the future, and instead of landing the job that gave him security and helped him to meet his wife, he takes everything for granted in a state of depression. This is not what won him the job in the first place, and he fails the interview. On his return to the present, he has no job and no wife, only memories of rejection and failure. He now has nothing for which he might go into the past, and not sure what went wrong, no choice but to accept these changes as the reality that always was. Believing that it will be truly generous to the future, he decides to commit every fiber of his being to the present, which in fact is a return to his former self.

In the next scene, everyone is naked and ashamed. They all stand behind rubber curtains into which they press to hide their bodies from one another. Across from them is another group of naked people behind a rubber curtain. They are equally ashamed and press themselves in to hide their bodies. As they do so, the rubber accentuates their charms. Each side notices the bodies on the other side, and sees that the other side is watching. They begin to show off. They try to get closer, stretching the curtain. As they do so, the curtain breaks, leaving a tight, rubber cover on each. No longer naked and ashamed, but rather excited, they pair off and head for privacy where they tenderly tear the rubber coverings off one another.

The next scene depicts a man who has spent his whole life

obtaining things. His soul is full of lust and greed, so much that as his possessions accumulate around him, when there are far too many things for him to use, his skin begins to boil, and something starts growing from him. It is a creature that is maturing on his body. As soon as it is complete, it drops off and takes on a life of its own. It quickly lunges into the horde of his possessions and begins to stand guard over them. As soon as this creature is free, the man's skin begins to boil with the development of a new one. Soon, it too matures and drops free. It lunges into the sea of his possessions and fights with the other creature. Thus he grows older. He continues to accumulate things. Creatures mature from him and break off, sapping his strength and withering him as they go into his wealth of poverty, fighting over everything, nothing of which is useful to him, until he dies.

An alarm goes off in the morning at the beginning of the next scene. Waking, a man who reaches over and pushes the button to stop the vexing noise. He goes into the bathroom and pushes a button that operates the light. He takes his electric toothbrush and pushes a button to get it started. Later, in the kitchen, he pushes a button on the coffee maker to start the brew. In the garage, he pushes a button to open the door and another to start the car. In the office, he pushes a button to talk to his secretary and another to take a telephone call. When he's leaving, he pushes a button to get an elevator and once on it, pushes a button for the lobby. In the street, he pushes a button to cross the street. Once home, he pushes a button to start his microwave oven. When he goes to bed, he pushes a button to turn out the light, and laying down on the pillow, finally takes a pill, pushes it on his tongue like a button, and goes to sleep.

In the next scene, a roving reporter happens to encounter a group of black youths enjoying a mud fight. They are having great fun. The reporter asks them why they are playing that way. There is a cacophony of responses. *We're having fun*, and *It's cool* dominate the noise, but the reporter hears one of the children say, *We like being black*. Hearing this, the reporter thinks, *Now this is an instance of racial pride. It's good to have this sense of pride.* Moving on, he comes upon a group of white youths who are fighting with shaving cream.

They are having great fun. The reporter asks them why they are doing it. There's a variety of responses. *We're having fun*, and *It's cool* dominate the noise, but the reporter hears one of the children say, *We like being white*. Hearing this, the reporter wonders at the hatred instilled by parents and the words spoken from the mouths of babes and asks, *How does prejudice begin at such an early age?*

The next scene is of a series of interconnected revolving doors. They are like cogs and wheels in a watch. There are thousands of these doors that revolve into other doors, and thousands of people pushing and shoving their way around. They go through one and choose another. They can go half the way around and get off at the next or do a complete circle and backtrack. There are limitless choices of direction, but not a single destination. The people move about aimlessly in the scene, changing direction and place while nothing changes. The land is filled with entrance after entrance, but there's not a single exit.

As that ends, a new scene begins showing that a young man and woman are rising to the top of the world, moving onto rungs of the ladder of success made vacant by the displacement of those moving either up or down. The couple moves into an apartment vacated by a woman who was just divorced after her child died. They know few details of the story. When they move in, the phone is still connected, and they receive a call from someone who says that "Dave" has committed suicide. At first they think they know who it is, and they feel terrible. Then they realize the call was for the previous tenant, and they breathe a sigh of relief. These others are just shades and do not impinge on the couple's happiness. Outside their window, there are other buildings, each equipped with a ladder that has people going up and down. As they look out to enjoy the view, they admire the sunset and toast to their success. They are oblivious to the backdrop that is the mirror of their own participation in life, and ignorantly close the shades that depict both their current blind rise and the painful faltering that will come in time.

I'd call the next scene, *The Hall of Famous and Forgotten People*, a place filled with extremely proud and effete statues of celebrated individuals. It is a wonderfully interesting place, for each statue is perfectly cast. Each separate monument stands on a floor that is beautiful in its own right. In fact, the floor is an essential ingredient in understanding the statues themselves. For you cannot help but notice that the base of each statue actually rests on a richly wrought mosaic of people crushed by the individual depicted in the statue rising to glory and fame. These mosaics are very nicely made. The statues sit squarely over them like stakes through their chest. The mosaic hands of these figures grasp at the base of these statues. Their faces cry out in pain. Each rendering is unique.

At this point the shrink said we should pause for a couple of minutes. He stood up and said it was almost over. Referring to the previous scene, he commented that he was amazed that people climb their way to the top without concern that they may trample others along the way up. His comment seemed to treat the scene as extant from my mind, and I was somewhat relieved that he could be so objective. It gave me some confidence that the final analysis might not be so intrusive or intimidating, and I felt a sense of respect for him. Perhaps he was a decent person. So I asked him joking, "So Doc, do you think I'm normal?" But he just apologized and said he could not discuss the material, and again I felt a cloud of ill will against him and wondered why he was there except to make me uncomfortable.

The next scene begins and shows a man sitting at the table. He is writing. He reaches for something. From a back view of him, he sees a baseball bat in the corner. Suddenly something clicks. A thought flashes in his mind. He sees himself holding a bat. At first, he thinks that this memory was from a dream. He concentrates on the thought. He sees himself holding the bat, but it fades in and out. It becomes harder to hold. Finally, it is lost for good. He can't seem to get even the memory back, dream or not. Looking at the bat doesn't help. He thinks it must have been from a dream. Then, he wonders what becomes of all fugitive thoughts. Now the scene switches to the inside of his head. There is a vault marked, *Forgotten Dream Props*. Two men enter. They are wearing overalls. "Alright," one says. "Let's clean some of this stuff out." They go into the vault and come out with a box. Together, they carry it over to the nearby stream of consciousness and dump it in. Many things come out. Everything but a bat sinks at once. The bat bobs up and down for a while, then disappears.

In the next scene, a man appears normal, but stresses make him more and more nervous. The stress waves become more and more severe. They cut through him. He is vibrating. The waves work through him and become separate elements. Working on one another, the puzzle-shaped pieces become less jagged. They become more and more round, finally turning into circles. Now built of circles, the man suddenly falls apart, collapsing to the ground and rolling away in all different directions.

The sequence that follows shows a failed photographer who is determined to go out with flare, to take one truly great picture to make up for so many years of visionless mediocrity. He decides it will be the picture of his facing death without fear. He goes to a jungle and stalks a tiger into rushing and killing him. He stands patiently, clicking off the picture just as the tiger leaps. He's torn to pieces with a smile in his heart, knowing that he's finally made a glorious statement to the world. Not far away from the tragedy, a group of natives hear the commotion. They enter the clearing and scare off the tiger. Not knowing what happened, they examine the scene. One of them picks up the camera. He fiddles with it, pushing and pulling until the back opens. Curious, he pulls the film out, exposing the whole roll to the light.

The next scene shows a man finding a small sprig growing out of his shoe. He takes care of it, watering it and pruning it, and for many years, it grows well. Then the tree begins to be cumbersome. They have grown old together, but while the tree is full of ripe fruit, ready to be picked, the man feels too tired to do so. The tree is always in his face, blocking his view. Because it's in his shoe, he feels crippled dragging it around with him all the time, as weighty as it has grown. So one day, he transplants his shoe with the tree in a field. He stands in its shade a moment, then turns to leave. As he does so, it falls on him.

Then there is a man sitting on the train. He sees a woman and thinks, *That girl's looking at me, she must think I'm good looking.* Then he remembers a woman who was unfaithful. They'd gone out for months, but he was forced to leave her. It was a horrible time. Now he looks back at the woman who is still looking at him. Then another man walks by, and the woman turns and looks at him. Now the man feels outrage and thinks, *I'd never be able to trust her!*

The next scene depicts a student who listens to an old Zen master's lessons with great interest. He is so absorbed in all of the mysteries and so filled with enthusiasm that he becomes distracted. Whenever a lesson is finished, he walks out so full of energy that he winds up playing ball to let some of it off. One day, he is outside doing just that when the phone rings. It is the old master calling. The student is holding the phone in one hand and throwing the ball up and down in the other, saying "Sorry master. I know it was due yesterday. I'll get to work." He sits down to write, but gets so beguiled by all the inherent power in the mysteries he is trying to unravel that he walks out in a trance full of visions and belief to get a ball game started. A short time thereafter, the master dies. The student becomes depressed. He neglects his work and drops out of school. His books become dusty. The papers on his desk go through a time lapse, yellowing and becoming covered with cobwebs. The scene switches to the student who is now an old man. He is pouring over his old books and papers, but neglect has taken its toll. He remembers the joy he used to feel, but he only feels confused and depressed. Was it the philosophy that he loved, or was it just youth running through his veins? He can't seem to remember, or has he at last figured something out? As he'd done so many times before, he was about to try to read some of the old books, but as usual, there are other things to do. In the next scene, he is saying to his grandson, "I had the talent and the vision. There's no telling what I could have done if I had put my mind to it. Instead, I wasted my life, just like you!" The grandson leaves. He goes upstairs to his grandfather's study to read the old books he found there some time before. Since he discovered them, his grandfather's bitterness toward him has increased in proportion to his growing fascination and enthusiasm.

In the next scene, a young man is standing on a forbidden precipice of an abyss. Just being there is a crime. To escape, he must cross to the other side of the chasm. He's been warned not to try, but he wants so badly to escape this world and start another. His people are coming to get him, to force him to rejoin their society, so there is certain to be punishment. He looks up and sees with great surprise that there is a giant zipper hanging over him like a vine just waiting for him to take a ride to the other side. What's to stop him? Why should they care? They're coming closer. It's now or never. In order to make his escape he prepares to jump up and grab the overhanging zipper, the teeth of which go clear to the other side of the abyss, holding back a bulging sky. He backs up a few steps, runs, leaps and grabs hold of the zipper. His momentum pulls the zipper open as he rides across the abyss, and out of the opening sky falls a myriad of creatures, a multitude of diseases and vices, onto the world. They all have wings and fly to either side of the abyss to wreak havoc. Realizing what he has done, the young man despairs and drops into the chasm just before he reaches the other side. His people watch in furious dismay from the forbidden rim of the canyon.

Then there's a scene of a man who thinks he sees something like dust falling from his fingers when he's in the middle of hard work, but only out of the corner of his eye. Peripherally, it just seems to pour out into a pile on the floor, but looking straight at it, there's nothing there. He grows frantic and stops working. He sits around unwilling to tell his wife anything. She gets increasingly upset. At the same time, he becomes less mobile. Finally, she leaves. He tries to get up to stop her but can't move a finger. He tries and tries until suddenly his finger bursts open, and the dust drains out of him until his clothes lie flat in the chair.

The last scene shows a boy who is mercilessly teased and then throughout all his life he doesn't say a word, just takes it and keeps it all inside. He grows up timid and gets a small job as a clerk and gets harassed by his boss. Married, his wife henpecks him constantly. Finally he runs away, and the sun beats down on him. When he dies, years pass until they find his skeleton with a big bottle in the rib cage. When they open it, out comes an incredibly long scream.

Well, the lights came back on, and that was it. The presentation was over. I felt I had actually gotten lost in it, almost like not even knowing it was there in front of me, all those images. I could say it was like being in water that is at a temperature where you cannot feel it is water anymore after you've grown used to it and stood still so as to not feel its viscosity. But now that it was over, that thickness of thinking came over me. What did it all mean? It seemed there were repeating themes. Yes, there seemed to be lots of people on the brink of death, or dying of boredom, or relationships out of whack and fear or the consequences of discovery. There were also broken plans and dreams, a general futility, or was it just my interpretation? I had some questions, but I was told the shrink had left shortly before the presentation ended. I had become so engrossed in the last couple of scenes that I hadn't noticed he'd left the room.

I thanked them, taking a copy of the movie with me, but I really had no desire to watch it again. It felt like I'd been turned inside out, and I was so besieged with images that I started wondering why there wasn't a greater effort to edit the damn thing, tone it down, and bring it down to a more palatable size.

Some of the images stayed with me and were like scenes from nightmares or an irritating song you can't get out of your head. In short order, it began to affect me so that I was less productive at work, and I wanted to shut myself away from people, but when I did that, the images annoyed me even more. I began to throw things around, and when I broke the glass on a painting my grandfather gave to me and damaged the canvas, I decided to do something. For the first time in my life, I wanted to seek professional counseling.

The one thing I did not want to hear was that this process of gathering data from my brain and developing a matrix embedded with facets of my personality had opened me up for the first time in my life. I sensed such a thing, but what I wanted was to close the hole, be what I was, go back into a state of insensitivity if that was what I was. I don't think I knew anything more about myself, but I felt neutralized, maybe even sterile as compared to someone whose mind was generally fertile. I was even afraid of having ideas that might in some way suggest vague truths about myself. I stayed away from books that one might read and become more sensitive, more self aware. I was as aware of myself as I wanted to be, and I did not like it. It seemed the better way to function, that everything about being human came out of ignorance and going with the flow. All the sudden I had a sense of what I was inside, and there I was, stuck in the mud. I could not handle it, so I called the company and made an appointment to see the shrink.

Of course, I took the tape with me so I could fast forward to any scene to help with any questions that might come up. I hate to admit this, but I had an ulterior motive, which was to find out exactly what he thought. I was never comfortable with just being handed something like a pile of daydreams for whatever they were worth. I wanted some kind of answer. Of course, I figured he would not tell me if I asked, so I brought a gun along to force the information out of him. Basically I would just laugh in his trembling face and say I didn't come as a patient seeking help but to extract his professional opinion, by force if necessary, so the best thing for him to do was cough it up, and after that I'd leave him alone. My palms were sweaty when the attendant called me into his office. The gun felt like a giant weight in my breast pocket. I felt certain it was pulling that side down and kept making unnecessary adjustments.

Once in his office when I pulled out the gun, he calmly took off his glasses and began to wipe them clean. He said there was no need of that, that if I wanted his opinion, all I had to do was ask. He said a good starting point might be the scene of jumping across a canyon and unzipping the heavens, releasing all those vices and diseases on the earth. He said that my visit to his office was a leap of logic in which my goal was to grab the zipper and fly across to close the wide-open sky and separate myself from the facts of life, from all the unpleasant truth that had recently come pouring out over me as a result of my leaping into the abyss in the first place. He said I was still young, but I was having one helluva growth spurt from what was ultimately a crisis of the heart and that the best thing I could do was think about settling down, getting married and having a family, and everything would take its course, that I was not a madman with a gun, and to please put it away.

I put the gun away and apologized. I admitted it was true that I did not like to look at myself, that I gave lip service to the truth, but experiencing so much truth all at once, some pleasant, some not, made me feel I was shrinking and realize how much I actually feared and avoided it. It was also disconcerting to not know what to think of some of the scenes. He answered simply that there is a balance in experience and dreams, and thought processes are generally so diluted that truth in proper measure weathers the soul such that we are ready for death at the proper time, worn out, but having lived a long and full life, and we are not so full of images that horrify us with meaning as much as memories that are themselves generally diluted. He added that I was not shrinking and that what I was experiencing was actually some significant growing pains.

"Let me explain it another way," he said. "You reach a point as you drive along in life that you are just a conscious gorilla in the front seat, and behind you out of your unconsciousness, if you are ready to listen, is an awakened sense of which way you should probably go. But you do not know how to listen. If you heard something, you would probably ignore it. You might even grow annoyed and tell the voice to shut up. But through our therapy here, you've learned something about that voice in the back seat. At least you know there is one, and from that point on, you may tune it in and track your thoughts and dreams. Along the way, your intuitive side develops, and over time you become more skilled in the process and more whole. If you are comfortable with that, you will evolve beyond the gorilla mindlessly following the world in all directions. You will go in a whole different direction, certain it is right for you without knowing exactly why except that you have learned to listen to what comes from within. It is like learning how to read. The letters come first, then words and sentences and finally more complex material, even truth. When you discover how to do that, you don't just find it in yourself but everywhere. I've gained much from other minds."

When he admitted that was the reason he was nodding and smiling during my analysis, I fully appreciated the fact that it was never about knocking me down to size, so I gladly made another appointment, and I've been seeing him now for fifteen years. We have the most interesting conversations, and I even give him some good advice now and then.

Dreams of Murder

One night I dreamed that I had killed my brother and put his body in a canvas bag which I then dumped into a pond. It was the day after the killing in the dream. I had nervously gone back to the pond, where I found my brother swimming. It was my brother as a young boy. I told him to get out of the water, and as he started for the shore, he made a sign that he had discovered something. His feet were touching whatever it was and he beckoned me to help him. From the shore, I tried to call him off as if it were nothing, while I knew that I should have been equally excited. I should have been telling him to describe it, to hold it, keep track of it and not to lose it. Torn, I woke, and for a number of days, I was occasionally uncertain if I really had committed a murder because the feeling of having done it was so real. Even in the dream, where I was thinking I had some control, I couldn't deep six him. A younger version's feet found the obtrusive sack protruding mysteriously that contained an older version.

In another dream, I was taken by the police to a building with a number of murder victims. My brother was one of them. Because of this, I was filled with the sense that I was somehow the murderer, but I was not sure just what I had done, or how and when I had done it. The corpses were upstairs. There were no signs of violence, but many legs and arms were sticking up. I saw my brother in the corner smiling at me. His eyes were open, and he seemed to be staring at me. I looked away. There was a woman there as well. The police were arresting her. From her glances, I could see she was interested in me. I had crossed to the other side of the room, and as I looked over to my brother, it was as if the eyes had followed me. They were still staring. As they started to lead the woman away, an officer suggested that I quietly go along and try to get close to her so that she would tell me everything. I agreed, and something else. I was not surprised by the suggestion. In fact, I was rather relieved to be going to jail.

I dreamed I was chosen for the lead in a play my brother was directing, but I didn't know the lines. I was given contact lenses to wear. My lines were to be written on the wall, and I would be able to read them with the contacts. As the play opened, the contacts started to grow. They were painful and too big to wear. I was afraid that I had broken them, but rather than take them out and be asked what I did to them, I faced the wall and tried to read. My eyes were watering, and I could only see that there seemed to be text, but I couldn't make out any words in the blur. The play went on around me as I squinted for what to say, not knowing what anything meant. Somehow I suffered through the embarrassment and carried scars with me off stage, only to learn later that I had given a masterful performance of a part my brother had written especially for me.

In a similar dream, I had shot my brother and was seeking refuge in a coffee shop where no one had heard about the shooting. They were discussing my brother as if he were alive, describing events so recent as to make me wonder if I had succeeded in killing him.

I ran to my car and drove onto a bridge. Strangely, I was looking at the back of my head from the back seat. A shot rang out. I saw myself look to the passenger side and heard myself say, "Ah well, it's only a small caliber weapon." I heard another shot and saw it rip into my head. I slumped to the wheel. I saw the ground fly by, the car going out of control. I was somewhere on the bridge behind it when it crashed through restraints and plummeted into the chasm below. As if it were a film, credits began to roll.

This dream was one of an endless stream of disjointed scenes which I remembered in pieces which made little sense. There once were days when I'd be filled with dreams I'd had the night before. They'd fill my space like the sounds of willow trees in an early June warm wind storm under a full moon. Those were days I could walk for miles and know what was coming. It was what I called being whole. But over the span of experience with my brother, my space became a disjointed series of days which hardly filled me, let alone offer anything through which my numbness could be reached and made to feel. I marveled at my brother's total control. After I thought I'd killed him, he was somewhere ahead. Not a scrape was on him. After adjusting his scope, he took aim and fired. The bridge crumbled between us. What I used to be lies below, beneath structures of his undoing. I had no control, as if I'd been shot, and I saw myself from afar. But as for who was to blame, my brother's name was the only one that scrolled before me. To him was given all the credit.

I had yet another dream that I had a key to my brother's apartment and walked in to find him making love with a beautiful girl. I left. Later, I returned, and she was reading in bed, alone. Her body language called for me to climb in bed. It was incredible that I was taking my brother's woman. That thought alone invigorated me to heights I knew impressed her. As we lay there, afterwards, my brother entered, acknowledged nothing, and left.

I was convinced she preferred me to him, and so became infatuated with her. Something about me pleased her more than him, I thought, but it was difficult not to act as I thought he would. No matter how I tried, I couldn't get a sense of what it was in me she liked. She was so cool and aloof. She smoked and fit her fingernails together, a sheet up to her waist. I thought of putting my head on her stomach as I used to do with Dahlia, but it didn't fit this woman's style.

As I look back to the dream, the way to have fit her style would have been to scratch my pits, knock the cigarette out of her mouth and grunt to her groans while letting those nails work my back. It was a case of my having idolized something ugly. It was clear until I woke that I was like a gold digger who found maggots in the garbage and thought he was frolicking with ingots and gold bars.

Even after I woke, I was filled with a sense that something he'd loved preferred me to him. But inside me was also a recognition of my blind sickness. To be satisfied at all was the contentment of a dog licking a filthy plate not out of hunger or in search of food but because it was his master's, and I knew that not even a dog would do that.

Another night I dreamed that I was having some difficulty returning to my father's car where I knew I'd left my brother's body in the trunk. The longer it took me to get there, the more difficult it would be to dispose of the body properly. It wouldn't be long before my father would open the trunk. It wouldn't take much to tie the murder to me.

When I neared the house, I was first disoriented, then distracted. I couldn't find it. Where the house had been, there was a store. I entered and found it was filled with pornography. I quickly forgot that it wasn't my home and browsed through the magazines, amazed at the depths to which pornographers had sunk.

On the cover of one magazine was a dog. His snout was all wet up to his eyes. God only knows where he'd been sticking it. The other publications were as bad if not worse. It repulsed me, but I was drawn to it for some reason. It was just another step in a regression but I had the comfort and discomfort of not being alone. There were many people reading the magazines as if they were used to them. I had vowed never to accept such things, but I looked at them anyway. I was shocked that I was excited, awakened to having compromised myself but wanting to see more. While pouring over this garbage, I drooled and guarded a feeling that I was a good person. Then I recalled that I was a murderer and had business to attend to. I tried to leave.

On my way out of the store, I saw a young lady in one of those photo booths where one can have pictures in a minute. Her smile was so friendly that I approached her. Our conversation was so natural that my inhibitions melted away, and I found myself, as in a drunken state, tied to all good things and believing that everything was possible.

As I kissed her, I wanted to pass on this sense of well-being, to convey my profound sense of trust. Intoxicated, I felt our soul strands wrapping us into one neat little ball, never to be undone. All these feelings shooting through me, were they shooting through her as well, or were they merely being mirrored back to me?

It was as if we were being filmed. A picture was developing slowly in my mind. As the resolution became more and more clear, the enveloping blanket of security unraveled, and I remembered the body in the trunk. How foolish to think I could find or offer any kind of peace! I suddenly began to recognize features in the building. It was my house, but it had been reorganized to throw me off guard. I heard a car engine start. My heart raced.

That ended the spell. Filled with guilt, I clambered like a crab chased out of the sea to scavenge the fetid flotsam and crustaceous defender of the jetsam on the beaches of a dog's nose. As I ran outside, I was blinded by thousands of flashes, each one making an exposure of one of the horde of confessions pouring out of my mind. The records were compiled and stored where I could be reached by the inquisition when it arrived.

Police Blotter

I was just reading a book that mentioned that Nero fiddled as Rome was burning. I wonder, what was he going to do as emperor, get in the fire line and pass water buckets? If Washington, D.C. started burning, you can be sure the President would take little part in the effort to save the city before being whisked off to safety. I have a certain sympathy for Nero, not because he was actually fiddling instead of taking matters more seriously, but because I believe he was just caught doing something normal but which just made him look bad, even crazy at the time. That image has stuck through history, and yes, I realize that Nero was extremely eccentric, that he enjoyed acting on stage and was far from being a typical emperor, but one could argue that once someone is tagged as nuts, he's scrutinized such that only negative data is collected.

I once did something that made me look stupid when I became a police officer. That career only lasted a few weeks because I just couldn't hack the pretense. My commanding officer, the Sarge, took everything so seriously that he never let up on me. Shoes had to be spit shined. Ties had to be perfect. I could only address him as "Sir," or "Sergeant, Sir." That kind of protocol was never going to change with him, but I guess I didn't take it seriously enough, and he leaned on me hard for making a few too many mistakes.

Then came my moment of fiddling while Rome burned. I'd only been on the force for a couple of weeks when we got a call that a woman had called emergency to report some kind of attack. It was not clear if she'd been killed or had only fainted. She screamed or blurted something about her attacker's escape through a window after barricading the door from the inside. We coordinated with the fire department, and they met us there with a hook-and-ladder truck. I was chosen to go up the ladder and climb in the open window to remove the barricade and open the door to let in the police and an emergency medical team.

So I climbed up, went through the window, and found the lady unconscious on the floor. She was breathing normally, it seemed to me, but she didn't respond to my questions. But I'm no doctor, and since help was on the way, I just put a blanket over her, then removed the barricade, unlocked the door and opened it a few inches.

Now this lady had a full-size mirror right in the living room, and after I opened the door, I caught sight of myself. My uniform was a little messy from climbing up, and thinking the Sarge was about to come in, I thought I'd better straighten up. So I tucked in my shirt, fixed my tie, took off my cap and was combing my hair when they all came through and looked at me where I stood frozen like I was some kind of total screw-up Elvis impersonator who only thinks of combing his hair when someone is maybe dying on the floor.

Well that was me being Nero. It was a perfectly natural thing as far as I'm concerned. Some of it was the Sarge's fault because if he hadn't been so damned demanding about my appearance, I would not have been so wound up all the time trying to make sure everything was in impeccable order.

Now in Nero's case, maybe he thought the Roman people felt he should behave in a manner consistent with leadership, that he had to show some kind of grace at all times, a fearlessness and a getting-on-with-life in the face of watching life going down the tubes. Maybe he looked from the palace all that he could until he'd had enough. And then perhaps only music could mollify his torment. I don't know, but it's generally projected and universally accepted that Nero was deranged for this action which may have been a harmless incident or even one caused by being in his position. In such cases as these, I believe it is the people who are culpable, not those charged, judged and sentenced without a trial. I did what I was told, all that I could do under the circumstances, but later I was treated as harshly as if I were the criminal himself caught in that woman's apartment.

I was slowly drummed out of the corps for that one. I could hear the snickering as soon as we returned to the station. I found a comb and hand mirror on my desk along with a new lipstick. Then the Sarge started to collect data on me that had nothing to do with my job performance. He and a couple of other officers went into my apartment when I was not there. He questioned my integrity because he found the bathtub dirty and towels on the floor. Once when I was getting out of the patrol car I tripped and skinned my knee, ripping a hole in my pants. I was put on report for improper dress, and twice that day barely avoided tripping several times when legs were deliberately stuck out from cubicles as I walked down the hall. It got to the point that there was nothing I could do right, and so I left the department. I didn't want anyone connecting me to the experience either, so I left town, and I never admitted to having been a police officer to anyone. I kept my scanner to listen to the emergency calls, but I started a whole new career.

Then one night I heard the department where I'd worked was on fire. I immediately drove over there as fast as I could and, man, that place was really up in flames. The fire trucks were already there spraying, but it was already so consumed that I doubt they really saved anything. I didn't want anyone connecting me to it, so I sat in my car in a corner of the grocery store parking lot laughing my head off listening to music on the radio.

When I read about Nero later, the details weren't important. Just the one fact itself was enough for me to identify with him personally, and I don't care whatever else he may have done during his reign. I'm not saying had I been with him in the palace at the time I would have joined him in a duet, but down with all petty-protocol authoritarians like the Sarge, and all hail the music of sweet revenge.

The Old Sun

Damned old sun, up there high and glaring. I don't care why. The last day of September was hot. Closing my eyes, it almost felt like July, but something in the breezes said it was the fall season. Then I looked to see that the colors of autumn had begun integrating the cityscapes. There was a bright yellow tree here, an orange one there, and some trees tipped pale like a hairdo.

I remember that day because it signaled the end of a long process of maturity. In these last weeks, the air froze, and the leaves turned brown and dropped. Now snow carpets everything. In September, I could watch many facets of a process unfold. Now, nothing seems to change.

But winter cleanses like fire. We wriggle in and out of shelters, shivering. We have no yearly parallel to the seasons. Age claims every generation in its turn, but what we really need is an annual winter scaling, a long sleep, a changing of colors all around.

September could be a month of kind goodbyes until the spring. The world could be frozen, razed clean, and the new spring would not be a picking up of last year's leaves, but the budding of new growth.

Too bad. We have all the symbols, but they are semblances. In our nature we do not gain peace from ultimacy, nor is there rejuvenation unless we let go of something, which amounts to everything we have in this world.

Number one I am not tired, so don't get the idea that this is. What I'm thinking has to do with this: that the way the world is

The Old Sun

crowded makes the work a person does completely different. Right now, if we were all up in the North Woods, then there would be no trees. But the point is that if you were to take a novel from a stranger, freshly written, and take it to your room in the city, you'd be so harried you wouldn't be able to give it a just appraisal. If you were to try to write one, it would be the same thing. Imagine it this way: you are standing in a space, and all around you, occupying all the other spaces, are the others. The others stand there, just waiting for your notes to fall out of your pocket. When they do, just try to get them back. They'll be read, and summarily rejected. What business have you, an ordinary person, to think you have the right to think anything around here? Let me put it another way. If you could see the way that you're limited by others, you'd wish to have it all back. I mean the world without bounds. We have all lost the world in which we can move without someone making us worry where we're moving. Something will stop us all. Frankly, nothing can save us. Do you think that there is anything you can do about anything?

One way to look at it is to think of vacuum-packing. Something has plastic wrap placed over it, and it is sealed by heating the wrap and removing the air from it. There are no gaps. Now take people. Everyone's mind is vacuum-packed. No one feels any gaps. A stupid person doesn't feel empty spaces waiting for knowledge to occupy. The spaces have all been vacuumed out. Even if this idiot went out and read a thousand books of interest, there would still be a sense of vacuum-packing, but a greater hunger to stretch out the packing, and increase the contents. Ignorance truly is bliss, and there is plenty in the world to keep it from trying to expand. Those who do acquire knowledge have to face the fact that it is a difficult commodity to pass on. It is a rolling ball with no holes to fall into, constantly in motion, bouncing off everyone.

I suppose I am somewhat tired now that I think of it. I exit the crowd and still exist in it. The crowd. That is really what is insane. Not one person, one murderer or any one idea. No excess is too excessive. A community of those who diverge greatly from the norms will tend to make happier freaks, and balance the unbalanced. It is hell for a unique entity to find no kindred mutant. There are hardened waves in nature, and the fresh dunes are doomed to be eroded. We need a synthesis of sorts, and when everything sorts itself out in its terms, the world will be no more or less broken up, nor held together.

Here I am dozing off to sleep again, quietly depressed. Why have I not accomplished anything? Now I am dreaming. A woman who lives next door to me appears. She is an aspiring actress, but in this dream she is a dancer. I am on stage out of sight, watching her perform. She's wearing a sparkling leotard, and her body is so very nice. I am admiring it more than the dance, or am I? I am admiring the way her body moves, and that is the dance.

She looks over to the side where her sister sends her ideas. Given these ideas, she struts them out, as if they are just occurring to her. It occurs to me that the audience must see her as spontaneous, while really, she is being fed. All this fear I had of being on stage myself was unnecessary. I was always afraid that I would freeze, but given instructions, there is not that problem. Even so, even the idea of getting out there turns me to stone. Only the sight of her body melts me. I feel my heart pounding.

Lately I haven't been remembering too many dreams. I suppose it must have something to do with my drinking habits. My face shows that I've been drinking to others just as my mind shows it to me. I am not the same man I should be. I am just self-destructive enough to take myself in chunks from time to time. In two weeks I can chip a good part of my soul away before recovering. Six months later, I take another chunk off. I'd really rather let life erode me naturally, but for some reason, I am like the powerless Ozymandias whose "vast and trunkless legs stand in the desert" and whose "shattered visage lies" near them. There is nothing I can do about what I am doing to myself.

I am carved from stone, and I am watching myself fall apart. I have locked myself backstage in the shadows of the dance, and the lone and level sands stretch inwardly.

What are the motions I am going through? With the sickbed and the grave somewhere in the distance, are not all these things I do meaningless diversions from the truth? What if I were to isolate precepts on the nature of living. Wouldn't those ideas be an obfuscation of reality, which is that I am going to die?

What else though can we do but live? We do not choose the era or the circumstances of our lives. In this ultimacy, we try to build a safe refuge in which we can see enough safe days ahead to calmly forget the ultimate reality that we face, and so we go about our lives, through the motions, getting caught up in the era's trends, in what we perceive as being important to others. Intimations of immortality may exist in childhood, but they evolve into delusions by the time we are adults.

Personally, my biggest problem is not being honest with myself. This carries over to others, who I never really face as I am because I've never really faced myself. What they get is a blurred version of what I should be. I have a constant sense of the disparity.

It is interesting that much of this stems from the privacy of lives around me. Due to the nature of individuals, each with his own insecurities, fears, hopes, doubts, experiences, there is raging caution and superficiality; and not much possibility of deep connection with any others.

I would say that to truly connect with anyone, I'd have to sit down and spill the beans, but it would be like tipping a cornucopia, endlessly pouring forth its immeasurable hoard, which is my cycle of delusions. Who could love me for that? And so, for fear of not being loved, I act in order to gain confidence.

Once any connection is made, it must be fed and fortified with new lies, such that soon I feel no great gain but the pain of having deceived. It is by then too difficult to explain how it all happened, and because even at that point I am concerned with how I seem, I find a way to end the relationship consistent with the role in which I have falsely portrayed myself. The irony, though it may seem cynical, is that very few people escape this kind of syndrome; only they do not feel the disparity in despair.

I have tried to make sense out of the syndromes that force us into such modes. It is frustrating when I feel I need to be with someone, to not be able to find anyone with whom I can feel comfortable about being totally open. People just don't want that. The manners we must adopt in socializing make us dupes. Once we set out in such narrow ways, the stage is set to nearly eliminate broadening and turning back. We become the creatures of customs which make us neurotic, but the customs are the opium from whose grip we cannot withdraw.

The sickness is that there is comfort in the shallows, in strangers that listen with interest to our exaggerations and watch in awe as we show them the high water marks of our experiences which are really no more than a finger dipped in a thimble. We turn our backs to our own recognition of our own base aspects just as we run full circle far from those who uncovered our lies right into someone new on whom we can spill our endless, fabricated stream. The motions we go through are of diminishing reliance on spirit and truth. We supplant feeling, communication, and honesty, thinning our lives to what society expects of us, with dissimulation and lies, and plow our hollow souls through our day and age.

We human beings, not content with living reality, try to recreate it. Whether it be in the form of entertainment on TV, in books or paintings, reality is all created from the mind, and depicts life, well or badly, realistically or unrealistically, seriously or not so seriously. Life has us talking about life. Reality is unspoken.

All of our attempts are removed from life. They are interpretations. When the entire human race is gone, what it will have left on the planet, though not all specifically designed and intended to be its archives (but very definitely its archives) will be millions of movies, books, sit-coms, soap operas, et cetera, to judge us by, as though that were a true depiction of life.

In the face of reality, we choose to escape and reward those who are successful at helping us to escape. One of the only ways an individual can hope to communicate is through entertainment carrying buried messages pertaining to life. Life's ultimacies are so heavy on us that we can only bear realizing the true weight occasionally, yet we spend most of our energies chattering about life in the general effort to divert ourselves in the (near) universal cover-up.

Life is a masquerade, and knowledge must go dressed to the party. Few can guess what it is, and it does not win the prize. Occasionally, knowledge streaks through naked and is arrested for indecent exposure. Mankind wants death painted up like Cleopatra so he can sleep with it and has painted knowledge to look like death so he does not have to look.

As a world race we have embedded all the truths in palatable forms of beauty, all the more beautiful because of the embedded truth, but we nevertheless enjoy it for the beauty, and with the same desire to enjoy, not to realize, we conjure a myriad of ways to keep ourselves occupied on cushions unembedded with any truth.

It's not an endless swim, but it's an endless sea. The human flow is the only flood I know. My mind and spirit amount to little in the vast desperation, but mean nothing outside of it. What words that might get through to link us must be true.

Someone has died. The family is fighting over what was left behind. The only thing that matters is they will all die. We all will make a desert equal to the vast silent deserts of the past. The nature that gets us fighting over a bowl, ignoring death, is passed on.

What messages get through to us? Everyone will die is a dusty slogan tacked on a placard somewhere in our thoughts. We do not sweep the cobwebs from it. Occasionally, a sudden *I am going to die* sign is seen as in a flash of lightning through a window. Briefly. That and the ensuing thunder may scare us. There may be a succession of flashes, uneasiness, and a sudden storm. But an intoxicating fatigue soon develops. Air through the window smells fresher, and sleep overcomes us. Dreams fill the mind. Light streams through the window in the morning, and the darkness, storm, lightning and flashing sign are not so frightening in hindsight. A warm hand then pulls us back into life. Hundreds of days pass. Someone we know well dies. We grieve at the loss and fervently claim a bowl promised us though it means a fight. Win or lose, we carry bitterness from the event, just as we remember love from another moment, until everything we carry is spread out like so many grains of salt on a sidewalk out of a

The Long Beat of the Metronome

broken shaker. The glass is swept away. Rain washes through the desert, dissolving the salt as it goes. By the time it cascades over marble cliffs, it perfectly matches and blends with the sea.

A thousand philosophies confuse me. My dreams are disturbing. I am enlightened by history to the point of disbelief in everything. It would seem that to our collective eyes, the planets and the galaxies are molecular bodies spinning like clockwork in gravitational balance, with an occasional stray comet, meteor or asteroid. We stand in momentary awe of the stillness of the universe which dissipates like foam when the rising sun evaporates the dew, and then we join the ranks of a weary army marching back from battle over the dead body of the element of surprise, which was our youth.

I know all this from experience. I took an interest during this era, my brief span, in my work, in my family, in wanting to change things, but eventually I took things as they are, which came as a result of not being able to take chances anymore. Why try to settle mysteries or dig deeper when there are bigger headaches, worries at work and problems in society? Why ask questions of the world when the world has its own way of working? A dog knows enough to take the world as it is, and it goes about its business. The stars shine above for the dog the same as they do for me. The dog does not ask what is really there. But I used to ask questions. I searched for the meaning of life, but what I found was that we merely adopted old ways rather than seek to discover the truth and follow its path.

So we leave the fate of the world is in the hands of fools whose political maneuvering is far from smooth and beyond stopping. The greater part of the world struggles to survive. It argues, not nobly, destroys the habitats of wild life and reproduces incessantly. Even the few who contemplate life and reach an understanding cannot change the world. The understanding they reach is that the world cannot be changed.

All around us is pressure. Each tries to exert an influence on everyone else. No one is a witness, few are believers, yet everyone is ignorant, shrink-wrapped in what is believed to be wisdom though it calls anyone who has an alternate point of view ignorant. One artist's poor try is taken by some as the truth, and another artist's profundity is missed, mistaken and taken out with the trash. In time, our body and soul are fraught with frustrations like the various markings and scars on a tree. The weathered trunk thinks it's getting too little sunlight that it doesn't even need. The branches argue about position and who's blocking their light. The whole forest complains it is besieged by hordes of petty bites chipping away at its bark and leaves. You can hear it if you listen closely. To our ears it's a most beautiful sound, a haunting rustle that lulls us to peaceful sleep, and in the morning, we brush ourselves clean of the residue of dreams that tell us an ignorant force is bent on eating us away. Alarmed, we head out blindly ourselves to chew on anything that seems to move against us. Whatever doesn't, like all those rocks inscribed with names of the dead, is there to focus our compass needle on passing through obstructions we cannot see. There are so many waves that would drown us, but we can raise them as Moses did the Red Sea. In the proper perspective, the spectre of our own death, once an army on our heels, is destroyed as the waves collapse.

What looks like a compass needle swings under the hour, not in seconds, but in increments so much longer that nobody can keep in step. It does not seem to move, but it has been wound to measure out one undulation equal to the length of our life. It is the timing as it comes to a dead stop that determines our forward motion, the one step at a time building of our lives over the long haul. Without a sense of the rhythm with no seeming sense or pattern to it, we have no real hope of mastering any pattern to our lives, and so we tend to drift with millions of others from paycheck to paycheck, meal to meal. The cemetery is a sharpening stone for the pendulum, honing our focus for a limited time as well. It increases the performance of the engine momentarily, even allowing us to sense the whole swing to realize that there is some kind of pattern, extending back through names we lost, and forward to our own removal from the field of play. A sense of panic and purpose obscures the reality and general distancing that defines our approach to reality. It runs one step behind us rather than ahead of us. We call the shots, and when the needle tells us that we're headed right for it, the mirroring is too harsh, so we find a park along the shores that crashed our enemy death into submission. We take a breather to sweep fear from the mind. We grow determined to live in the moment and forget trying to leap from one era to the next. We give up the dream of using the needle, seemingly stalled under the hour, as a guide for a single thread to pull our life together just once. We open a bottle and raise a glass to the sea, turning red as blood gushes from the gaping hole in us onto the beach. What we don't realize is how this awakens the water to respond to prayers on the other side for the waters to part, just as they did for us. Others will pass safely as we did and bleed out for others who will come. We find the needles are connected, that we are sewn to others we do not know.

Even so, there is an innately-embedded desire to require no connections; to be able to subsist wholly independent so no loss can shake us. There's a mystical promise of such a state acquired through faith, but it comes in the midst of also being linked. It is promised that when these links are broken, the greater understanding will relieve any sense of loss. When I am threatened with a loss, I sense how great a thing this peace would be. When a link is cut from me, I cry for the benefits of this great promise, yet my only way back to peace is to acquire new lines that will draw out blood for the sea as compensation for the loss. So again I stand with my line cut, turning the sea red, and across the sea, an act of deliverance is in progress. I can feel them reacting to the emergency, having cogent dreams, feeling clear upon waking, crossing safely where there was deep water a moment before and watching death destroyed behind.

If it's true that there's a chamber where my bones will be interred, is it not true that there is a place where one day I will be able to contemplate all mysteries of life and death, peacefully alone? Why do I not desire a state in direct association with what the world offers and instead cry to be whole? Where is the collective cry that goes generally unheard, whose signal originates on the red beach in moonlight? Rather than listen for it, we angle for position and nip at one another ad infinitum until one day we require peace. And so we find ourselves at a wall of water where we acquire a sense of how to live our one long beat of the metronome through a simple pattern so painfully clear. A transfusion enables us to cross through parted waves; once there, we'll return our life's blood to the sea.

All of the things I have on my mind cluster like fingers of a clenched fist which is my brain as I lay down to relax and sleep for the night. Slowly the press and struggle of pressure begins to ease up, and by degrees the fingers separate into figures in the darkness of my distracted thoughts. They have been infused with different personalities, unbeknownst to me, representing the characteristics of those things that were on my mind during the day, those things left undone and all that I soon must do.

As they finally don the dream garb as I begin to slip off, I become a mere listener to their incessant bickering. I exist somewhere in a central darkness as they waft around me at each others' throats on principle. They do not have faces, but I know each voice and must learn to pry open my mind from the combined force clamping down. In my freedom as I listen to them fight, I am amazed at my disinterest in their words.

I find myself only wondering what costume I've supplied the actors this time because the language is beyond me. My interpretation is strictly intuitive, but it goes something like this: I am a stage for their dance which will be forgotten, and even their motivations, personifications, will fall behind me in tomorrow's new waking drive to do something, anything, of merit in this world. By nightfall, in symbolic disintegrative drifting toward death and the spirit world beyond life, I will witness my own stiff pride detach its seals and release itself. The actors will take shape in the release, and in their embattled pictures I'll find indications in vague or lucid memories, intuitions of some strange meaning pertaining to my life, resolutions that will aid me without my knowing how or why as I sense symmetry in the enigmas. The stress will be eased by this far more than sleep, and I'll find more room in the daily armor into which I slip my bones. But the day will be as unbearable once I hit the road. I hardly ever consider my journals of these strange shapes and symbols that I keep in my heart. Before the front lines of the world I must face, I wouldn't even admit that I keep such things.

A New Moon

Dark the night, so damned dark, with specks of light. The new moon is what, a night without a moon, and so we start fresh from a void. What is a beginning if it carries with it everything from before? Landing somewhere but receiving packages from a previous life to bring you up to speed. That does not count. But let me tell you something. Being born isn't the only way that such a thing happens. Yes, it certainly does not require the same force of argument as it is fairly obvious. Whatever you are began with your birth. It was a true beginning, and no other beginning you make in your life can be compared as having the same clean surface of the tabula rasa, as both the mind and body are fresh into the game, never having been here before. But somewhere along the line, there is a at least the possibility of a total change in spirit, an awakening if you will, and it is this kind of beginning and only this that might be said to compete with birth as it is a new spirit that emerges, nothing like the old one, nor does it require any of the baggage that still may be present. Even if everything is kept, it does not impede or weigh down the new spirit.

How would I know this if I had not achieved it? Can anyone trust the witness, or must they witness something for themselves? All the directions of where the path lies and how to follow it are concealed in paradox, but there is inherent beauty in the words such that one who is ready to hear and follow them is able to distinguish the true melody from the song of the sirens, constantly calling, and paddle through the various signals into the deep night, almost as if the way to go is marked by darkness. Avoid the light. Avoid it all costs, it

A New Moon

seems to say. This is the way. It is the way of the new moon. Begin the journey in total darkness, and do not fear tripping over anything as you walk because you will not be using your legs, nor is a paddle necessary. You take with you only what was given to you in your birth. Nothing else is required. That is the beauty of it.

Another facet of its glory is how it can envelop you without warning as if it had a mind of its own to cast a net over your life and capture you. The darkness is sudden and total, even horrifying, but there is nowhere to go, no way back. It is the same as being born into the world for the first time except at that moment there was no direct consciousness to compare the state of existence to anything previously known or unknown. Now, you have everything before you, years of memory and consciousness, to bring to bear on what is happening, but none of it can shed light on it because that is the darkness, paradoxically. The darkness is everything you were, all that you knew. But all that is an old sun, gone from the sky, overshadowed by so many years of a life developing an opaque totality that may at some point undergo the black flash point, whereupon it becomes a whole new sky, a new canopy without stars or light of any kind, under which this whole new beginning may take shape.

And so it is required that one live for many years in utter ignorance that the light he thinks he sees is false. The prerequisite for the epiphany is to live a lie so long that it may ignite in the same way that a black hole, having collected all that it possibly can becomes a pathway to another dimension. So it is impossible to declare to anyone what path must be taken when he does not have enough baggage to undergo the transformation naturally. The saddest thing that can happen is that one will somehow manage to avoid the experience of the metamorphosis, to go from broad daylight to total blackness and know suddenly and all at once that finally he has been born. The darkness of a new moon stands ready to pervade. All one need do is live, accepting this or denying it. It does not matter. It is all up to unknown factors operating in such a way such that all at once from out of nowhere the whole process suddenly starts rolling, and there you are, without any bearings at all, realizing that your whole life, everything that stretches behind you is a total lie, and all that awaits you is all that you were ever born to receive, which is the first point of light, not visible in itself but realized intuitively, and becomes the first thing in an empty hand, not the hands themselves but a spirit in the shape of a beggar, needing something, anything, to explain what has happened, but unable to accept any explanation, only able to discern what is true, even if it be that nothing makes any sense but this total shroud of darkness, and the hope that everything in the new life will begin to take shape, and that understanding is real, substantial, and not the equivalent of the enveloping shroud.

In and out of the endless riddle I go, speaking of a cloud in the distance as it moves overhead in response to what appears to be a call I've made by the mere consideration of the endlessness of it all. I find myself listening to the crickets that will be gone by the first frost, and back again next summer, but these are unique lives, singing together, and at the same time repeat beings, like us, equipped with something that makes them what they are and distinguishes them from all other beings even with so short a life. I have realized there is something to pondering the mountain of external insect skeletons that comes and goes into the dirt. If such a thing were to exist, we might pass it in awe and compare it to coral in the sea, as a reminder to the brevity of life, and wonder why we had bothered to collect them all. In the end, we are not able to gather in the immensity of the plankton. Surveying the heavens, we consider ourselves masters somehow, set up here for a purpose when our own bones however the handling is an improvement, still sink into the earth and are forgotten.

The immense formations in the distance do not belittle but rather magnify me and force me to examine what about me does not match up against these wondrous backdrops. Should I not fear them and keep the children warm when I should be preparing them for the coming Ice Age or would that just fly in the face of evidence suggesting the end will come before they come of age? What does it mean to recognize the future as a fulfillment of the continuation of all things? Why do we need to express it as an unexpected explosion caused by our not properly preparing the smokestacks, which we have retrofitted with funds that would have made schools better, but what use are schools after we have choked ourselves suddenly and violently to a sudden end?

I am working the vault of a new heaven today, chipping away the pervasive blackness, hoping to unveil what is underneath, but the spaces fill in where the dark chips have fallen, and before I can collect them, they have already been swooped up by worshippers in the sanctuary for the fact that they are part of the new revelation, a thing to hold that is not a vestige of the past when things were held to the degradation of the soul. These are rather things that can be held up to those still walking in under the old sun, lenses to peer through to get a glimpse of what might come when the weight of experience finally presses in and reaches its dark flash point. There is a community of souls that have changed, only they do not necessarily live together. Most are long since gone, but the shards they have left from scraping the ceiling are still tightly held, even regulated in some places, and still in others, banned under pain of death.

An ancient angelfish, or something very like it, found between the rocks, its bones embossing the stone, is far away now, so far out in a kind of space that we add it to an already huge nebulosity somewhere in the back of the mind, where it wanders, nipping in its day again, in its pond, not in an ancient world, but swirling in our thoughts, somehow compelling, not for any clear reason, more like the way a dream hangs on in the morning looking for interpretation, a cracking open as it were to reveal a crystalline cave in miniature that took thousands of years to form in a bubble until it became an object of desire due to some connection with its being different, conveying something of eternity, of beginnings, somewhere, that might in its presence, in its calling, hold a key insofar as it awakens a quest, a yearning, an inner search that discerns something distinct, not nebulous, though it is anything but clear, and nothing that can be put into language, possibly not even approximated well, and yet one knows when one is near it, when it is being detailed or tracked, which is happening at this moment, and if you have come this far into the darkness, and detect within yourself an agency at work gathering what amounts to less than an aura, then you have an awakened intuition, a spirit that feeds on such rarified suggestions, diluted as they may be, detecting the distillable intensities as being already fathomable in the complete silences within, that these are all waters of the angelfish, falling to the bottom, packed in the silt, and lifted out once again in a splitting of slate into a splash of wordless pull as if on a line held out for survival, for food, something to be stripped down to bone, the bones removed intact and buried respectfully next to the fire, embers sailing upward against the black vault of the night sky, tiny super novas turning to nebulas as wide as the crab itself, scurrying across the bottom nearby, its claws nipping at the tiny lights reflected on the surface, dividing them up into millions in concentric waves. Such a moment as this is the end of all specks of light and heralds the rising of a new moon.

Legion of Ghosts

Robert Frost said, *Good fences making good neighbors*, but these days we need more than that. For me, a fence is not enough because local code restrictions do not allow one higher than six feet for basic privacy, and there are instances where the best you can get is your typical low-to-the-ground, white picket variety with a cute gate. This style is more of an accent than a statement, and with my neighbors, I have to be on the lookout constantly, and the Middle Ages serve better for ideas than my local hardware store.

The neighbors across the street are pathetic, and though I have good reason to attack them, to do so would only make them slightly more miserable than they already are if it would do anything at all. It is enough to know that there is little I can do to make things worse for them, though I can't help but look out the window and sometimes feel the anger and disgust for them turn to pity. There's nothing anyone can do to make them happy, so pity is not appropriate. I hate feeling sorry for them. I try rather to ignore them, which is hard when I'm angry. It makes me want to look at them.

As for bothering me, from their perspective, there is a river between us, more like a moat that actually surrounds my house, and there is a moat around their house as well. More than me, they are the kind of people that enjoy sitting out front with a line in the water, but they wouldn't dare even come close to me, not even to look into the water. They stay where they are. They have their own water, and I can see they look at me like some kind of bait. Yes, all I am to them is a mud slug that has ventured out of the water onto the opposite bank. Nothing would please them more than to capture me and put me on a hook and dangle it in the water, but they also know that they would have to cross the water first, and they fear what might be in the water, so they pretty much keep to themselves. It could be a nice neighborhood, but the whole street is a winding river full of leeches, hungry leeches, out for blood. Nobody around here would ever think to communicate with reason and intelligence, preferring rather to wait for emotion to force them into outbursts of profanity, with lots of yelling. Yelling is necessary because of the fences, the moats and other barriers between dwellings, and since nobody can stand the fact that others will quickly open their windows to glean some new gossip, arguments are kept very short, and only rarely can one hear any long shouting, and it usually turns out to be kids arguing in the park.

My main adversaries are Jack, the head of the family that lives across the street, and Barry who lives on the other side of me completely. Jack loves power toys. He has a motorcycle that turns into a boat the second he rides it down his driveway. The thing has a powerful motor on it which he gives full throttle the second he hits the water, at which point he puffs his chest out at the helm. Again, this is good for mud slug picking, and his wife and children usually run out to the bank and collect the fresh batch just waiting to be scooped out. I can't go over to see their moat because it would indicate that I have some kind of interest in their pathetic lives, which seem more than anyone around here to revolve around that water.

Paula, Jack's wife, can hardly bend over to pick anything up. She looks like a pair of olives separated by a marshmallow, with two toothpicks for legs. The clothes she wears are so bright and tight, that the mud slugs must wonder what monster it is above them as they catch a glimpse of her through the shallow murky water. They must burrow deeper into the mud whenever she is near. It is not beneath her to stoop solely to smash mud slugs into the mud. She likes to kick them out of the water onto her lawn and twist her foot over them until there's nothing recognizable. It is like her face after she covers it with all the make-up she uses, bearing no resemblance to what she looks like without it. The mud slug paste is very dark and slimy and works very well as both mascara and eye shadow.

These are people who know how to live off the land. The river is their life, and it provides for them.

It is almost a religion with people like this to use everything up and count on nature to replace it. They come out in the morning to wash their laundry. The filth brings up the mud slugs, which they pick off as they wring out the water. They dump all of their garbage into the water as well, and they have a dog who bounds up and down the shore picking spots where there are plenty of mud slugs to jump in to swim around. One would think they would give the dog a bath since it stinks of the muddy waters, but to them, that is the smell of the earth, and they like it.

The three kids, two young girls and one little boy, are generally unhappy and unsupervised. Strange, but children seem to have an innate grasp of a situation's absurdity before they completely adopt it at some point. The girls have looked for years like they were waiting for a riverboat to arrive and take them out of that hole, but now they are expert mud slug attractors. The boy is lonely beyond words since the family has carved itself such a life away from civilization. It is obvious he just wants to be a boy, and Jack cannot understand why the mud, the dog and the river aren't enough, and so he yells at the boy constantly and is miserable with a fat wife though he's fat himself. He mistreats everyone but himself, whom he rewards with plenty of beer, sitting on the front porch sulking and throwing the empty cans in the water, which the mud slugs only love too well. As the evening draws to a close, he staggers off the porch to the riverbank and takes a piss into the school of mud slugs swirling in the lamp light at the end of the driveway. This seems to drive away more mud slugs than it draws in, or perhaps it's that they instinctively know to swim from the net he dips in to scoop them up on shore. These are not for bait but to feed the dog, which has been waiting nearby for just such a treat. Done for the day, Jack stretches, belches, and heads inside for the couch where Polly forces him to sleep when he drinks on the porch to all hours of the morning. Even she can't stand him and insults him by calling him a mud slug.

In the morning he attacks everyone with his mighty hangover. The girls cry, and the boy picks up on how the adult male behaves and goes out with his pellet gun to shoot mud slugs. He watches the river as various boats go up and down. It's a fairly active stretch of water, and there are lots of boats, but none ever stops by to visit. They're all on their way to other destinations. He takes potshots at them when they're far enough away to give him time to hide. He's broken a few windows, but he has never been caught.

Enough about them. I want to mention Barry, who is worse. Years ago, when I was building the fence, we had a brief conversation about the method of construction, but he seemed more interested in whether my permit was filled in correctly, and I was filled with suspicion. Sure enough, when I was constructing a tower in the back, which is technically a two-story shed that is higher than all the houses, offering a good vantage point to look into his yard, he complained to the authorities, and they came over for a surprise inspection only to find my permit was in order. After that, he goes out of his way to turn his back on me. I've ignored him for years, but it's still irritating to see a man waiting for me to notice that he's staring me down so he can turn his back. If he's far enough away, he just stares and stares, but when he's close, he turns his back, looking over his shoulder from time to time to check my exact location in order to make adjustments. He likes to keep his back perpendicular to me.

Now, what he doesn't realize is that the tower is my way of watching him. The structure is the symbol of my superiority, my never flinching desire to face him so as to force him to keep his back turned to me. The building is also set in perfect position to block the sun from his garden for many hours in the afternoon, and I know this has had a detrimental effect on his yield. But despite the fact that the tower is within the compound surrounded by the fence, I have extended the moat and equipped the tower with electronic listening and monitoring devices. He used to come out front more, but now he spends his time in his back yard, so I'm beginning to feel like I finally have the setup I need to sit back and relax. Maybe I'll write a book about an army that storms across the moat to tear a castle apart when a king dies, only to find that they are a legion of ghosts who can do nothing but watch helplessly as a new king is born.

The Power of Hate

I have managed to have as much power as anyone could ever dream of having, enough to dispense goodness over countless millions of countrymen, and if I desire, evil on those who have in any way offended me in my life. My signature is all that it takes to fill a fleet of cargo planes with provisions to bring relief to an entire state in distress, but at the same time, I am in the unique position to separate an enemy or two from those benefits if I happen to be so inclined. On the whole, I would say that my general feeling is of kindness to all, but I do confess a certain unremitting and unforgiving coldness to a few I will never forgive for what they did to me, and while others enjoy the sacks of rice and boxes of cheese I send to their flooded city, to the others, what I deliver to them will be served very cold, you can be sure of that.

Now we are all facing a terrible disaster. The president has selected me to decide who is to be saved and who will die when the asteroid crashes into the earth. I know already who won't survive. I have made a list of names of all those I warned that one day I would get them. I've spent years making them miserable by my success. As manager of public works, aviation and recreation, I had their land condemned and built parks, or a yacht club where I have placed my own fine ship. But this is different. I now have a chance to see them come begging to try to make friends again and be one of the few to join my entourage to escape the blast. But I have a surprise in store for them. I already invited everyone I have selected to be spared, and all that is left is to express to those who cannot go the deepest and most sincere apologies from the government that life is about to end for them. Of course, there are some that I do not know, people for whom I am sad that we cannot find a place for them, and I will meet with them, but to those others I hate, there will only be a form letter, and it will be mailed the day before the disaster so that they will not receive it in time. They will be in darkness before the darkness falls. Isn't that scrumptious?

I am feeling nothing but happiness that I'll be among the leaders of a whole new civilization on whatever planet we colonize. The fear is that earth will be destroyed. Our ship will survey the destruction, and if it can be determined that it will recover, we will stay on the moon for as long as it takes before returning. There is already a secret base there that will sustain us for years, so our greatest hope is that some day we will return, maybe sooner than we think.

Now, as our ship is getting ready to take off, it suddenly occurs to me that these enemies of mine might do something to sabotage the ship, that they might place something in the engine or shoot at us when are going up, having no regard for the ultimate preservation of mankind, so I put out the word and have them arrested and taken away to prison. I have signed the execution papers so that there will be no chance that they will pose a threat, much as I am sorry that they will not be present during the cataclysm and experience the ultimate in fear and pain.

Only a few hours before blast off, I receive word that scientists have found a way that the asteroid can be thwarted. If it can be done before we leave, then we will not have to leave after all. I have called the prison to ensure that the executions have taken place. I don't want these people released with as much anger as they will have for me after all this, but word is that not only have they yet to receive any last meal or meet with a priest, but also there is an uprising in progress since word has gotten through of the possibility that destruction can be averted.

The maneuver was successful, and the asteroid is no longer a threat. It passed several miles from earth, and is headed back to deep space. I am amazed at how quickly everything can return to normal. The paperwork on my desk has already piled up, and it includes work from those days when work was suspended. Usually, having so much to do relaxed me, but after all that has happened, I am preoccupied with thinking about what my enemies may be planning against me. Since the close call with destruction, broad powers have been curtailed and restricted pending a review of all activities leading up to dodging the bullet. They haunt me. I've been told by my lawyers that it's very possible that I might face some kind of trial. I asked in dismay how such a thing can be possible given the state of emergency, and he shook his head, but I think he has information that it was personal between me and some of those in the prison. I have sent feelers out through contacts to determine if there is any chance that some kind of deal might be made. Not everything that happened can be traced to me. If I've learned one thing in high office, it's how to keep a straight face, show no emotion. It will be easy to say I had no hatred for anyone, that there was nothing personal. In fact, given the relief that the risky voyage to the moon has been cancelled, I would say I am feeling quite chipper and forgiving, and I sense I might be able to extend my powers of goodness over everyone under the circumstances, call a truce as it were, only I'm not sure what it will require to buy them off. I have heard some of them want seats in the government of their respective states. Some of these people are considered heroes in their locality. I doubt whether any deal like that would turn out well in the long run. Who knows whether someone might surpass me?

Before this all happened, I couldn't see their faces, but I could push them around, and I enjoyed imagining the stupid looks on their faces, and even their clothes that they used to wear, how shaggy they became under my administration. But now I detect a certain look of rehabilitation even though I cannot see them. The way they have managed to rise up by chance against my authority is due to another force more powerful than me, and they have been more influenced and shaped by that force than me, and with that in mind as a factor to be considered, I believe it's fair to say that as a result of being dipped in a miraculous effusion, they will extend a drop of mercy to me out of the sluice that opened to them. So I really have nothing to fear at all. Nothing.

The Old Bullfrog

Harry was a bullfrog. He appeared in the guise of a man, but ultimately I realized he was a frog, back on his haunches and settled into form amphibious and slimy. He may be some kind of pooka, one that generally maintains a warm front but whose purposes are as cold as the water in which he was spawned. The first time I met him, he had a book in his hand, which was made from tall swamp grasses woven into leaves and ironed flat to pages. He had made the book painstakingly in his hovel near the center of town, a place I only heard about much later. What I did not see was that the book was presented as holy, but Harry used it as a repository for his daily intake of insects, some dead and dry, others kept alive in several compartments in the book. If I'd had a camera with a fast lens, I might have been able to capture an image of his tongue flashing into the book in the middle of a conversation to pick up a tidbit. He was always eating from that book, and in church of all places. It was a shame, but nobody recognized that he was from the swamps as he freely declared that he came in the name of the Lord.

In the world we are all fair game. We sit outside, the bugs attack. They're on us in minutes, and we brush them off. In daily life, too, we have annoyances, some larger than others. Harry had seen it all. As a young man, he had been to war, but he managed to steer clear of combat by using his amphibious power to hide in the water or between the rocks. He made roll calls and mess, and he marched with the squad, but when the shooting started, he could make it to the water in a few leaps and wait in the weeds, eyes just above water, until it was safe to come out.

The Old Bullfrog

Once out of the service, he became a lawyer and thrived in this profession, and it was here that he grew large, spotted, and fully conditioned as a bullfrog, meaning without any remorse whatsoever for what creatures he encountered, cornered and devoured. He married and had children, but as the years wore on, he began to wear on his wife, and she finally left him during a scandal that cost him his license. So he looked for a refuge where people were as vulnerable as a client clueless about the law, and saw the field of religion as a good area to feast upon.

He was penniless after the divorce and fines, but he was fine with a tiny rented room in the center of town where he drew on his experience as a soldier to survive. He kept the room humid and wet in order to keep his skin slimy. He started an organization with himself as holding every position, and using only a typewriter and the church's photocopy machine, inundated the pastor and every elder he hoped to influence with daily ramblings about people to pew ratios and the satanic influences of his wife. He lied about his past to visitors, speaking as if he had been present at the groundbreaking, saying "we" did this, and "we" did that, when he had only been attending for a few months, and he handed people condensations of the Bible, which were the first few words of every verse, and he claimed that he had largely memorized the book in this way, and he cited how many verses total there were, and how many chapters, and divided these numbers by the number of apostles and what not and generally made no friends, but as anyone could see with a strobe light and fast lens, he was always eating, and sometimes licking the faces of single, older woman as they appeared in the narthex after services.

To men, Harry always spoke of still being married, of using his fingers to say prayers for her and each of his children every day. He wore a large ring on the ring finger of his left hand, and he would slide it forward to reveal his wedding ring intact, that he still honored his wife though she was deceived by Satan, and that one day they would be reunited when she saw the error of her ways. To women, it was anything but this story. He needed to get out of that room at some point because it was hindering him as the sunning, rock sitting beast that he was. Selling himself high in every situation was easy enough to see through, and everyone did, but he'd settled into his true nature long before, and was immune to any kind of whispering. Light breezes are nothing to a hefty bullfrog. But sooner or later he knew some honest and unsuspecting, lonely female would come along and be flattered by his attention and believe he was important from the fact that everyone knew him. He concocted and staged so many appearances and taped himself speaking and handed everyone copies of the tapes that it was universally known that he was an idiot, but to this woman who finally came along, he was just universally known, and so he took the rings off and let her buy a new one for him, while he filched one off a dead woman's hand at a wake, had the inner engraving changed and the ring sized, and presented it to his new wife. He never told anyone he was getting married, but he sent a letter to be read to the church, filled with bombast and high import, and everyone laughed and said good riddance. Harry left the church and his hovel and went forward with his new wife's money to greener pastures.

The last time I saw him, he came over in a broken-down, rusted-out van filled with empty plastic gallon milk jugs that he needed filled with water. He'd made similar visits previously, bringing tubs of dirty dishes and silverware that it should be my honor to clean for him because he was poor. So my wife would fill the dishwasher and let it run, and Harry would sit and tell stories of his life and war experiences, the sins of his wife and estranged children, never with any indication whatsoever that he might have been responsible or culpable in any way for their estrangement or the losses he'd incurred. He brought a ukulele and played tunes, which would have been acceptable except that he had not worn underwear. Perhaps they were being washed by someone else at the same time, he never said. But he played without any shame because he loved having an audience. It allowed him to lick up the various dead insects hidden in the pages of his music. He needed to be furtive, to have this be a hunt. That was in his nature, and so it wasn't enough to sit in his hovel and eat flies freely. No, he had to hide a bug collection and go out and eat in public because it excited him that nobody knew what he was or what he was doing. Neither did I for a long time, until that day when he came to my house in that broken-down van. Like the dishes, which he had a system of using, the water was the blood of the plan. He explained as I brought out the hose to begin filling the jugs that he would use this water I would give him in a preset proportion each day, both for bathing and for other needs, and it would last him a specific length of time. The dishes also were tubbed and made to be used and stretched to a specific number of days, the same as the water, but he had them staggered so he would only do dishes one day a month, and collect water one day a month, and he would prevail upon the elders of the church, each in his turn, to perform this wondrous deed of helping one so poor and profiting from it in the eyes of God.

I was standing out front with a hose filling the jugs for Harry, and we were down to the last few. All of a sudden, he grew quiet. It was as though he was receiving a message. I listened, and I could hear frogs in the distance. It was spring, and the swamps had thawed out, and though it was still cold, the sun was warm, and the cold-blooded ones were singing. Harry thanked me and said he had to leave. The van chugged away with all that water, and I decided to follow him. He turned right at the stop and drove over the railroad tracks about half a mile down the road, then turned down the gravel road that leads to the swamp where the sounds of the frogs were, and they were very loud as I parked by the road and walked down the rest of the way. Frogs will generally quiet down when someone approaches, but they were louder than ever, and Harry was standing on the shore. He was communicating with them. I managed to get out of there without being seen and went home.

As he'd exhausted his need for me, I never saw him again. He found another community of vulnerable believers to fall for his soothing manner and practiced delivery. One day I ran across one of his old speeches posted on the internet, and again felt the tongue on its mission in the manure fields, dispersing and feasting on the flies such that nobody could detect his silver tongue was darting around as he spoke, swallowing some and storing others in his cheeks to paste in his book later, not being one to miss a beat or meal.

The Shadow State

There were a lot of things playing on Judd's mind during that last week of his wife's pregnancy. He felt like he could fill empty bottles with pure and powerful concentrations of his various emotions. The pregnancy seemed to be acting like a prism on his mind, separating the general mix of consciousness into the full spectrum of feelings. Anger seemed to be the most prevalent, and it was a wall compared his other emotions, which were more like thin seams. It dominated the strata. Anything could upset him, and with the birth of his daughter at hand, it was all coming to a head, his head, and he just wanted it over with so he could get back to his life. But even with only a few days left for the baby, after nine months of stress, he was starting to crack at the seams, not that the wall of anger would be coming down. It was built so well that the bricks could hardly be discerned. But there were bricks and mortar, both of the same material, both built high and casting a huge shadow, and all together ready to collapse under its own weight.

One brick was the fact that they were having a girl. Judd wanted a boy. He'd always wanted a boy. His wife said the same thing,. They were in concert on that. They both felt it was almost a kind of imposition to have to get through this pregnancy so they could start over and have a boy. And what with there being no guarantee they would have a boy, coupled with the fact that Judd wasn't making a lot of money, he was angry at the vision of having to stop at two girls without a son when one child was all he wanted as long as it could be a son. That was just one brick in the wall.

Another brick was the enduring anger of his brother's senseless death a year earlier. He'd never gotten over that. Another was his self loathing, which was not divided into any spectrum but mixed together like mud swirling in a heavy rain. It wasn't just who he was or where he lived in this chapter of his life. It wasn't just his job or the kind of car he drove. It wasn't just the bad breaks that turned the course of his life away from what might have been. But all of those things together muddied his outlook on everything as well. He hated the ties in his closet, hated it when one dropped to the floor on a pile of boots, which he hated for not being properly arranged. Looking in the mirror as he tied his tie, he hated how some of his hair stuck up in front. He hated his face and teeth and said so consciously. But he didn't call himself by name in his mind because he hated that, too, and hating it was on his mind.

Just the day before, in church, Peter and Judas were brought up for comparison. Why did we relate to the one and not the other? They both betrayed Christ, didn't they? But people could see themselves more in Peter's shoes than those of Judas, who did it for money and then killed himself. But for Judd, sitting there listening, it was about the name, how nobody was named after Judas except in slightly changing the name to something like Judd. He'd never actually met anyone else with the name, and the occasional celebrity only reminded him how rare it was, and he felt singled out, almost like God was saying, "Whatever you're going to do, do it quickly." Other boys were named after apostles, each one of whom had a known weakness or failing, except perhaps John, but his namesake was a traitor to them all, which is the Bible lesson that sunk into Judd over all the others. He didn't really admit it to anyone, but the gospel had always been mostly about Judas for him.

There were many other bricks that made up Judd's wall of anger, but the mortar that held it all together was the stream of thoughts wafting in and out between the bricks and around the walls. It was the way he thought about everything that held it all together. Angry, negative thoughts just ran through his mind for no reason, from one into the next for throughout an entire day. For example, in those last days before his wife delivered, he thought a lot about the rest of mankind. He surveyed the world from his mind (which was all he could do really, for he wasn't well-traveled), comparing areas where people lived with animal habitats, some expanding, some shrinking, but all of them ultimately encroached upon by a larger force. As real animals, regardless of their current state or location, must ultimately deal with man, so does man have to deal with a larger force that takes a swipe at him, deals him a heavy blow that could wipe him out though most of the time he bounces back. Judd experienced this in having his car broken into repeatedly. He lived in an "up and coming" neighborhood in the city, which meant it was still lousy, and he was sick and tired of everything from his neighbors to the glass on the street from shattered car windows. It was the whole look of the area that he despised. It was a wasteland that old ladies would try to make look nice by putting a vase in the window with a flower in it. Judd would walk by for several days waiting for the flower to die and then realize it was fake. That was the essence of his neighborhood. They didn't even have real flowers to brighten up the place. So he went back and forth to the train that would take him into the city, the days and years passing quietly as he collected a paycheck in a dead-end job, suffering the same humiliation every day, fighting for parking spaces and not talking with neighbors and not being able to count on the police to follow up on any of the car break-ins. It was all a muddy blur until he met his wife who took it all with him, even rode out in front to try to absorb the brunt of it as she recognized the damage it did to him. As much as he felt trapped, she helped him to see the possibilities of working their way out of it together, and when she told him she was pregnant, he quickly realized how important it was to start trying to make changes. At first, the pregnancy energized him, and he squared off to meet the challenges with renewed hope.

Judd's wife was actually glad to see him come to his senses and fight back, be a man against the machine. He said he wanted to take them out of the city, that the environment was dead. He felt cordoned off from the rest of the world like a frog pond between two developments that would eventually usurp it. The pond would be drained and filled with a concrete base covering up whatever it was with something modern. Whatever particular tribal life in the century was worth anyone's attention would have been recorded, perhaps in an issue of *National Geographic*, that anyone who lived there and read the article would never see as truly representative, missing the point entirely. But when were stages of development in city neighborhoods over decades of change ever considered of any cultural interest? Who really was present to preserve the way of life that Judd had grown used to and sick of over the years? Dickens captured the filth of Victorian London so well that it was sanitized, romanticized into musicals. Its moment in history was granted the same status with Caesar's Rome. But the world of Judd was just so much swill to flush and watch swirl down the bowl. Nobody was recording his life, and certainly there would be no musicals down the road to make his experiences seem worthy of background music and a wonderful duet to bring out the true angst, and turn the pathos of his pain into art, and of all people, he wanted it to see it all go away.

Even if someone did come along to document the cultural significance of this useless moment in the days of the life of Judd, he would not be one to do anything to help them or explain anything. They wouldn't understand that what Judd meant was how whole sections and regions can seem to be left outside history. Dead to what is good, they turn into a Sodom without consequences, a place where cab drivers take people looking for action; a city without exterminating angels stopping by for a visit, full of thieves and sexual slaves but offering no excuses for any of it, contributing nothing to the general good; and until someone would do something to clean it up, or until the value of land rose high enough to drive out the bad element, nothing that happened would be missed or singled out historically. It would appear on maps, but unrecorded, it would be largely forgotten like so many bad sides of any given city.

So the renewed sense of purpose, much as it was wrapped in a canvas bag of depression, tied with the ropes of anger and dropped in the thick mud of his current setting, didn't stand much of a chance to climb out on shore and evolve, besieged by the constant downpour of his daily life. Within a few weeks, the thing that was draining him the most was the pregnancy. In short order, the hope wore off, and he was alert to the coming birth as another thing he couldn't possibly do anything about that would only add to his troubles It became particularly clear when the ultrasound technician told them they were going to have a girl. Until that moment, the wind in Judd's sails came from a sense of connection to the past, to his fathers and grandfathers. Believing there would be a son to continue the legacy, he was able to part the muddy sea and see a dry spot in the commotion and struggle. The dry spot was his home, his place in life. He recalled stories his mother told him about the Great Depression, so he knew it had been hard for others. But when he learned it was not to be a son, the walls of water collapsed, and the mud blew up, forming bricks and mortar that reformed the wall of anger, but how can a small ebb of promised good wash away what a tanker has collected and dumped on shore over a lifetime?

He was like the operator of a junk yard in an orchard, where after a while the operator can get used to the taste of rust in oranges and sell them off as having a special tang, but still nobody will buy them, or if they do once, won't a second time. Judd's focus was not on himself until no one was left, and then over time he came to realize what a flat plain of simple shambles he was, with a thin façade of being strong and whole. Then he came to the thinking that it did not matter what anyone else thought. But he really didn't know what he thought, and while that might seem like it was going around in circles, it was more like going around in the dark without stumbling, having memorized where the clutter is, but it becomes awkward as one becomes so accustomed to having to step over all the junk, where that becomes a part of one's gait, so that when one is in the clear, walking straight has an uncomfortable feel to it.

Judd's lay of his own land was that it was environmentally unsound, that so much of his surroundings had leached down and poisoned the well, but still he had hope some bucket was coming to pull him out, but beside the hope there was so much anger for people he didn't want around him. There was nothing really he wanted from anyone, but his need was so great, it was some kind of hunger gnawing in him, wanting them to come for him, to call, to knock on his door, for no reason at all. But only a few had come during his greatest pain, and those who had, though he let them in, he wanted them gone behind the handshakes and the smiles, and he tried sending them all away with feeble commands, with thoughts, nothing vocalized. It would be too embarrassing to say in a public setting for the sharing of grief that you want to be alone. But that was it. He wanted people to come after he had sent them away because he didn't want to be alone, but he would say that a second time just to get rid of them. He realized it was anger, but he wasn't quite sure why except that he was at the bottom of a well being poisoned, and the whole point of his life, the promise was that such a thing would never happen to him, that he would not wind up stuck in a dead-end corner of the universe thinking *Nothing matters.*

Judd had his own way of affirming life, which had advanced to being all that he could expect it to be while getting the most out of himself in the best spirit he could generate or offer for all the tasks at hand. He affirmed his emotions and tried to keep them in check. He did not drink or smoke and lived so that if he had any children, they would stand a better chance to have a better home to come back to when they had a family, better, hopefully it would turn out, than he had had, looking back. But in his attempt to live as some kind of model were only the supports necessary for the outside appearance. He never considered that his emotional state would be even more important as a model, and that what sank in over time and made him unable to escape what he had become was just as likely to permeate the home when it was time for nurturing new, tender beings. The difficulties he had controlling his inner life was only beginning to sink in. Judd felt he was a kind of sunken ship from the start that had to be raised from the bottom, and while he was surrounded on all sides by his neighbors, he didn't feel that close or able to open up to any one of them, feeling he was at war with the world not with them, that they were entrenched in their own foxholes, doing the best they could, all on the same side, but that they could easily become casualties of his friendly fire if they did not watch their step. Life for Judd had seemingly passed the point of his nearly being able to get to know people and become a dear friend because he was no longer of a mind to just give anyone the time. He was too perspicuous of what mattered to him, too intent and focused to relax, and too demanding of his own time and energy. At social gatherings of any kind, he quite quickly began to feel taxed even in ordinary conversation with people, and he did not go very deep, deliberately, though he felt that in order for there to be anything between him and others that things would need to be deeper, and the boredom of shallow conversations drained him more than anything else. Once he started out on that note, he couldn't put things into words, found that people weren't comfortable either on those topics that didn't really matter, so he keep turning to the snack bowls for a nibble and moved away to chat with someone else. Then, when he'd get home, he think what a lousy time he had.

In those last few days, he had strange dreams, and it made him angry that he couldn't remember them. He showered and shaved and went through all the other motions of the day trying to remember them because they gave him a feeling like the dreams had been trying to tell him something. Then he woke up with a very clear memory of one very lucid dream. It was very disturbing as he felt totally vulnerable in it. He was packing his bags to move when he realized in the dream that life is not real like we think it is, and only real in a way we don't entirely recognize. When he understood this in his dream, he felt overwhelmed with emotion not just for the meaning experienced in the revelation but for how he had missed the point for so long. What suddenly came to him was that life is a shadow state, a place in which our lives mean nothing except in how we live them for others in the same state. Our lives are transient. We pass through here believing there is something substantial. We hold the rocks, and they are hard. We search for gold and fight over it. We grind ourselves away in fruitless efforts while the spiritual reality is left to suffocate. Judd sensed that a sword was hanging over his head and could cut it off at any second. But he saw further than the inevitability of his own life ending. He saw into the chain of being, the connection of all souls with another, or rather the disconnection of all souls from one another due to sharing the false perception that the world has a greater reality than the soul. The shadow state in the dream became even more clear when he took this new knowledge into the world of the dream and continued trying to justify himself before others. There was a woman who recognized two thugs and tried to remind them of her association with them. They laughed and insulted her, leaving her in tears. She was ugly before them, but when they left, she became beautiful before Judd and began to insult him. He tried as hard as she had to justify himself to her, and he woke feeling more ugly than free of the shadows of his wall due to what he'd seen in his dream.

    He didn't say anything about it to his wife. It wasn't something he would easily forget, but there was so much going on, he just went back into his life and discounted it as something that resulted from an excess of emotion. He didn't have any neighbors he could confide in since he'd stopped talking to them after his brother died, not so much out of his own pain but because of their seeming insensitivity. Judd wrote them all off for something only one of them had said. A raspy old lady said, *Que Sera, Sera,* when she heard about it, and the wall went up for good on her and all the rest of them. He went about his business as was his right, in every avenue his time allowed, and focused solely on making sure over the coming decade that he would have the means to have a family, to have a boy to name after his brother, that as the hopes for enough money to even have one child faded, the unwanted pregnancy now suddenly made it the most crucial thing, that all the months and years of slow time didn't matter. He would wait it all out for the long-term objective. Now the near term said he was about to be saddled with one more bolt to keep him down, a sense that didn't come at once, for in the first weeks there was hope. But they agreed to hear what the ultrasound had to say, whether it was going to be a boy or a girl. Before the pronouncement, he said a prayer. It didn't seem like a long time to him since he was a boy looking ahead to the idea of growing up. There was a time when all he thought of was having a family. To have a couple of boys and a girl was his dream. But now a boy was all that mattered, the only gender acceptable in this moment, in this focus, which was his life. Somewhere in a black cave for creatures blind since birth there is a balance where whatever comes the way for a creature, life or death, being eaten or defeated in battle, there is balance for the cave, and if opened up to the light of day, even after a thousand years, there will be life inside because there is balance. Judd couldn't be eaten or defeated, but a girl would throw him out of balance. It would be the last straw. It had to be a boy for sure, and though there was a chance it could be a girl, somehow he knew it was going to be a boy without the ultrasound. But his wife wanted to know, so he agreed, and the ultrasound operator asked what he wanted, and he said he wanted a boy, and the ultrasound told a different story, and he was disappointed to say the least.

His wife admitted it, too. But she went through the passing months bravely. She wanted a fresh start to infuse her husband with new life. For her sake, Judd put up the appearance that this was to be the beginning of a family, that it is wrong to say we have been shortchanged when the path before us stretches beyond what can be seen. There is no poll or questionnaire provided on childhood or guarantee all wishes granted, and so he accepted the roll of the dice. But secretly Judd did feel cheated, that the nine months he had to wait were in themselves too long a stretch of days. It was like getting all the light from the sun you would ever get in one day, and only getting darkness after that, all the time. Judd couldn't see any light at the end of the tunnel, and the promises he believed were true in the past all seemed like lies to him now.

Then one day toward the end of her term, his wife complained she didn't feel the baby moving, and she became frightened that something was wrong. So they started a drive to the emergency room, before which she ate some ice because the doctor had told her early on that doing so would stimulate movement in the child, and sure enough, just about halfway to the hospital, the baby moved, so they called off the emergency and went out to breakfast.

That afternoon she had a regularly scheduled stress test, and everything was normal. Judd sat reading a magazine, listening to the booming heartbeat over a speaker. It would only be a few days more, the doctor told them. But the days passed, and nothing happened. She was late. They asked about inducing labor and were told that would be a necessity at some point but the process itself was not without risks, that it was better to wait, but they planned to induce her a week later when the birth would be more than ten days late.

The Shadow State

Finally, two days before inducing, her water broke. Judd thought she had a strange look about her that day, something he would only go back to later and consider as any kind of signal anything was wrong, but there was something seemingly almost dead in her eyes, as if she had an aura only a channeling person might be able to see. But Judd swore later he could almost feel it, and his wife said she'd seen it too, but just thought she looked like hell.

At the hospital they strapped her in a bed and connected her to a monitor. Judd was almost aggravated it was happening. It seemed to take something out of his day. There were other things to do, and this was just a girl being born, and there was another aggravation, a student training to be a nurse started asking all kinds of questions which both Judd and his wife found extremely annoying.

Then the nurse started to adjust the monitor. Something didn't seem to be working right, so she left and came back a few minutes later with another nurse and the two of them couldn't get it to work. Judd asked what the problem was, but they wouldn't answer. Then there were five or six people in the room. His wife looked at him and they both rolled their eyes, starting to feel something terrible was in progress. They called the head doctor who came in with an air of complete authority. He told everyone to clear the room, for now twenty people were gathered around the bed. He spent one or two minutes with a stethoscope, looked over to Judd and his wife and said simply "I'm sorry, there's no heartbeat," and then he left.

Judd and his wife were stunned. He tried comforting her, but there was nothing he could say. They waited for the doctor to come, and some four hours later, Judd had a stillborn baby boy. It was a terrible shock to learn that the ultrasound early in her pregnancy had gotten it wrong. The operator had seemed so certain, but the doctor said it was an imperfect system, and results were sometimes misread. The old lady down the street who'd been on the pregnancy watch with everyone else heard the bad news and said, *Que Sera, Sera* again. Judd was instantly inflicted with a sense of the burial to come. How could this woman live well into her seventies without more sympathy and foundation? Maybe it was going through the depression and the war, that maybe she had cut herself loose, through her own problems or losses, that everyone sooner or later has so much to deal with. But Judd couldn't help thinking of his poor little boy who didn't even get the chance to live, to see all that is here, not even for a single day. He never got to see what light looked like under the sun, only whatever light might filter through his mother's tummy with eyes not even developed enough to focus.

And Judd was suddenly struck with a sense of a great emptiness if life is the only thing, and how little life means when there's nothing after it. People said it was a shame his son died, and he thought, *There's no difference between me and him. Life is here, but he'll never know about it. Being here is meaningless except that it keeps me from nothingness, but once I die, it's all the same.* And Judd realized that the universe is no delicate bubble, but a bag of rocks, and without something to realize and describe it as such, not even that. Without that single, precious thing, it was nothing at all. He began to find nothingness impossible to fathom; and yet it was nothingness that had given him an idea that there is something more, along with a clear sense from meaningless death that there is much meaning to life.

Judd stood without a child to impede him, nobody to name after his brother, but despite the clarity of the memory of the imposition of a daughter, he was certain this was not what he had wanted, and he was ashamed. But he didn't turn away. Through it all, remembering the dream gave him strength. He felt a shattering, a crumbling of the build-up of negative experience. It left him exposed and vulnerable, but no different than anyone else. He knew it now: only spirit is substantial, and the purpose of life, if one resists the blinding lure of things, is to serve others in the shadow state. He'd had it backwards all his life, and though the length of the shadow he'd cast ran parallel and intertwined with the dream, he didn't feel anger. If he had, he would have seen himself as a Judas in reproduction, a traitor to the very fabric of life, but he identified with the Apostle Peter, who made the kind of mistake anyone might, threatened and confused, desperate in broken spectrums of light flashing in a clouded mind. So Judd resolved to move forward and concentrate on light that delivers purpose to the present, to leave behind the darkness of an old self in muddled shadows, ruins of a previous mind.

The Cry Room

If I'd had the choice, I wouldn't have signed my daughter up for church day care. My wife was working, and I'd all but tapped the great family joke of a legacy even though I was milking it one last time in the hope I'd do better than just make ends meet. I had hopes for this project since there was no solicitation on my part. It came to me, and it was better that someone else wrote the book. Going over all these family photos, I realized I was just too close to the subject. All I had to do is go through and make key selections, but even barely five minutes into it, I'd already gotten worked up.

My daughter didn't understand the idea of being left with other people. She cried before coming over, so I told her I wouldn't leave. Down the hall there was a cry room overlooking the church sanctuary. She had been in it during services, so she calmed down when I explained I'd be close at hand. I grabbed the photo albums, got her settled in group, and went to the cry room to start working.

I suppose I should be grateful somehow for being the child of such famous poet-parents, but I still don't get how they could each become so engulfed in the poetry *field*. I don't know what else to call it. Once they became well known in their small circle, everything about them became part of the poetic picture. I've thought a great deal about this, and the only way I can describe it is that they had a knack for this great unknown quantity, and becoming known verified their perception that they could see something better than everyone else. And they entered the inner circle of a number of key people who validated one another's sense that they had this special intuition. The problem was that poetry is the kind of field where the sensibility in the poetry is held high, and the modern poet who has the ability to get the perception out is painted up with wax and given wings to fly. Then not just the public eye but the consciousness of it ignites the sun. Soon, they fly too close and fall into the sea. I don't know why this was so in their day, but there was something about the *Confessional School* that brought not just the private lives of people into the picture but their souls as well.

Anyway, as a child of the "marriage of true minds," you would think that I would have been a witness to the marvelous unravelling of ideas to be hung in the balance and gather people up like a great tongue, but what comes to my mind out of my experience is fly-covered paper twisting down in a smelly highway service station rest room. They didn't touch anyone, only mangled one another. There was no room for me between the two of them, and I was put into private schools to free them up. I published the letters they wrote me about how they loved and missed me, telling me to be strong. Meanwhile they were tying themselves together with wires to a powder keg. I only wish I'd been around to see them go up in smoke. Well, I have a tendency to let my anger affect how I see them.

My always being away from home is one of the reasons I didn't want to put my daughter in day care, but I don't believe it's only because I had bad experiences. I can't fathom the attitude that poetry was more important than family, but to them, it was everything. And what is it? I think my father's words said it best. *The long edge to the night is actually soft, and so vast that you spend your entire life wallowing in its deep cushions, falling toward some terrible prick of light.*

When I look at the two of them in these pictures in the photo album, I can see the mixed message in their faces. There are the pictures before they were famous. They are human in those. After they were known, they were always putting on some kind of a show, a more thoughtful and perceptive pose. "Wait honey, let me get my tweed jacket and pipe, and a book to put on the table." Actually, the best phrase that comes to mind to describe my father and his work is *Heaven's Orderly*. What I like about it is that it describes his compulsion to force things to make sense, but in the vast scheme of things, he would be akin to a janitor. My mother's personality was the opposite, and this is why I don't believe opposites attract. The phrase that comes to mind that best describes her is *Horsing Around*. I only saw them on holidays, but I could see what really interested her better than my father could. If he wasn't blind to her indiscretions, he certainly turned a blind eye to them.

Other people seem to see more in my parents, or they can find what is essential, what they were truly about in terms of poetry, probably because they can separate all the private life information out of it. Maybe people are grateful to find dysfunctionality shared. It might make them more comfortable with their own, and if people can have such a keen sense of the truth, or of the unknown, or that "nothing" that every human being senses is more than nothing, while being completely screwed up, maybe there's hope in being an intellectual after all. Again, it's hard for me to be objective.

Sitting in the cry room with all the old pictures, I remembered my father taking me to the movie theatre cry room with a friend of his to watch the old silent movies he'd seen as a boy. I was only about eight or nine. I remember that he talked with his friend in a normal voice, and that was something you couldn't do in the regular seats. To me, the old movies were strange, full of old cars and people who walked funny, which was due to the film speed, but to my father and his friend, it was like going back to their childhood.

Some of this is in the pictures in the album when my parents were children. These pictures, old as they are, are very clear. My grandfather became a photography buff and was one of the first to get a box camera. After taking pictures, he had to send the camera in where the film was removed and developed. After a wait of a couple of weeks, the negatives and printed pictures were returned with the camera loaded with fresh film. Later in the album, in the early 1950s when my parents were young adults, there are a number of Polaroid pictures, all very faded. I remember my father had a Polaroid camera, too, and most of the pictures he took with that camera are inferior to those taken with film. But it was all about the thrill. The results were immediate. I looked at those pictures and thought of how many things in my life are about immediate results. It seems that camera was only the beginning of a whole Pandora's box of technology designed to save time, but which is really taking it up.

Life used to be much slower. Up until my grandparents' generation, people traveled through life almost as if on a barge where only three generations would fit. Everything essential about life, all that one needed to know, was passed on through people on the barge. When they grew old and fell off the back, their faces were lost as well. Most families have very dim recollection of their history. But now we can record everything, but who is going to care about any of it? We still float on the same barge. In time, most everything will get thrown in the landfill and be forgotten. The world can't and doesn't want to remember everything. Most of the pictures in the album aren't marked. There are many faces I don't recognize, and there is nobody left who can tell me who these people were.

Looking out through the cry room glass into the dark and empty church sanctuary, I could see my reflection. It suddenly occurred to me that the cry room is the metaphor for the single mind alone and detached from God and Time within itself, where all it can do is cry and not be heard. Thinking that actually got me started writing poetry, and I started working on three in the cry room, one about my father, one about my mother, and one about myself.

Hardly in the World

Father sick still cleans. I let go, leaving hair on the floor
While he uses even a spare few seconds to pick up
I lag in the back of the mind, searching for vague clues

I do not expect to ride any waves on heavy cleaning days
Just advance an inch at a time, though I'd take a mile
And cross the vast expanse to leave the present tense

And they're leaving me in vast numbers, by degrees,
All my old friends, each in his own rigidity
Facing the wall ahead. Is that a slot for passage,

Or does it collapse at the end and finish the bug?
If I could be taken above and over it all to have a look,
On returning I'd find some new right words for it

Nobody listens to the same old. Does anyone see it,
Head turning tumblers through a keyhole, fearless
Of arrows from the valley, hair growth in the grave?

Where does one gather the heart and find the time?
Seems I'm hardly in the world other than to probe my fears
As he rips the oxygen mask off before the room is clean

I remember spending time with him in his last days. He said he didn't want to leave a mess for anyone to clean up, then left one.

Dark Stallions

Five dark stallions cross from sparse woods
Glaring and snorting, here in this crowded space
Where one hardly sees a deer anymore
And block the road for an instant. Amazing

The first four are all that the horsemen would need
To carry out their mission: complete the apocalypse.
Their own weak steeds have held them back across history
With these they finally could destroy the world, utterly.

But these have proved themselves to be past capture
Wild and untamed, always a step ahead. Four unbroken, free.
The one with bridle and saddle, the fifth — my mother's, once
Kept hidden in a clean barn and loved far more than me

Riderless in the stall, awaiting passage, like some rare bull,
It charged through my every house. Put out to pasture,
It tracked and dragged me down. Now that she is dead,
It casts the shadow of my reins, spurring me, grazing quietly.

I'm not sure why, but the impact of a mother is great on a young man. I identified with Hamlet then, and I remember throwing chairs at the cry room window in those days, trying to lash back at God for leaving people free to ruin innocent lives. As I grew older, after they both died, I've come to feel that I wouldn't have the sense of things that I do without things having gone the way they did.

The Long Beat of the Metronome

Sparks

    I used to bark because I had the knack to crank
The terms without the meaning. I only wanted
To be launched crewless into the swell
    Where I learned, as the boat was spinning,
In sickening panoramas, smeared in 360 degrees,
To focus on the waving beacon of her hand on shore
    And from there were deeper journeys, places
Of strength derived from the dead. I returned
With a new slang but slurred it all away
    I wanted only to take a big breath to connect,
Radio my position and surrender terms through static,
Encode familiar music with subliminal fire
    But I lunched while the tide went out. Then
Eruptions everywhere, sparks flying upward
Forced me inland, no beacon anywhere in sight
    My hands will tie the knot or sever the tie
I'll launch the ship or I will die. A star so still
Will guide me, there, in the evening sky
    Now someone take this down for I've no time —
Light counts, not dark nor sparks, but long guiding light —
And plugged in, I'm sparking, spouting darkness, barking blind

    I realized that my poetic excursion was merely an extension of personal feeling, and as such has no poetic merit. I accept this even if it begs the question how one separates the essential poetic ingredient out of all that is personal in Catullus for example, or Sylvia Plath. There is just so little isolated to explain what characteristic is being sought. You have the intuition on the one hand, and the projection or encapsulation into poetry on the other. It would be like having a bottle of darkness in a room of light where the light doesn't scatter the darkness but the darkness penetrates the light. The issue ends up being that it would seem the decisions are made not by readers because there are too few for it to be a popularity contest. Instead, it comes out of the society of poets themselves, who in all fairness, shouldn't have to be social. In any case, my parents were, and they passed the mustard test, and their whole lives, even mine, became part of the literary frenzy tacked onto the fame. I've been interviewed and hounded for the tiniest details, as if that could add anything to the dark impact. But whatever it was that fascinated everyone, I'm not sure it hasn't become everything else, or that the original poetic part would survive if it weren't for all the salient details of my father's awful suicide, and my mother's drinking herself to death while screwing every English professor in the ranks.

So I figure if I supply them pictures to feed that lust, I'll be doing myself a service as it will facilitate sales and increase my cut of the project. I have mixed feelings about revealing facts of life in this way, however. It's one thing to report on a life close to yours where an injustice has been done. As long as it won't hurt anyone living, you may reveal a secret when people who concealed it as too painful to bear have died. You may even be compelled to do so if it rights a wrong, or opens the eyes of the reader to present-day truths. To merely dig into their lives for new information is one thing, but this is more like a fishing expedition into the tarpits to drag out anything that smacks of moral turpitude, which I'm saying is an immoral exercise in itself. I used to think poets were immune from this kind of probing, but the world has become a place where even the corpse is a handy thing to use as bait. They drop it in the water and leave it there. After a while, they pull it up and set it on the dock. After a couple of minutes, the eels start slithering out. Oh those delicious eels. The photo album must be full of big juicy ones.

My barge is down to two generations. My wife's parents are also deceased. Everything there is to say to our daughter that could be said to have come from the long ride will have to come from her mother because I was pushed off the front and received love in the form of words under a stamp. I suppose they thought there was a greater legacy to be excavated, that they were on a mission of some kind. Then why all the focus on their own lives, why the selfish lust and trying to keep it clean? Was it that the impact of what they saw or found drove them in ways that would suggest possession, and did they need therefore to deal with it by going the way of dispossession, of me, particularly? I must get past the anger somehow if I'm ever to see it clearly. And even if I reach a point of getting to an understanding that surpasses theirs, it isn't likely that I'll receive any literary attention. Nepotism doesn't work in poetry. There's so much of the dark matter that there's a scan for something else to go along with it that makes it interesting. My parents are more fascinating than their poems, but it's because of their poems that there's interest in their lives. And yet I don't know anyone who really cares for poetry that receives a benefit along the same lines from knowing it.

Eventually there's no room for crying, even in the cry room. I learned to stand outside my own life and watch what it might and should have been. I've stood and watched it all from a distance, believing that being the son of famous poets made me somebody. It has only come to me late that my barge went aground long ago, and if I continue with this photo project, I am contributing to a lie, unless believing in poetry is the lie. Whatever we hold to be the truth, it's only held in the head or the hands for a short time. We have a sense of sharing, and poetry is a repository for all that makes us human, all that we share. Those who encapsulate it must seem repositories themselves, so all that spills over is fair game, fodder to better understand what it's like to understand. When it turns out to be worse than our lives, so much the better, unless it's my life and I do understand, at least as much as can be understood. Couching the truth in terms like *The Horror* or *The Wasteland* might work better on the soul than *We're all gonna die*, and *Life is meaningless*, but it's still a rhythmical regurgitation of what our ancestors passed down on the barge, except from accounts I've heard they did it with love.

Again, I can't get past my parents' impact. Others see more, and less, than me. Maybe all minds are beautiful in concept, and all lives ugly in open book form. All I can do is close their book and hope I see the bigger picture within. What is the world that it would want such things? Real poetry does not feed such appetites, but if it were an herb, it would be considered poison. The barges would pass it by.

My mother once wrote, *If we turn to poetry out of a decreasing attention span, we'll find it deep and murky and drain the pond to eradicate those 'real toads' everyone's so excited about, and the new garden will leave nothing to the imagination.* Then she went off and slept with a stranger, and the prick of light imploded on me.

Waiting for Voyager

It was an amazing sight, earth and its moon, seen from millions of miles, the sight one might see coming home from deep space. None of the pictures from the Apollo missions had that perspective, not to say it wasn't wonderful to see the earth rise with the surface of the moon in the foreground, but the image of earth and the moon in the same frame as seen from a great distance was an entirely new perspective, made possible by the launch of Voyager, which would in time, send clear images of all the planets back to earth, and though it would take many years, Ed Philips, already 34, didn't want to miss any of those pictures of Saturn, Jupiter and Neptune.

He pinned the best pictures available of the planets in his cubicle, and then worked and waited. The days went by in bundles, and then there was news Voyager was going to make a pass, and then the pictures began streaming in. Those were wonderful days, seeing Saturn's rings, the red spot on Jupiter, and discovering that Neptune also had a ring. Ed could look at the pictures for hours. He poured over the space magazines with a sense of awe and wonder at what was out there. He'd managed to make it through the entire Voyager program, and he was happy that he didn't die along the way.

The days of looking at a vague blur had passed. Even the moons were clearly visible now, and soon came landings on Mars along with wonderful, colorful landscapes under strange skies. Ed could place himself there when he saw these pictures, but Voyager was the one that had commanded his loyalty. The internet came along, offering access to thousands of pictures, but Ed didn't much go there except to retrieve pictures from the old missions, from the early days, like the picture of the earth and moon together, taken at the very beginning. It was still his favorite.

Once Voyager crossed into open space and went out beyond Pluto, Ed seemed to fall back to earth without any real connection to anything uplifting. He'd passed the age of fifty and had read all the books he'd wanted to read. He'd given up on many of his dreams and accepted his lot in life. He found himself grumbling at the younger generation and at politics, which reminded him of his parents and grandparents, but he didn't much mind that he was growing old. He was comfortable with the slow advance. The days didn't so much go by in bundles anymore but passed in regular intervals. He didn't look back as much and took things as they came.

But at the same time, Ed was beginning to become aware of his lifetime accumulation of junk. He was a collector of many things, and there were rooms in his house that were so full of odds and ends that he would sometimes stumble, and he could never find things. Something in him said the time was coming when he would need to consider not being here anymore, that he should not leave it to others to weed through his possessions, but thin it out himself. He stood in front of his bookcase one day and started to throw things away, but each thing he touch represented a memory, a connection to something in the past, even to the day he saved it. He had old day calendars from past jobs, but looking through them, useless as they were, reminded him of days in his life that he wouldn't otherwise remember. These were symbolic of bundles of days, but each stick was inscribed with specific events, and were perhaps his only means to remember specific events. So he stopped trying to throw anything away for fear that it was an inner piece of himself that the truck would take to the dump. Going the long way back through his life, these were the markers in empty space in images analogous to those Voyage sent back, and in the present tense he was granted a greater sense of wholeness by the presence of all the things he had touched on his passage through time and space, and yes, this was just stuff that someone would toss in the end, but until the lights went out, it was a kind of map of the constellations, the present by itself being a void in which the seed of creation germinated, expanding into all the heavens, into a fantastic living thing in itself, where we establish our range in all that appears not in constant motion but fixed, and remain fixed in the sense that we are moving by leaps and bounds, spinning circles on a grain of sand and existing all in a billionth of a click in a giant time keeper.

Ed used to sit and ponder the immobility and futility of life until Voyager lifted off, and then his own spirit soared. When the missions were over, he descended again into the pages of his life, into his work, into the minutia, the daily tedium, not so much with relish but with dignity and concentration, feeling there was something to the effort of putting his energy into his prescribed moment in time. The weather of the thousands of days of his life were already in whatever cycle there would be, the droughts and warmer winters just the way it was for him, each temporal being allotted whatever portion is polished into the saddle he will wear while ridden by the events of the days of his life.

He was thinking these very things one summer day in his yard when he saw something in the clouds, a little white bead jutting in and out of sight. It wasn't long before he saw three of them, too tiny to discern at such a height, so he marked the shape of the clouds and ran inside for some binoculars. When he came back and found them, he realized instantly he was a witness to unidentified flying objects, three huge shapes somewhat oval, in formation it seemed to him, and completely alien from anything he had ever seen. He watched until the clouds covered them over, and when the clouds opened up again, they were gone.

Ed spent the next few days searching the sky and news for anything, but he saw and heard nothing. He wondered how it was possible that he could have been the only one to see it, but he'd gotten a clear view, no more amazing than a clear photo of Neptune for the change it can make in someone waiting for change to come from that general direction, someone who had hoped he would get a glimpse of what was between heaven and earth, and experience an awakening as the unfathomable breadth of totality separated him from the masses without giving any detail or providing an explanation for whatever it is, just by chance.

In that moment, Ed became Voyager, a finger taking the pulse of the moment in the endless stream and touching the heart in a way. He felt that a rich history would one day begin to unfold and lift mankind out of a long, dark age. On internet UFO web sites, he found pictures of objects quite similar to the ones he'd seen along with descriptions that matched his experience. He watched television programs on the subject of extra terrestrials with great interest, wondering why greater attention wasn't given to them, and he concluded that governments knew the truth but had determined the information would be dangerous if shared with the general public.

What is the general public, Ed wondered, that it should be kept in the dark? Rather, what is the government that deems it preferable that people should be kept in the dark? Ed thought that left to his own, man was able in separate instances through history to form complex societies that were similar in many ways. The Egyptian and Mayan cultures, for example, were very alike. They built pyramids, used pictures to communicate, and their rulers were gods. But while we may marvel at these cultures, in many ways we think they were primitive and ignorant. They were often brutal. Except that we have developed technology and debunked their religious myths, how far have we really come to say we know anything more or whether absolutely there is or is not a God?

Ed thought enlightenment was a bulb with a number of clicks on it. There is just being conscious. Man is still smarter than animals. There is being educated within a culture. There is having clear scientific understanding of facts and how to reason. There is faith and belief, intuition into what turns out to be true. And finally, there is being a witness to that which is true, which entails being changed beyond one's peers who are not witnesses.

Ed didn't think he was a witness so much as he had an open mind. Perhaps it would turn out that what he saw was a natural phenomenon, or an experiment of some kind to be revealed at a later date. All he knew was that he did not know, and in having opened his mind and having it opened more for him, he was knowing less and less. He was beginning to realize this was also a form of enlightenment that ultimately entailed bowing to everything but nobody.

Losing Face

Einstein had it right probably, saying something to the effect that the most incomprehensible thing about the universe is that it's all comprehensible. I can understand that in terms of the Periodic Table of the Elements, P shells and relativity, how time and gravity work together, but what I can't figure out, and what someone like Einstein would probably have to admit he would never understand, is the stuff that makes the heart tick and how nature touches us like we are children, and how we know how to read into it from having been parented all these thousands of years, like it's been ingrained. There will be no laws or scientific explanations for everything, so Einstein was just looking over his papers and considering that the spaces in his unfinished constructs would one day be filled in. It's a nice thought to think that when we understand everything about the universe, we'll be able to explain ourselves as well.

But will we have changed along the way in how we deal with being in this universe? Will comprehending it all improve our ability to say goodbye to the place without any fear or regret? Seven more stories added to Einstein's building, even seeing from the suburbs, towering over us all won't make much of a difference when news comes that the wife was sideswiped into driving through a railing over a cliff, now will it?

Today the ginkgo biloba tree is going to lose most of its leaves. For some reason, it holds onto them longer than other trees. I mean that other trees lose their leaves over many days. They change color and fall for several weeks. But the ginkgo holds them better, and then one day, all at once, they come down in several hours. Oh sure, some of the leaves do come off earlier, but it's still a significantly different manner of distribution for this longest living and oldest living species of tree, that I wonder whether it got something right when nature was a much younger parent. Then again, what difference does it make to me? It's just another living thing doing things in its own way. *Vivre la différence*, as they say.

It's a relatively young tree, maybe thirty years old. When it's very old, a thousand years or so, it will come to have stalagtites that can be taken off, turned right side up and planted into trees themselves. I wonder where it came to acquire this ability. If we were to live so long, would we have acquired so much knowledge or experience that something would just form on us over time that might be seen as a slow drip, perhaps even become an extension of ourselves, able to begin a duplication process right there on the spot? The female ginkgos produce a rather smelly fruit with a large nut, often in abundance, so why the secondary form of reproduction, and again, how did the tree come to acquire this ability, and how did it survive the cataclysms of history, and why does it live so long? Does Einstein mean that someday we will comprehend all this?

I wonder something else far more petty today. Last year I added a face to the tree, features purchased from a store that children enjoy especially. In the package, there are two eyes, a nose and a mouth, and you hang these on nails to make a face. The features actually have been manufactured for trees, and are surrounded with what looks like bark so that when placed on the tree, they have the appearance of having grown out of the tree.

Now, what I don't understand, standing here as the leaves are falling all around me, is why this tree is losing face. There is only one eye and a mouth left. A few months ago, the nose was there, the eye having fallen about six months earlier. Is the tree kicking them off? I have placed faces on other trees, and they are fine, all intact. But the ginkgo is dripping prosthetics. I imagine the painting by Dali where the clocks are wilting. I'm sure I could drive long stainless nails in and solder these things on, but I am not going to fight it. By the end of the day the leaves will all have fallen. Did I say it wasn't windy? Sorry if I forgot. Yes, no wind today.

Did you pause to think about that before I take it back? I wanted to strongly suggest the ginkgo was consciously making the decision itself, not using the wind as a facilitator, which does not negate the timing. I've seen this process many times, and each year, regardless of any variations in the weather, there comes a day when the leaves all do fall off, wind or no wind, but the wind does blow many off before that day comes. Even so, how would this diminish any further our already diminished sense of all that surrounds us? It has become easy to say that we can understand the universe, amazing as that may sound, but what in setting matters of nature aside, aren't we saying they are not relevant? Once you define *intuition*, you can assign it to an elephant recognizing the bones of a companion, and move on to the composition of a star's hydrogen furnace. But can one say that all of what makes up the veins and brains is naturally occurring, that from an enzyme in slime, what can account for life at its most basic tending toward the development of eyes and ears?

Why in all its thousands of years did the ginkgo not develop eyes, or does it just have eyes that we don't yet understand? After a thousand years, why couldn't a tree impart to each individual seed some ability beyond that of a normal tree seed? Imagine one ancient tree that managed to survive reaching the capacity to impart this ability in its young, while its very surface had become like the sagging skin of an old man, but only over hundreds of years of slow motion, of imperceptible, slight change year to year was that stage reached, that to say we could ever find it comprehensible is ridiculous; an entity of such long life, so different from us, that we ultimately look to something we can actually fully fathom, eventually at least, like the mathematical formulas that describe the clockwork movements of galaxies, rife with dark matter and black holes.

The leaves don't suddenly decide to fall, and it takes longer than one day, so I've distorted facts, but I've only done so to increase a kind of cogency that does not depend on a one-to-one correspondence with reality. In posing an alternate reality, the concepts of truth are visible in new combinations and are often more easily extracted and much more embedded in the story at the same time. For example, imagine for a moment that I have acquired a strange new mutancy of mind, that this is my complaint, but it turns out to be my strength. I say that I am losing face, that I used to have an acceptable outer appearance, something terrible has happened to me. I have become stricken with strange growths all over my face such that my face looks like something out of a strange vision. The growths are made of the same flesh as me, and protrude from my features and even obscure them. But they are figurative themselves, recognizable in some way as having human qualities even though they are quite distorted, and though I am distraught at the horrible metamorphosis, at the same time there is some compensation, which I know to be related to the growths. My insight and intuition are greatly improved, to the point that I would probably decline any surgery to remove them because this is what I have always wanted.

I also realize that nobody will have anything to do with me in this state, but I am content in that the insights relate to a perfect sense of harmony in the universe, and though I may be so repulsive as to drive people away, my roots have taken a deep strangle hold on truth, and I draw everything up and refine it, even such things as anger, frustration and confusion. These only improve my vision and I gladly absorb them. Soon I will reach a point where I will have many things to say. I can feel the wisdom pooling, and I am beginning to feel as though I am ready to drip new life. I realize it sounds strange, but all one need do is turn my offspring upside down and offer something to sustain it. In exchange these new but ancient entities will surge and bear much fruit.

I may have distorting some facts, twisted ideas to extract truth, but it is not losing face to admit that we cannot know everything there is to know about everything, but we do have a gift to surmise the *glory of the sum of things*. Losing face comes only when it means more to us to save face than accept the truth. Life is a beautiful truth of many things we cannot explain. Some people beat their heads against it, some so hard and with so much frustration that they lose an eye to see, a mouth to speak, but we can take heart and realize these very extensions of the senses have emerged from the ginkgo, which is putting them to good use in a grander scheme of things.

A Spider Pays its Respects to the Dead

Putting his arm around her, he asked, "Did you hear about the spider paying its respect to the dead? You drop your driver's license on the floor. A draft blows the hollow husk of a dried-out, dead spider onto it. It sits somewhere next to the numbers indicating your date of birth. During the course of the afternoon, a living spider marches across the floor and onto the license. It stops at the carcass of the other spider and stops. This is when you look down and notice what is going on." He recognized that she was not very smart but seemed to recognize his intelligence. She seemed to melt in his hands whenever he spoke to her like this. "Now you ask yourself, what does this spider understand?" he continued. "Can it detect a fellow spider, now deceased, or is the husk merely an object to a presence of mind so beneath ours that consciousness is hardly an issue? Yet, for us, intelligence and understanding abound."

He lit up a cigarette, two actually, one for each of them. They sat and smoked for a minute. "The license has meaning," he said. "There's a direct relationship and connection to you. Your picture, height, weight, date of birth, even a number corresponding directly to you according to the state's method of tracking you is there. That spider stands on a bridge to human society next to a dead comrade, but what does it know? The numbers mean nothing. It doesn't really perceive the picture is of a human being. For the spider, the plastic lamination is just another floor to stand on. The husk isn't food, so the spider moves on."

The Long Beat of the Metronome

"I hate spiders," she said, wrapping her arms around his neck. "At home I always call my father in whenever I see one. Actually I scream," she chuckled, "and he comes to my rescue."

"Yeah, that's great. Do you want me to continue or not?"

"Yes, I'm sorry. Please."

"No problem. So there's a whole order of an entire world the spider doesn't know about, which is our world, right there in the same room with the spider. He's been within sight of all the indicators on a single item, but it doesn't perceive any of it. In fact, it doesn't even have the capacity to begin to fathom it, eight eyes or not. So we pick up our license, and the story is over, except for the blind pride we carry with us that we aren't walking on a surface full of indications of a much higher order, perfectly coherent, that is above us watching the way we pay our respects. Maybe everything we stand on is something like a license, but we're satisfied we see everything or are incapable like the spider. But even so, it's all out there."

"So you're saying it's like we can't help our limitations, nor do we have the perceptions to fathom the greater order?" she asked him, nibbling on his ear. The front window of the car was starting to steam up a little. He started drawing a picture.

"Right. So maybe this here is our house, but the cloud above, right there, is a kind of mist that comes and goes, which has meaning, is a way maybe that higher beings communicate. And this line in the middle is night and day, and add this cross to show the four seasons, and all of it plays in as vital signs of another world above us where perhaps even the planets are just atoms connecting into a thing that someone is holding, maybe an egg he's about to break for breakfast. Yes, the universe is just an egg, but it will be billions of years of time to us before that egg breaks on the side of the pan."

Now she tugged his chin and pulled his head so their noses touched, and she started to kiss him, holding him until he melted there. The drawing on the window began to drip. They stayed there another hour, and the longer they kissed, the deeper they both began to swirl in a whirlpool of sensations. He felt like he was floating and had the distinct impression that the spirit was empowered by feeling to explore further than ever before, but at some point, it became so inundated by sensation that it lost that power and became totally absorbed, consumed with a desire to reach the limit of sensation. When they were finished, he looked at his watch and realized it was time to go. "Your father's gonna kill me if I get you home too late," he said.

"Relax," she said. "He's asleep by now anyway. I'll sneak right in."

As he was wiping the moisture from the windshield, his picture going with it, he remembered their earlier discussion, and he started thinking that the human spirit has the capacity to sense a greater order, something that is real, not just a fantasy. "You know," he commented as they were driving home, "I could scare the spider off the license by waving my hand. It wouldn't know what you were, just that you are bigger, and it had better run. We sense something bigger too. We don't know what it is, but we know it's there. We're gifted with a special sense, but we also have the capacity to cloud that sense, even to deny its existence."

She was just finishing restoring the luster of her lips with a gloss. "I don't get it," she said. "What's any of that got to do with anything, really?"

"I thought you liked it when I talked about things like this."

"Not after. I'm hungry now. Let's get something to eat, and stop talking about spiders and something watching everything we do."

They had some pizza, and he dropped her off. When he called the next day, she said she wasn't feeling well. In time, he got the message that she didn't want to see him anymore. One of his friends said she'd been saying she got tired of his philosophy and he was a lousy lover. "Didn't anyone tell you how she likes to chew people up and spit them out?" he asked.

But the worst came when he found out she was pregnant. Despite the hiatus, they were brought back together and married for the sake of the child, but it was born prematurely, and not long after that, they split up for good, but she asked him at the end, "Did you ever consider that the spider was up there above us, unable to recognize the order down below, unable to see how it stomps and rumbles around making a mess out of a whole world?"

He said he hadn't but that anything was possible.

Orpheus, Looking Back

I must protect people here, so I've had to alter key facts. If I was ever able to make wonderful music, it must have been a long time ago, the talent tied directly into a beautiful, happy spirit that I only vaguely recollect. It is almost like a dream. I see myself running around in childhood. My mother let me do it without shoes, and the bees. Oh the bees! There was so much clover in the yard. I can't count the number of times I was stung on the feet. And I was sensitive to the sun, I remember, and my shoulders used to get so sunburned I had epaulets of crusty skin peeling off all the time.

But I don't recall any of the pain. It was a glorious time. I soon learned to capture bees in bottles. We punched holes in the lids and called them "radios," fascinated by the buzzing inside. It was a trick to add more, but we managed, and we learned to outrun them if any escaped. We'd often engage them, try to get them to chase us, and the rule was keep running, make lots of turns, and don't look back.

I had this one friend I'll call Phil because he always wanted to be a philosopher, even way back then. I don't know where he even heard about such things, but that was what he said. He didn't have a father. His mother just showed up one day with him and rented the house across the street. I remember she drove off one day leaving her purse in the middle of the street. I retrieved it and brought it home. So later that afternoon she was at the house telling my mother her life story, how her husband had committed suicide, and how he couldn't get a job. She said Phil thought he'd gone away to think, and I figured that's where he picked up on becoming a philosopher.

Anyway, Phil and I became great friends. I was taking lots of music lessons, and I used to watch Phil out the window playing in his yard. He liked to grow things and tear things apart. He had a great garden full of gourds. He was good at drying them out and making maracas out of them. Those he gave to me to dry out always rotted for some reason, so he gave me some that were dry, and I was always fascinated with them. But as far as tearing things apart, Phil hated bugs and would do anything he could to smash any that were in the garden. Usually grasshoppers got the worst of it. He even used to tie firecrackers to them and blow them up.

There was one plant in the garden that Phil adored. I wasn't sure why it was so important to him until many years later, which I'll explain in due course.

As I mentioned, I was studying music while Phil was outside blowing up bugs in his garden. My father said that Phil would never master philosophy that way, but that my study of music and the other arts would develop my latent powers and make me famous someday as a man of great understanding. My father was a man of business, and at that time I could not see the disparity between what he envisioned for me and his own life. I couldn't ask why he wasn't such a man himself and how he could know these things. At the time, I thought he was such a man.

My music studies advanced quickly as I evidently had a gift, and I delighted in all the forms. But during those days, my father tried to involve me in his own pet projects from when he was a boy. He'd apparently shown talent as a young poet and had composed a children's story that was a failure, but he used to read it to me when I was a boy, and then he would make me read it out loud to him. He would sit there across the room saying as I read, "Why didn't this story succeed? What did I do wrong?" And he was always sending it out to publishers hoping someone would see what he did, but it always came back rejected. Though I had known it all my life, I was his only reader, and I didn't have any critical sense to give him an honest opinion. But my enjoying it was all the proof he needed to keep sending it out. His cover letter told the story of a boy who loved it, and he hoped someone would give it a chance to reach other children, and he finished by saying that it would prove itself in time for it was a magical tale. But competition was tough in the publishing marketplace, and it never saw the light of day.

Despite some terrible things that happened in my life, I managed to save a copy of my father's story. It's yellowed and has many literary flaws, but through it, I learned to believe in miracles, but at the same time, such belief led to some very bad decisions. I won't bore you with the whole tale, but I've included a brief description because of the influence it had on me.

The story basically is about a man named Earnest who dreams a beautiful song and remembers it when he wakes. He also dreamed it would become a great national anthem for his country, so he goes to the capital to make it happen. A corrupt politician recognizes both the power of the song to uplift and its having come out of a deep sleep. Tapping into the latter, he rearranges the song and uses it to put the nation to sleep so that he can take power. Only Earnest is immune, and he wakes everyone with the original song, which goes on to become the national anthem. There was much more to the story, most of it ridiculous, but that is the essence of it.

The strange thing is that I latched onto the more ridiculous aspects of the story. My father laced it with all kinds of convoluted anagrams, and like the corrupt politician in the story, took a perfectly decent premise and put people to sleep with it. My father had a blind spot and saw great promise in it because I enjoyed it. He used to refer to it as his "Earnest Song," and said it represented what was best in him. Frankly, I only discovered and connected the dots of the story much later. It was so convoluted, it was hard to pick out the basic story. But when I was a child, I showed great promise in music, and my father always taught me to put my guts into my music and present it as an earnest song, promising me if I could do that, I couldn't fail. When I was more successful, he brought out the story again, hoping that I might use my influence to get it published. But when I read it, I realized it was hopeless, but I didn't know how to tell him. Reading it again just now reminded me more of that plant I mentioned earlier, the one in Phil's garden that was so special to him. It is as if there are stands we take that take on a life of their own and affect our lives. The garden was like the sea serpent Apollo sent to kill Laocoon for his warnings about the Trojan Horse. I felt that my father's story was a heavy weight around his own neck. He was asking me to lift it off for him, not to keep him from falling into the deep. He was calling me from the bottom to turn it into a life preserver and bring him to the surface. I so much wanted to do that, but going into the heart and mind of one's father is a very complicated journey. I did not feel it had the right merit to publish, and so I sat on the story, delaying as long as I could. Then I had my own problems, and it was easier to sweep it away.

After many difficult years spent pondering how I lost my wife, matters I don't like thinking about and won't discuss here, I took a trip back to my old home town and walked around one afternoon. My old house was very different. It was full of trees. I stood there remembering how much I'd wished there to be trees on the property, and then I recalled planting them before I left and realized these were the trees I'd planted. That was a pleasant memory, but on the whole, I hadn't been thinking how much I liked the trees because the shade was killing the grass. Besides that, I used to have the run of the place. I remember how big the yard felt to me, but now there was no place for a kid to run around. It seemed I had changed the yard for the worse. I stood there pulling leaves off branches and thinking about my childhood when I heard footsteps behind me in the street. I turned around to see a man I didn't recognize but who knew me. It was Phil, after all these years! His mother had died many years earlier, and he had kept the house. He invited me over and apparently wanted me to help him with something.

It was that plant of his. It had been growing out there for more than forty years and had completely taken over the garden. It had mushroomed over the entire yard and was full of thorns. I walked around, searching for the trunk and could see it through an impenetrable mass of thorns, as wide as a tree. Phil wanted me to help him remove it. There was a pile of branches he had cut, but it looked weeks old, and he said that it was a day's work and two days of growth had replaced it by the following day. I could see many things caught in the bramble. Phil said that was nothing, that there were hundreds of things that had gotten swallowed in the brush. I said it was just things, and that this was something that could be removed by professionals. He said it was his life in there, and he wanted it back.

Phil explained that over the years the plant had grown at a normal rate, and he'd always kept it pruned, but he'd followed my music and my career, and after his own wife died, he'd played my music in the house constantly, and the plant had taken off from there. "I'm not blaming you," he said, "but look what your music has done."

I had stopped performing. I didn't even play anymore, not even for personal enjoyment as music only reminds me of her and the harsher recollection of how my father's silly tale nourished in me the foolish belief that I could alter reality using only the power of an earnest song. It is true that my music had a powerful effect on others, and it is true that my music was an earnest song, but I would have to admit that much of it came naturally, and I didn't have to force anything. My father's work had the smell of his sweat on it. You could feel it was constructed and almost trip over the seams they were sewn so badly. My father had great hopes for his personal work. He always hoped one day to quit his job and devote his time to writing, but his job took so much of his time that all he had in the end was that early story, and it had "don't quit your day job" written between every line. Unlike my father, I was able to write my own ticket, as they say. I don't remember putting much into it, and I took it all for granted, and while I milked it for all it was worth, in the end success went to my head, so much so that it was not my music but something in me that brought me down, and I realize now looking back that a bush of thorns had filled me up in the silence that I forced on myself during the bitter years that followed. It still does in fact, and it continues to grow, and when I try to scale it back, the same as in Phil's garden, two days worth of new growth fills one day of pruning. The one thing I had was music, and now it's the single thing I refuse in my life, and unlike Phil's garden where music is credited for the growth, in my case the bramble inside me is due to the lack of it. It is like I have put a spell on myself that music has no power, and people are flawed, and though music might break that spell, it would break my heart, so reclaiming me out of the bramble is a delicate operation.

On the other hand, another kind of song is not singing, not playing, not falling so fully into music's grasp as to make it your own; or in my case, to abandon it and fall into the common fold of everyday business to forget beauty, truth and things to love. That is the crime, and my father had the stronger heart. He was only forced into business to make a living, whereas I chose it as a refuge after losing my wife. Phil found solace in those same songs, and a bramble surrounds him. I suppose that's preferable to being eaten from within and blocked both ways on a path to and from hell.

Some things stick in my craw. First, all those years when I was performing, it didn't matter what I played. My success was in interpretation and rendition. I had the right touch. In my father's story, it is apparent that there was magic in the song. The melody of Earnest must have truly been wonderful, and quite frankly, I am ashamed to say that I never really tried composing anything of my own. There was already so much out there, and I always took the easy way. My father did not. I was not present when he was dying, but I heard stories about his last week. Something in particular has stayed with me all these years, and I am only beginning to understand its significance. He knew the end was coming. He said he was not afraid. My mother had died many years earlier, and he'd remarried. I never much cared for this new wife of his. I met her after I'd lost my own wife, and she was always trying to get me to get back to playing music, and she hardly knew me. Her efforts actually helped solidify my will against music.

But after he died, she told me these stories of the last week they spent together, much of it on a soft mattress they had placed on the floor near the fireplace, almost like they were at a campfire under the stars. In those last few days, they shared the essence of life in the struggle that no one else wanted to be around to share. She helped to lead him forward into his transition, into letting go, holding his hand all the way. They looked into one another's eyes, knowing what was coming. It did not come at once, but gradually over several long and painful days. With her being there with him, he did not suffer but grew in peace as the final moment approached. When it finally came, they were watching one another, face to face, down to the very last breath. She said there was a sudden sound behind her at the door. She looked up to see who was coming in, but nobody was there, and when she looked back, he was already gone.

What I want to do is compose an anthem to go along with my father's story, something so beautiful that people will understand the meaning better. I have contacted several publishing companies about the idea of including a song with the book, but none has been interested so far. I think I'd do better to compose the anthem and include it with the query, but I have no talent for composition. You can't just pluck random notes and stir feeling, but if the feeling's there, you could almost lead the dead back through life's door. Everything swings on whether they have your attention or you have theirs. For music to be great, you've got to get their attention and not let them get to you. It's like opera where you don't even need to understand the story, just that people are in pain.

The Choir Master

The choir master was a lonely and belligerent man who had a grand vision to build a spectacular band shell in the hills above the city. He bought the land and had architects draw up the plans, and the only thing left to do was build it. During the months of preparation, however, all the various pressures had brought the worst out of him, and he had driven everyone out of the choir. Many just got sick of him and left. He'd insulted others during practice, telling them they were unworthy to perform in the new band shell. At the same time, he had become so immersed in the project that he'd put his own family on a back burner. Everything about them had begun to irritate him. His wife had a family reunion coming up, and for the first time, he made it clear he would not attend. There was simply too much he had to do. They had three children of their own and had adopted three others, and six kids in the house made a lot of racket. It was difficult to concentrate. He said he needed the time alone. This was unacceptable to his wife. She said he had no right to leave everything in her hands, that his being the choir master was getting in the way of more important things. She said finally that he needed to make the right decision, not the one that was convenient to him at the moment.

At about this same time, he had met a woman with a truly wonderful voice that he wanted to kick off the first season of concerts when the band shell opened. The worse the pressure put on him at home, the more he started idealizing the vocalist as a woman with personality traits more suited to his own. He did not know her very well, and the time he was with her was generally spent discussing business matters, but he had begun to see her as a replacement for his wife, as an artistic counterpart to him, the other pole of the magnet, the yang for his yin, and it wasn't like he was swooning inside. At least he didn't see it as a romantic obsession. Nevertheless, he was becoming obsessed with her in his own peculiar way, and one day he determined that it was the right moment to drive to her house and lay everything out for her.

She came to the door very surprised to see him. He came in and started talking about the future, about realizing their full potential together, how she could quit her job as a voice instructor at the community college and enjoy a brilliant career as a soloist. He also declared that he was building the band shell for her. He said it was going up in the hills above the town because the town wasn't fit for it, that the human race was a sick lot that just sat around breeding and passing on the breeding rules. But the two of them were made for greatness, and together they would light the world with music.

She had never seen him in such a state. She also didn't know him very well and thought this was a clear sign of how he really was, so she very kindly said she was not interested in any of it and asked him to leave. He did, but he also kept coming back. He'd park in front and watch her house and bother her when she came out until she finally succeeded in getting a restraining order. His wife left him and took the kids back to her family, and this all happened around the time the band shell was completed, which everyone found laughable now. It was all a big joke. There was no choir, no schedule of concerts, only a sick choir master who had lost control.

On what would have been the night of the opening concert, he went up to the band shell and sat there in what was the most acoustically perfect setting, in the perfect spot in the rocks overlooking the village. He didn't think about anything that happened, only about what might have been, the amazing concert that everyone in the valley would hear. Then he heard them, the voices from below, the kids crying, the cars honking, it was all coming up to him, amplified by the shell around him. "I wanted their ears, not this noise," and he sat there crying. But loud as he was, the valley was louder, and nobody could hear him.

Bad Time Stories

Chester Himmes started an internet blog under the pen name Josh N. called *The Way It Should Be*. He thought he had some good ideas for stories that were tense but positive in tone. The web site was a test to see if anyone found his material interesting.

His first post to the blog was a story about a single father whose daughter became sick. He called the doctor who phoned a prescription to the pharmacy, but she was too sick to go with him. She was also very young, and he'd never left her alone. But he told her he'd be right back and not to worry. Everything went smoothly until he was almost home. The gates were down for a passing train that was coming to a stop. After waiting ten minutes, he left his car to look in both directions down the tracks. There were train cars in both directions as far as he could see. It was not a far walk from the tracks to his house, so he backed up the car and parked it off the road. He could walk back and get it later. He pocketed the medicine for his daughter and climbed on the connector between the cars, but as he started to do so, the train started moving. He could easily have jumped off, but he froze, not knowing what he should do. As it picked up a little speed, he decided he must jump. He looked for a soft spot, but by the time he saw anything, the train was going much faster, and he was going further from the house, but he finally jumped. After rolling when he hit the ground, he did not move.

This is how Chester left the story on Friday, not quite sure of some of the finishing details. But he made no indication that there was more to tell, and on Monday when he returned, he was flabbergasted to see there were many hits on the page from readers who thought it was very interesting. He'd intended it to be about heroic struggle through pain, that the father would wake and crawl home to his daughter even though his leg was broken, but now that readers had responded with kind comments, he let it end that way.

His next post was a story that was supposed to end when a rape ring was arrested by the police, but instead he ended it abruptly to see what kind of reception another troubling end to a story would receive. This one had a young man surprised to find his girlfriend not at home when he came to visit. Hearing noises in the back by the train tracks, he discovers that she is surrounded by a gang of thugs who are raping her. He pleads with them to let her go, but he also is stripped and forced to have sex with his girlfriend while they watch. He is unable to perform for them, so the gang ties the couple down and leaves them on the tracks.

This story also received rave reviews from readers, which prompted him to show some of his family who were appalled at the kind of stories he was writing. When he explained, they said it was a bad idea, but he said he wanted to see where it would lead.

So he continued writing stories that were sad and troubling. His next story was about a man with a heart condition who had many disagreeable qualities that made him vicious whenever he saw them in his son. Later, he attacks his son for being different. One day at the park, cursing his son under his breath, he sees his son across the field in trouble. Other boys are ganging up on him, so instinctively he runs to help him. Because he is running and images are jumbled, he thinks he sees that they are killing his son and that he'll never make it in time. He's so far away, they will have time to finish him off even when they see help on the way. He stops to try to get a better look, but it is still too far away to recognize anyone. He also begins to feel faint, and he collapses there having suffered a massive heart attack. In the original version, he rescues his son.

Readers did not seem to mind how similar this was to the first story. They pleaded for more. His next offering was a tale of a young girl who was abused by her parents and befriended by a neighbor who was always very nice to her. The parents became upset by the relationship and told their daughter that she must tell lies about the man. She did so, and he was arrested.

Again, the messages poured into his web site to keep it coming. So he wrote another story about a bad marriage where a man who was very faithful and kind was henpecked constantly by his wife. Meanwhile, she started cheating on him, and she was not very careful about it, so he found out about it. He became very angry and confused. His appetite disappeared and he grew dangerously thin and weak, so weak that his wife started bringing her boyfriend home with her, doing nothing to help him, and he wastes away.

By the time he added this one to his blog, the number of hits had quadrupled. He did a search on the site and found that people were posting links to it on chat boards. He began to pour over some of his ideas for those that were easily chopped to have the same kind of impact. All of them were ultimately very positive, but there was always a place where the tone shifted out of negative circumstances, facilitating the editing of his stories for the blog.

He then posted a story about a man who did not interact in life but was a collector of things. By the end of his life, he had spent all of his time adding to his house in order to display his things, not realizing that he was becoming a great cavern himself. When he died, he was not found. His house was emptied of the junk, and people were surprised to find the cavern in the back, which was nothing more than a dank emptiness. Still, it was unique in the village, and became a popular site for visitors. At no point did anyone realize that the cavern had once been a man.

When Chester's family read this on the blog, they questioned how it would have ended in the original, more positive version, and he refused to answer them, saying only, "It is complete as is." They characterized what he was doing as "serious." Chester answered that it was nothing more than a serious joke.

The next story was about a man of God who started a church under the slogan, "Ten Thousand Days of Peace," and for just that long the church was friendly and peaceful. Then, on exactly the ten thousand and first day, the minister went berserk, tearing up the town, shooting from the bell tower until an armed unit was called in to take him down.

It was at this point that Chester received a call from a television network about his blog. They found him listed as owning the domain name for his blog. He said he was merely hosting an artist named Josh N. who wished for the time to remain anonymous, at least until enough was published in the blog for a first book, at which time he would be looking for a publishing deal. They asked to speak with Josh directly, but Chester wouldn't give them any information. When the story aired, the report only said that the web site had established quite a following with stories that were very tragic. "The Way It Is" blog was compared to "News of the Weird," strange but true stories from around the globe. These also were an internet sensation, but there was something interesting about the fact that these stories were fiction, and nobody knew anything about the writer except that he wished to remain anonymous. Chester was expecting much more but the piece only ran a minute.

His next story was about a man who was overly focused on the health of his children. When they got sick, he always feared the worst. Fear often overwhelmed him even though they may only have had a slight fever or cold. He experienced a hurricane of emotion, a sense of the full terror awaiting everyone at the end of life, and he cursed God, if there was such a thing, for having created a state where we seem to have ample time to linger, write songs of love and sing them only to face the horror of the inevitable in due course. When the children felt better, the bitter winds died down, and once again he was capable of joining in the chorus of joyful hymns praising life and its benevolent creator. In time, his children all grew up healthy and went away to start their own families. Then one day he was in the station waiting for a train and started coughing. He felt worse and worse, like he was suffocating, and he reached a point where he crumpled to the ground against a roof support, unable to ask anyone for help. Nobody offered assistance. When people near the scene were interviewed later by police, they indicated they thought he was just resting. The fact that he was bleeding from the ears and foaming at the mouth did not come up.

At this point, Chester's blog was getting thousands of hits a day. He also noticed the sudden appearance of numerous messages objecting to the content, but the positives far outweighed the negatives, and he passed it off as being related to the story on the news. For the first time, he was also starting to write new material without any thought to its needing to have some kind of positive ending. He just wrote the intense, sad and tragic beginning, and a weight seemed lifted off his back. Having to build a story with structural counterparts of good and evil presented a problem. It was like having to create a perfect balance. Before the blog, it was difficult to finish some of his ideas. He had always appreciated the art of telling stories. When he studied classic fiction, the moral sense was always very clear. They seemed to always make life make sense. When he first studied some modern writers, however, there were stories that challenged his beliefs. He thought they ended badly, but the instructor would ask how life ended and discuss the role of literature in telling the truth rather than preaching the message of the writer. He might be an instrument of the church or even the government, famous, in the end because his books were found acceptable. Some courses traced the history of thought without regard for the artistic merit of the books. Chester had naively thought the books chosen for study were naturally only the best works with ideas still worth believing today. Finally, with this blog, he felt he understood. He had found not only his niche, but the truth. There was no right or wrong. The only truth in the greater picture of life was the graveyard. All the pointing to the way we should think and act treated the world as a child. Chester no longer wanted to be a writer if it meant he might be compared with a preacher or a moralist of any kind. The stone cold truth was obviously very appealing to people. They were sick of lies, and even libraries had sections full of them.

Since these stories were easier to write, Chester started posting several at once, all without thought to a happy ending. The first was one where a man drives by the hotel on the highway where he first met his wife when she worked there. He recalls those happy days and nights, then how she left him. The story ends abruptly with the man driving through the wall into the lobby and killing himself.

The second story was about a family. A mother is diagnosed with cancer and starts to actually flatten down quickly into a seed-shaped blob like a clam with eyes lit up in the darkness between two shells, and underneath her are the even flatter shapes of her parents who were dead, and beneath them a greater but less recognizable flattening that takes on the general look of layers of sedimentary rock. It is a time of sadness for the children, and when she dies, the effect is subtle, but they are each noticeably flatter.

Then he posted a tale of a church on wheels that drove around snatching children from the bus stops, driving into the woods and dumping them out the back down a ravine.

Chester checked his blog the next day, and the negative messages far outweighed the positive. Some regulars were suddenly saying he'd lost it, that the blog had gone south. This story really incensed his father, who was a pastor. "Why are you writing this kind of garbage?" he demanded to know. Chester wouldn't answer.

Chester got angry and wrote a story in which the world was a dumb, self-destructive giant. He lives alone, worries about every little thing and destroys anything that gets in his way. In the end, the giant trips over the very things he builds to keep the pests out, and dies in the very traps he sets for them. He festers into a rotting mass that pollutes the atmosphere and poisons the rest of the planet.

Chester received mixed reviews for this, too, and rationalized he would always have detractors. But is was downhill from there, and a month later, he was publishing anything to get people's attention. His father called and advised Chester to go back to writing real stories, to follow his original plan, not the course that hooked him when he'd gained a following. "Rip a hologram apart, and the whole image is still visible, which is why your first stories were popular," he said. "The faith was still there even though you ended them suddenly. No matter how horrible a picture from life, the photographer can't remove faith from real life. Remember the minds that read your work are transient, like yours, with fierce, sharp claws scouring the earth for hope, like you. Give them a rock, and they will drop it on your head, but offer the truth in any form, and though they may say you've laid an egg, they'll be the first to sit on it until it hatches." So Chester went back to fix his stories, and the long, silent period of incubation began.

The Minister's Garden

Despite what some have to say about the ephemerality of this place, this thing called life, things we say and actions we take do stay behind for other minds to consider, and what we make, unless it's destroyed, will be there as well for other hands to hold. This place has a memory, and it has a desire to consider what those who came before have said or done, and to hold things they have held or made. Perhaps this explains why Interior Minister Glorp took so well to his garden in later life.

It wasn't always that way. The minister as a young man was anything but interested in such things. Even by middle age, his back and knees were causing him great pain, so the idea of bending over or kneeling in the dirt was absurd to him. But even much later, there he was in the morning digging with a spade on his hands and knees, and spraying it all with a hose by sunset.

Glorp had risen to the high rank of Minister of Interior with brutal efficiency. The power it gave him might have been rendered more compatible with God's commands had Glorp been more attentive to them, had he been a compassionate being, but he was not a religious man. As a child, he tortured insects, turned them to soup using a broken lawn mower. The starter cover had come loose and fallen off. The spring that rewrapped the rope broke too, so now he had to insert a knot in a notch of the exposed cup and wind a rope manually and pull to start the mower. Once started, the rotation of the cup made it a centrifuge in which he dropped crickets and grasshoppers, or anything else he could catch alive. It all became a blur into which he would place the snipped end of an old hanger, liquefying what did not come flying out of what quickly became insect soup.

Glorp started this with crickets because they would sound off from hiding behind the walls of his room, stopping momentarily when he made any kind of noise or attempt to silence them by running a hanger under the base of the wall, resuming their racket once he got back into bed. There were times in the summer that he thought they would drive him mad. His parents were not very sympathetic, though they let him spray insect repellent around the base of the walls, but until the first frost, the crickets kept it up at night, and so by day, he flushed them out around the house, captured them and liquefied them in his soup centrifuge.

Years later, when Glorp was married, already a minister, he made up his mind that his sons would have an aggravation-free childhood, and so he commanded his wife to leave things alone in the big yard. He wanted the boys to have room to play, and if she put anything up or tried to grow flowers, no doubt they would knock something down and be punished for it, so he gave her the front yard for her interests but said the back was off limits.

Each year, however, Madame Glorp managed to do at least one thing to undermine the Interior Minister's standing orders. She would do something like put a swing in a tree for the children, and after doing that, she would do something like plant flowers along the fence. When the minister complained, she would say the flowers were a wild variety, and it did not matter to her if the boys knocked them down. And so by degrees, over many years, the back yard became filled with a variety of physical and organic objects, many for the children, and many for her. And by degrees as the boys grew older, their range had grown smaller, and they were reprimanded whenever they knocked down a plant by kicking a ball into it. The yard was so filled up with her stuff that the boys hardly played there anymore. The minister himself was too busy to remember his original plan for the boys or listen to their complaints. By the time the oldest was ten, the standing order was that they should stay out of the yard and play at friends' houses if possible.

Then one day the first subpoena came, catching the minister by such surprise that he actually started to shake uncontrollably. It was only by going into the solace of the garden that he was able somehow to steady himself, and he sat by the arbor for several hours working out a scheme to rid himself of a scandal in the making, which he succeeded in doing, turning the tables on his enemies and dropping them into the centrifuge for a little stirring up. The business files he accumulated and kept in his house for just such an eventuality came in quite handy, it turned out, but after that, he sought refuge in the garden on a regular basis. Some people were clearly out to get him, and the garden became his sanctuary. He even began to limit his wife's use of the place and gradually took over the daily maintenance, and drove home at lunch on hot days to water the plants.

Still, by the end of his career, even though nothing had actually been pinned on him, there had been so many scandals and indictments, one after another it seemed, that he was finally just glad to get out of the robes. The newspapers said he had been forced out, which was true, except he had gradually let it happen over the years, giving up this power to that person and delegating so much of his work in order to insulate himself that by the time he left, it didn't matter much to him. His career had been over for a long time.

But this is where the fact that the world in which we live has a long memory comes into play. The minister, too, had a long memory. He could still see the faces of everyone he railroaded, forced out of office, sent to prison or had killed one way or another. He would see them when he was out for lunch alone. They would come to his table like shadows seeking to lure him into an extra slice of cheesecake to clog his arteries. Each would whisper facts of his case in his ear, hoping to raise his heart rate, urge him to put more sugar in his coffee and have another cup. They would surround him when he checked the time and got up to leave, walking with him down the street hoping to maneuver him into the street in front of traffic, or at the very least just generally make him feel terribly ill at ease. Glorp always saw them, but he never flinched or twitched or gave any indication that they were succeeding. He reasoned they were created by his own imagination, that he was responsible for all that dredging up of old history, but how detailed it all was. Clearly he did not forget his transgressions. He had lied his way out of every trap ever set to trap him, but he was keenly aware of the truth, that was certain. And as his reputation hung on a thread that would break if so much as one bit of truth of his misdeeds came to light, he embarked on a journey to bury it so deep in his heart that it would be neutralized to not eat away at him from within and die with him in the end.

How was he able to achieve this? With the garden. He retired there, spent all his days in the grasses and flowers making things grow. His boys were grown up and gone, and his wife had made new friends and spent most days shopping with them. But Glorp wanted to be alone and was happy to be in control of things. He made them live and watched them die, and they all went back into the earth. It wasn't that it brought him peace, but rather that it was his answer to history and the memory of the world, which has a keen eye for anything of value, physical or metaphysical. However innumerable may be the population of organic life forms at any given time, the number of antiques and ideas floating around far exceeds it, and these are kept alive in such a way as to even impact the way the world functions, much as it had driven Glorp to his garden, though he would argue it was his choice, that the world had nothing to do with it. But Glorp was only deceiving himself.

The garden has always been a place of ideas. From the beginning it was where good and evil first squared off. Nature magazines will often show a picture of a creature in camouflage like a viper hidden in the leaves. We clear away the brush and make a habitat for ourselves, not just to kill everything that lived in the jungle, but to eliminate the fear and danger in a dark unknown. Still, we have all the mythology of the hunter with painted face stalking his prey. Without a real jungle, we create a jungle within our society and ourselves. and the laws of the jungle are like a carnivorous plant.

Take Glorp for example. One day in the hot sun, he got dizzy, started spinning and was unable to move. Something like a stick in his garden cup, liquefying him and his interior into Minister Glorp soup. Later, his wife turned his files over to a nice, young reporter.

Momentary Loves

Did you see the movie? I just did, and I'm still reeling in the images. I choose that phrase deliberately because I'm both swirling in them and picking them out of the swirl. What a flick!

I loved the interplay of the two relationships, how they never intersected but revealed not just one another but another that was not even discussed, only alluded to in moments of guilt.

There was Anna and Hafez. What a passionate couple they were in the three days they knew one another. I loved the seduction scene, the way she washed and dressed so carefully as if she knew it was coming, wanting it to happen. It was like she was guided by intuition, by some unknown waves that one feels. How easily detected by the heart are things no machine can be calibrated to measure! And Hafez was such a gentleman, dancing and holding her so gently while so ripe and ready to burst. The peak of love about to unfold is such an intense experience. There is nothing else like it in life, and while we don't really even see the couple beyond that first kiss, we'll never forget her white scarf blowing with the same lightness as the fabric of the curtain in the window where the camera took our eyes as they gently leaned in that wonderful kiss toward the bed.

I'm not sure it was even so sad when they finally said goodbye to one another a few days later, knowing they would never see one another again. He spoke of the palm branches painted on the window of the shop where they first met, how whenever he saw a palm tree, he would think of her. And he lived in a land full of palm trees. There was one just outside his bedroom window at home. He was telling her that she would always be that close. And she told him that whenever there was a breeze of any kind that touched her face, she would feel his face close to hers. And she was from the coastal region where the wind blew in or out every day. You knew he could imagine her walking the beach in the breeze, remembering him.

But underneath all of this, we knew watching why they were saying goodbye. They knew it couldn't work. The world was too set against them. They were of different faiths, enemy faiths to the very soul. This did not matter in the least to them. Like so many individuals who meet, they cared nothing for the traditional politics that made their countries enemies. Not only that, but their skin color was not the same. This did not matter either in the three days they were together. Everything about their cultures was different, but why should they care? They experienced everything one can hope to, gave everything they had to one another in their momentary love. That was all that mattered. It is all that matters. They knew more than the world, but in the end, heading their separate ways, we understood what they did, that the world would be too hard on them if they stayed together despite that world.

The second relationship depicted in the film is even more illicit because one was married. Elsa and Thomas met because of business that Elsa's company was conducting with Thomas, and from the moment they first saw one another, there was a terrible tension and irritation that could only be remedied by a removal of clothing and passionate lovemaking. It took almost an hour of criticizing and bickering before they finally gave in to the forbidden taste of one another, and like Hafez and Anna, it only lasted a few days.

But it's amazing to realize that Elsa's marriage is not bad, that Elsa loved her husband, and set in the nineteenth century, not only was it harder for her to break her vow because of the terrible pressures of those days, but her own marriage, even if it were to last another hundred years, is over because everyone is dead. Elsa and Thomas make it clear how all human love is momentary in the larger sense. Some loves are stretched out more than others. Some affairs may be kept going for months and years, all in a kind of rejection of the higher forces that ultimately dictate our general actions, but not the feelings in our hearts. We can do what we want, follow where our hearts lead, but just as we know intuitively before we kiss that we will in fact kiss, we also know when something will be short-lived or even doomed from the start, and we don't need to speak about it to our momentary lover for they know it too as a correspondence and contradiction of all that stands against them. Even in a kind of blind obedience to it, there is not merely a rejection or repudiation, but a proof that it need not be that way, and this is directed by the film and understood by every heart watching it, which makes it all the more amazing. Each person in each enemy land weeps when Anna and Hafez say goodbye. They know it could be them. They know they could find someone to love in that other country, and they know it's just a political situation perpetuated by the sense of the mind of the larger group, not by the heart of the individual.

Even so, the relationships end. Elsa goes back to her husband. A note at the end says Thomas got married, but he named a daughter after her and when he made love to his wife remembered his brief but fulfilling moments with Elsa. The other issue was that Elsa was twenty years older than Thomas, and when he did finally break down and try to get in touch with her, much as she yearned to make contact, she had gotten gray and did not want him to see her that way, but remember her as she was in the last days of her prime, which was another reason she had the affair to begin with, because she was facing getting old and wanted to live again for a moment.

The film reveals that people mingle in an intuitive repudiation of conditions that the world imposes. Lovers make the statement that politics are unreal in the face of individual feeling. They are saying it's senseless for countries to hate one another when loving someone of a contradictory value system is possible. But in the end, people fold, not because they could not handle any tension they would face, but because love is such a long haul, and sooner or later we settle down into a daily routine, which is slack, and slack is not just the environment that tests relationships, but a key influence in the hatred of distant neighbors. The world cuts no slack, then there's too much. One night we steal a moment, then we submit to our culture where we can safely weep at depictions of forbidden love, then join hands and tug hard as we can, tightening all that slack.

Henry Collins

One of my colleagues in the English Department mentioned that Henry Collins was laid up, not doing so well, and suggested that we go down and see him before he died. Word had it that he was getting worse, that he had all kinds of bed sores and was going down the tubes, but for some reason he was talking more. There were all kinds of images coming out, and people want to know what he's saying, not knowing if it was cogency or lunacy. For both of us, it meant meeting him for the first time, not just seeing him, and given what a great writer Collins was, I felt both inclined and intimidated, especially the latter since we'd be walking in on him at a bad time. But Don made a few calls, and heard back that Collins agreed to see us, so we drove into eastern Kentucky down some back roads, made a final turn that took us deeper in the woods until we came upon a mailbox at the roadside where if you looked hard you could barely see a gravel driveway overgrown with weeds. Through the thick brush we could just make out what might be a trailer up the hill.

It was not the dilapidated trailer we saw, but Henry's little hut, which is how he referred to it in a couple of his stories. And it was a super hot day, just like in his stories, the kind that makes me feel heavy like I wish I hadn't had bacon with my breakfast. I wondered how I was going to make it through the next few minutes, wondering if I was really seeing things right, like there's some kind of optical illusions going on, and the eyes can't quite seem to focus, a strange, almost hypnotic effect. There was a smell too, like everything was about to turn bad, to rot, and the insects were so loud but nowhere to be found. The whole place was boiling. It was so humid, and there I was, not feeling so well, and it was only morning, and I was heading up to visit someone who is supposedly very sick, barely hanging on here, and I was feeling like I had it worse. So I tried to keep in mind that I was there to visit this legend, this man who was so successful at writing local myths and stories, so well known for his story of the marble hidden in the bookcase, *The Growing Marble*, and *The Flower in the Chair*, which was also a good one.

It was a long walk up the gravel road up the hill, and there was siding everywhere like a tornado had taken bites out of the trailer, in different colors. There were lots of rusty cans, some buried half stuck in the cracked dirt that must have been mud at one point. And getting to the top of the hill, I could see down the other side was a river, the Big Sandy, which was running low, and over the bushes and vines were old appliances dumped there over the years. Further down were loads of plastic milk jugs, spray cans and bottles all piled up in places where the river had run out of room pushing them off to the side when it went down and left them all there until it would reach that plateau another time.

In all this wreckage, next to the trailer, there was an arch that was covered with clematis in bloom, carefully tended with weeds pulled from around the posts all dried up around it, the withered giant leaves of that grapeless ivy knocked off the arbor but covering everything around it. We went through it and up a few stairs to get to the door, then waited on the welcome mat after knocking.

Even on that small landing, I felt like I was going to fall. I started to lean on the handrail but thought better of it. There was a slight tilt to it, and when the door opened to a darkness in the hallway that took my eyes some time to adjust to from the blinding light outside, I could feel the floor was askew as well. Leaving the rank jungle and that terrible glare of sunlight, I was so glad to get out of it. But the hallway was an oven though I could hear the sound of an air conditioner, and since it had become the primary sound in the trailer, I could remember it hidden within the sounds I'd just walked through outside, buried under the hissing *dit-dit-dish* of the insects.

My eyes gradually adjusted to the darkness, to the strange brown coloring of the whole place. The walls, the rugs, and the hallway were all brown. The woman who let us in had just made tracks through the hallway to the back, so we followed, and again had to deal with the tilt of the floor. I felt like I was walking sideways, and I kept one hand on a wall to guide me, and I could tell by looking at it that it's pressboard, and it's starting to fall down in places since they used brackets instead of drywall nails.

Then we came into a large room, that looked like the only room, which had a kitchen area to the left and next to it was a a bedroom set. I could see the windows were dusty through the nearly closed curtains. I could just see the glare, but not the colors or the life, but I could almost feel that right outside the glass the vines were creeping all over the back of the trailer, everywhere in heat, that was coming through the walls, stifling except in this room. And there was Henry in bed, and his wife, the woman who let us in, so much younger and in good shape, or was that his daughter? Looking around I saw a still life of bananas and fruit in a bowl. Beyond that were lots of dishes in the sink, and the ribbon tied to the vent of the air conditioner blowing my way, toward which I wanted to lean because I could detect a larger bubble of cool, slightly drier air to my right, and I was standing in the full fringe of a wet, warm stench before a very sick man, and I don't know how to describe it, but the smell was lots of things pertaining to Henry and his condition.

We said our hellos, introduced ourselves and thanked him for seeing us, to which Henry gave us a dying look as he tried to move, then gritted his teeth and whirled his arms for help. "Sit me up," he ordered. "Get me out of bed for my visitors. Put me on a chair." The effort was excruciating enough to watch. I was horrified to think we'd come all this way to put him through such hell. Henry's lips were parched and covered with sores. His legs looked as if he'd been bitten by hundreds of mosquitoes and had been scratching the bumps open. His few strands of hair were all grey and nubby and he looked so tired. As he was easing finally into his soft chair, there were so many bottles of pills I was just beginning to notice in various places. As bright as it was outside, the whole place was so dark. I looked around for a light of some kind, a pole light or something, thinking how a skylight would light the whole place up, something, some kind of opening, and then thought how that might make me feel if I were in bed most of the day, looking up most of the time. I wondered when the last time Henry had gotten out, whether anyone ever took him out at all, and whether he could navigate the tilt in the floor without falling over. There was no ramp at the door, and it was obvious his legs weren't much use. But I had this idea of taking Henry out on a wheelchair down a ramp and a clean, paved drive for a walk around the premises, if you will, and engaging him in a lively conversation. This occupied my thoughts rather than what was in front of me at the time. Rather than stare at his lips and wonder how it felt to have so many sores, I thought of Henry absorbed in watching the sand hornets jet about quietly and suddenly engage another for a moment before resuming their steady flight. I thought how he might sit there and imagine his days there as a boy. Sitting in the room, it was easy to think he'd lived his whole life in this awful room, but just outside the door in that horrid light and heat was once his great domain along the river. He wrote about it quite a bit, and there it was, just beyond the door, that legendary idyllic domain.

And here in this room, we sat in the other domain, equally famous for images connected to it, particularly the one he wrote about the flower that grew out of the chair. We heard before our visit that he'd been talking about that, almost as if changing the story, arguing with people who asked him direct questions about the meaning of the story, not so much contradicting them but adding to it, and they didn't know if he was saying the original story needed to be changed or more likely that he was just off on some tangent.

In the original story, a flower grows out of the chair. Everyone is amazed, and nobody wants to sit on the chair, and people in the house grow straighter and stand taller. Eventually the flower bears seeds, and the family collects and sells the seed for people to plant in their chairs. Sooner or later everybody in the community is standing up better. Sitting becomes a thing of the past, and they eat standing at the tables. Then one day a preacher comes and tries to get everyone to church, and they come but want to stand, not sit.

The Long Beat of the Metronome

But the preacher says they have to sit, even kneel down, and when he learns about the seeds he preaches that it's the work of the devil, and that people may think they are standing up but have become lazy in spirit. So he orders them to bring their chairs out to be burned in a big fire, and as the smoke goes up, everyone sees a big flower in the sky. Later, no matter how they try or kneel and secretly pray for it, nobody can get a flower to grow in a chair again.

People said that when Henry started talking again about the flower in the chair, he said everyone in the room was a lazy dead plant, and the chairs were all shined up from constant use. And he asked why nobody remembered his sister who died when she was little, how he brought a flower and put it in the chair next to him in church, and the preacher that day said that the world was full of different points of view, but there is only one right one, getting God's point of view into the mind was the issue, to plant that seed so it would take on a life of its own, and those in whom the plant had grown stood for things in ways that others did not, and stood together with others who stood for them too. Then the preacher saw the flower Henry put in the chair next to him and said it was like that flower, only man had turned the seed into a bomb and dropped it on a city, and a great flowering cloud went up. Everyone kneeled and prayed, but somehow the age of flowers was over.

When Don told me that Henry was talking like this, I had no problem at all with it. In fact, I liked the idea of listening to him and said I didn't have any expectations but hoped he would feel free to expound on whatever came to his mind. Even if he was completely out of his mind, I wanted to hear what he had to say.

Finally Henry was settled in his chair and squinting at us like we were giving off a bad smell. He said, "I never could play the rhythms, so I was stretched paper thin over a tin, you know, like a chamois tied around a coffee can, turned into a flat turtle, if you will, with head, arms and legs sticking out, but my heart and soul were held over this great emptiness, held hostage to something who knows those rhythms, playing me, making them pour out of me." After saying that, he patted his belly a few times, showing no musical ability whatsoever, and he smiled, then winced in pain.

"Mr. Collins," I said, "If you don't mind talking about your work, I was thinking of one of your stories on the ride over here, about the man who finds a marble he threw into a bookcase behind a shelf of books, and as he pulls the book out one day years later, he sees this little marble, that it must have been thrown behind the books, and thinks nothing of it except he remembers it as smaller. Later, he sees something big between two books, but it couldn't be the marble because it's so much bigger, and he can see his face in it, which seems to cause a growth spurt because all the sudden it engulfs the bookcase and then he's trying to put the book back, and it encroaches and it grows bigger and it knocks down the bookcase and fills the room. Sorry, I'm not exactly sure where it goes from there, but I don't see a bookcase here anywhere, so I was wondering..."

"You got it backwards," Henry interrupted me. "That thing got in my eye and started growing, first like I could see better, then bigger like I had to look through it to see. Then it started to hurt, and it rotated like to turn and look at me, but I had grown connected with it, and all I could see was what was in me. I was blind to everything else. Then one day it popped out while I was sleeping I guess, and I put it in the bookcase, into a special book and if it started growing from there, it was in your imagination because that was the ending to that story."

I knew that wasn't the ending, but I didn't know how to respond other than to nod and thank him. I looked at Don, as if to say, your turn to ask him a question, but Don just looked at me.

I told Henry there was music in his voice, and even though he had a fairly strong accent, he spoke slowly enough that we could make out every word. Then Henry just started talking, and we listened like we were at a concert. "I'm like a singer from rough beginnings who was about to have his bubble burst. The singer was meticulous," he said. "He had to be, with all the competition out there and his faults being sometimes observable in practice and in competition. He had to work doubly hard to ensure that he would be recognized, so he cultivated an attention to detail and polished his appearance and style and was extremely professional in every way. Some people predicted the rough beginnings would eventually show through. Even the singer could not forget the dark days, but he had so much natural talent, trained meticulously and had achieved unquestionable early success, that most gave him the benefit of the doubt. Then one day, while singing on stage, a bubble formed in his mouth and grew bigger as he held a long note. He noticed it along with everyone else, and watched it grow with horror and fascination. Then, seconds later, at the precise moment when the conductor's signal should have cut both orchestra and vocalist, he kept on going until the conductor walked over and popped the bubble with his baton. This ended the singer's career, and the course of his life changed. The incident was replayed thousands of times on various networks. It made him look ridiculous. The seriousness of his demeanor changed to that of a buffoon, much to the delight of his detractors who said they had seen it coming all along, but there was an interview shortly after the concert where he discussed what had happened. He said as he watched the bubble growing, knowing the moment of truth was approaching, he made a conscious choice to keep the bubble alive, and that to the true artist, the bubble must come first. If you don't put the bubble first, there's another kind of pain, much worse than nobody knowing who you are. I always handled that pain well and wrote well under duress. I did a lot of things better because I let the bubble form and blew past the stops, where there's pleasure that makes it easy to forget the pain of being unknown. When I'm gone, the world won't be as thankful for the pains I went through as saying it's glad I'm going through them anymore, and all they'll have left is the things that they wanted from me, the fruit from my tree of broken limbs, which in a higher sense are used to make boats to sail on the aforementioned bubble." Saying that, Henry smiled.

"Now these boats I remember were in a race," he continued. "I was in my prime, only just a little out of my element, didn't quite have my sea legs, when all the sudden the signal went up, and the boats started moving out. Oh they were fast, but I knew mine had the best of everything, only I wasn't barking the right commands. We fell behind quickly, and the better captains were already far out in front before we got everything going right. I was watching from the bow, and they had such a big lead I figured we couldn't catch up. But we were a faster ship and were gaining on them. There was just no way of knowing if we could do it in time, and a bit later on, the word came through that the lead ship would have crossed the line at its pace, so we settled into port to drink our sorrows away. If everything were as it should have been, we'd have won.

"Now close your eyes and ponder with me for a few minutes, examine your own mind, you'll see many of the nuances that would be mentioned to create a true picture of who you are. All the things. Nothing left out. And why bother describing it at all if there's no aberration, nothing wrong with you to fill the minds of others. Only there is if you look for it. Even if you don't look. On one side you have the constant stories of people going over the deep-end, jumping off cliffs, picking up guns and shooting every stranger in sight. That's in you somewhere. So how does it happen to come out of them? What happens? How does one go from just a happy afternoon and reading a book, to becoming an alcoholic because your mother dies? What building blocks are in place with experience that you become unable to reflect upon the concept of God at some point because you've been taught to become a fanatic from an early age? Or are there some that can withstand the pressures, reflective personalities just as there are obese personalities, and people who punish themselves, who can't get over an incident, who are humiliated rather than inspired, who can't step up in front of the stage and speak, but crawl into a closet and delve into thoughts that eventually bring them out of the closet as something different from what anyone has known before? What is the personality anyway? All is being discussed in a thousand ways in various forums, and it's not the job of a writer to discuss any of that directly. There's plenty of self-help books and discussions, but meanwhile, writers undertake something else, delving into what the mind is in other ways, maybe as the mind should be, even if due to many factors that cannot be attributed to life itself, which comes at us as what it is, the question being how do we adapt to it or how might we have done better if not for some flaw, some blind spot. So for better or worse the struggle with the various stages of consciousness in experience has also been reposited in literature over the centuries, and this is in effect prose on that subject, but not prose as you typically think of it. This is not non-fiction. This is fiction. So these are in effect stories, elected in deliberate ways to infiltrate the soul, out of myth for example, out of something like Ulysses at Circe's, a little bit like Circe's, yes, the island he visited. For how many years was he stuck there? Then all of a sudden he wakes up and exclaims, *What was I thinking? Can we leave?* And he realizes Circe has changed his men to pigs. She did this and that to make him forget his mission. Well, how often do we swirl into eddies? And how many years does it take us to swirl out of them? How often do we forget the larger mission and take on the task, the new mission, of escaping from the clutches of something where we work to save our souls, give our lives back the meaning it once had, saying to ourselves, wow, what was I thinking? Whether it be a bad marriage, or a bad job, how long does it take to shake off the impact of that, or of the influence of our parents? How long did my mother live under my grandfather's shadow before she eventually was able to say he was a jerk, only to realize in later life how kind he was as a father in so many ways, just flawed in so many others? Or how long will it take my own children to shake off the effort that I put in to mold them? When I think about my own experience of becoming a writer, how long did it take me to shake off the influences of the world trying to get me into the mines, into the box, the dark dread of daily life that everyone complains about then brands anyone who rejects it as a traitor? But it's hard to shake the mold. Some think eternal life must make us willing to waste this one, to give up the race, that for even promises made to us by the oracle, we would make our own calculations by the stars and pull into port for a witch's brew.

And so it was that word came to that port that became our home that the lead ship hadn't made it, hadn't crossed the line at all, but had gotten lost in a deep mire in shallow waters that receded further to muck and dried out. This was great news, and we went down to the dock for the first time in what suddenly seemed ages to see our own fine ship buried deep in the mud. Knowing nothing about excavation, a new race was on, to dig the ship out and get her back to sea. My first mistakes had been due to youth, and it was pride that drove me to assume that all was lost, I suppose, but I did not have the tools or expertise to pull us out, but I felt if we could dig around it, then use water to remove the mud and expose the hull, we might learn by proceeding and find ourselves back on course. Amazingly, the crew didn't look back. It was like they were just glad to have me back, and I knew where we were going and who was going to lead."

Henry stopped and rested, wrestled with the top of a prescription bottle, which spun out of his hand. I reached down, picked it up and handed it to him as he popped a pill into his mouth and took a sip of water. Leaning back in his chair, he looked over the the window and said, "We're under way now, but the witch kept the anchor. Can't you feel the way she's listing? We had everything in the hold balanced with the anchor, but I stole the eye. The blind hag won't realize it for a while, but she won't be able to hold it to her head to see anymore. I've put it behind some books in my cabin."

Henry took another pill out of the bottle, set it carefully upright on the food tray, removed his hand, and the pill quickly rolled off the edge. He tried to catch it but knocked over his glass of water, spilling it onto the floor. The woman got a cloth from the sink and started cleaning it up. Henry watched her for a minute, then said, "That's like me after I'd melted. I was in Japan, had to leave my wife here and go serve, and I met this girl who turned me into a pool, a puddle, after what we did. It was hard to scoop me up and pour me into something to try to hold me together. They tried spatulas, and it wasn't so much the holes in the spatula that kept me dripping back, but the holes in me. I was like mercury, the messenger. *Kill the messenger*, I kept saying, not wanting to hear what I was trying to tell myself, knowing it was messages from my own mind to myself that kept sending me back to the floor because I wouldn't listen, especially when I was with her, the story goes. That was what they told me later, that when I was with her, I grew the heaviest, and though I was telling myself as the unread letters piled up that I was lifted up, although I told myself that I was full of joy and passion, I was always putting a deep depression in the bed, a big depression that transferred itself to me. I melted where the spatula couldn't pick me up because I drained into the depressions, and the flat edges that reached for me to pull me back up just sailed overhead, hardly grazing me, almost like hiding in a cave while the rescue operation of helicopters goes on in the distance. You can hear the blades and see the lights, but you're still lost in the caverns. They'll never find you, actually, because the closer they get the deeper you go. It's like you see them as egg beaters, and you've come out of your shell, which is why you're all over the place. But they're only saying while you're collected in the depression that they're coming to get you, just reminding you that it's your job to beat yourself up about it. And I did all this for just one moment, all this as if to recreate a dream of being young and in love like I was with my wife, to have the heightened sense of passion and power felt in youth, that carried you over through school and all along your years the sense of love, though this is the opposite of love and the negative of a force that flattens the spirit and presses it out. But again it's a melting like mercury, you slap it and it goes into globules everywhere but with a little nudging eventually pulls back together, poisonous to the house it's in, shifting back and forth, always escaping, until finally it all recedes, when it's done whatever it's going to do, when you can say it's long gone, evaporated, and you find yourself back together on your feet at ease, and the only thing missing is your youth, and the natural innocent look in your eye is missing something, just a little thing, which is the tear you cannot cry because it's gone out of you with her, and there's nobody to feel sorry for you, not even yourself.

"Scientifically, you've become what is called a nebula, an exploded star in the process of unstoppable expansion at a rate much faster than the universe, which some think has made us giants compared to toy-sized ancestors of only a couple of hundred years ago. Your rate is faster because it's the expansion of experience in the gvmind at the point that by the time you hit fifty you know so much you have to hold back so much. You're this big expanded thing with experience taken in one bite of the fruit of the tree of good and evil, which you're just realizing has really worked its way through your system (hear the gurgling, feel what's coming?) so there's a mismatch between old men and young women, the expectations, the

Henry Collins

honesty of women in their fifties, the way they talk about personal experience, laughing at bawdy jokes. There's this slow fanning outer expansion, a dissolution of brightness of the compact star vs. the explosion of the red giant that in the end by old age we reached this kind of being a nebula after the fantastic expansion from an explosion of experience burned in days over a lifetime, but at the same time, what is it but a great emptiness in a loss of once being a source of light? Sure, looking through a telescope, a nebula is a wonderful thing to behold, but in the mirror quite another thing. It is a kind of emptiness just looking at it, a reminder of a former self, no longer the pinpoint and the focus that it once was. It's also the sign of an entry into the age of knowledge, or the age of metaphor because now we can talk about the importance of rules from having broken them, we can talk about qualities, the riches of youth, for having lost them. It's as if now having been covered with bugs we wished we wouldn't have let them in; now having been lost to all that sin affords (if you can say sin affords anything) but lost to specific sins that we chose, wishing we never held our finger out to those things, that we had the awareness that has come from the emptiness, which only came because we did not know such a thing would happen. But one day you'll awaken to realize the mass of emptiness was that frozen tear, which in space is made perfectly round into a marble, but it can only be placed into a book for safekeeping by breaking it down into words, such that it becomes the very book in which you would conceal it by cutting out the text and leaving the margins intact. The marble is the story, one slap at which sends it flying into thousands of globules, all of which are eagerly assembled again into the sphere that runs hot and cold, basking in sunlight and darkness, refusing to be summed up in anything less than...Finish the sentence." Henry paused and looked at us. I looked at Don. "Finish the sentence," he demanded. "The world refuses to be summed up in anything less than...?

The woman spoke up. "Are you showing off again, Henry?"

"Sho 'nuff," he replied. Then he glared at us. "Are you listening?"

"I heard every word," I said. "It would seem that you've made a marble an eye, a droplet, a book, and a planet, and if you're going to sum it up, you obviously would need to do it without losing any aspect of what it is. But even as any one of a number of things in summation, you've left the door open as long as you're able to look at it another way, so nothing less than the mind, I'm guessing. Nothing is anything without the mind, so anything less than the mind is unacceptable."

Henry smiled. "Boy, I don't know what you were listening to, but you're going to put your class to sleep with that stuff. I hope you won't be teaching anyone how to read me. I like to think of everything as a day in late fall, where the leaves are all gone from the trees, blowing in the cold wind across the roads and open fields. Anything I am or perceive once I process it becomes made of that same dead stuff that piled up becomes everything we stand on, build our houses on, fight our wars on."

He was getting kind of excited. I wondered if the pill he'd taken, whatever it was, had started to kick in. He swung an arm and knocked down the whole tray, and said, "nurse" to the woman, and for the first time, we realized she was not family. She came over and started picking things up, and I looked at Don and twitched my head ever so slightly toward the door like maybe we should think about leaving, especially since Henry was starting to cry.

"It was a beautiful dream, being in another culture, Japan and being with this family, teaching me to use their connections to the truth. We were conquerors, with the most powerful of weapons to bring them to their knees, which was the hardest thing to do before a nation, but before a single soul like me, they did that naturally, willingly. And here was this girl, their daughter, who I was clearly made to feel without a word of any kind, rather in movements and utmost respect, that the way was open to her. I said that I'd been doing these things associated with the arts, with writing, with particular interest toward local culture with treatments and imagery designed to evoke the spirit of the living and the dead. To which they opened up an arsenal of brushes and paper, and showed in simple characters what I can't convey in our language, where the marble is the word itself, and a stone in the stream, the egg in the nest, and there's no book though it sits on your lap. And as it happened that I to came to understand such things, to appreciate this world my eyes had opened to, the father finally said that a son had come along, and as his father, he would let me have all these things. I bowed down, flat on the floor, and he apologized, said that they would be taken away. I said I was just happy to be allowed to have an interest in the family, and he paused for a moment and said if I married his daughter, then there will be no reason for any of this. I looked at her face and I don't see any major happiness, and I said I just didn't know her feelings, at which point the father and mother pick her up and reveal something to me underneath her kimono. It's a scar from a terrible injury, and I realize she's been hiding this from me, that even with this flaw, everything about her has been spiritually arranged like tissue around an irritating intrusion in an oyster, wrapping around that sharp and painful thing and turning it into something else, a pearl. Then the father put the whole world of the family poetry on the floor next to her, her inheritance, her dowry to me, which was the extraction for under the neatly arranged clothes of the history of the family, the soul of all its ancestors, all covering the wounds and scars of life and death, turning into a subtle thing, a beautiful thing, and I could see the whole culture not just in these moments, or in the family, but in that moment, during those seconds and in that connection that it was like her inner beauty was suddenly all revealed to me, that though this girl had said nothing and was completely shy, the orb in the haiku, the moon I thought, had suddenly lit up to reveal the larger soul that has no physical counterpart or representation, something you only know when you realize it for the first time, when it's revealed. And I just became filled with joy and tears of happiness to be a part of all this, the culture, the experience. Even now, it traces itself back through me and into all the things that I've done and everything from now on that I'm ever going to do, though I could do nothing but back away out of that house and stay in my barracks, venturing out only when ordered to and keeping my distance from everyone. It wasn't until we were shipping out that I saw them in the crowd, and I acknowledged them with a slight bow and felt my shame of lies that I'd packed into a ball of spikes deep inside of me where nothing can be put into words and where it could never come out and be put into a book unless I took its place in the hole it made in me, unless I melted where no spatulas could find me, and unless they did, there was nothing I could do but grow old scales and scabs and cough it up as I do now, wondering how it got so smooth while wrapped in such misery. I carried the culture of peace as if it were a thorn, and everything I delivered, everything I thought was alive, was shed skin from the beast I was really holding, growing inside of me until you can now see the scales protruding all over me. And the only thing left for me to do is deliver the pearl, but it will have to be cut from me, only it is not a physical thing, so I live with it, tossing it around in the folds of my spirit that has softened it into a wonder to behold, but only I can see it, and it has her face, that white, white face, and my only peace is that I took her wound on myself, that I carried her pain, but I cannot know anything, but such is war, and the war is almost over."

Henry started motioning to me while he was talking, pointing under my chair. I looked and saw the pill that rolled off the tray and retrieved it for him. He popped it in his mouth, took a little water and kept right on talking. I was getting tired, and I wasn't sure what Henry was doing, whether he should be taking another pill or not, and while he was getting more animated, starting to sound more intense with a look of lucidity in his eyes, I failed to see any clear objective or focus in his conversation, and thought he was just drifting from thought to thought, which is what we expected.

Then he looked at me rather sternly and said, "Let me tell you something. If you ever visit the Parthenon, remember to go in your bare feet and slide around on the floors. First, you'll be amazed when you go in there that there's nothing they hadn't thought of. The floors look amazing enough, even more beautiful than anything we have, but if you slide around on them, you'll hear the intonations of music and voices ingrained in the marble surfaces, and the floors are tilted in just the right way to let you do that, and hearing the music, you're transported into a vision of beauty that corresponds to the intricacies of the pieces you'll find in the museum." Then Henry started to cry. "I always wanted my floors to sing like that, and I never saw anyone more amazed than the people listening when I was sliding around in that temple. It brought the whole place to life, made it a living monument, not a dead one, but I've gotten too old for physical structure. It's not my desired thing, and the desired thing is what keeps the end game from being successful. I thought I had it beat when I realized this, that I could suppress my desire by throwing myself into building a passage of some kind in my mind. I'd done a lot of harvesting and gathering things there that I wanted to push through. But as I was digging this tunnel, my neighbor there, an alter-ego in my dreams, the one I was shutting out of my passage, kept looking over the fence asking what I was doing. I just told him he better get going on making his own."

Henry was getting agitated, and he switched to present tense now and then. "I tell him it's got to have religion," Henry said. "And a lot of other concepts, and he keeps asking what's it for. So finally I tell him it's a passage into the next world, that everybody needs to build one, that it's what life is all about, that it's about gathering the materials to build yourself an end game. You lie in your bed, and you die, and if you don't have it, you have no where to go. That's a terrible end, so you have to build a passage from which you know and see the direction to go in at the last moment if at that time you have no sense of the answer. By having found the answer, you tack it up in the passage like lights so you can find your way through.

Then I came to realize watching my neighbor that he wasn't doing anything but watching me like he was waiting for the right moment to just come over and steal all my work and take my place. So I yelled over the fence that it wasn't just about the passage but who was in there, that he couldn't take my place. And his answer was that this was my religion, not his, and he was just as much a part of the soul as I was, and that I was just the slave part, and when I was done slaving, he would take his rightful place in the transmission to the next level, and I'd just go poof. That would be the end of me. So I started to guard the place, to dig down my heels, plant myself dead set against him. I became a sentry on my side of the fence, marching back and forth for when the day came that one of us would make the trip. After marching for some time, I started to hear a strange sound on the other side, like there was an animal following my every move. It was a strange sound of scratching, and as I walked along the fence it's was very pronounced. I got the feeling somehow that it was fierce and fearless, and I was afraid to even look over the top of the fence. So we started playing this game. When I walked, it walked. When I stopped it stopped. Simple enough, but there were other things, like in daylight it's much more furtive, while in the evening it's more pronounced. I got so used to it that I was almost afraid when I didn't hear it, and I had complex feelings of wanting it gone at the same time that I didn't want to scare it away. Once in a while it wouldn't be there, and I longed for it. I would say to myself, *Come back little thing, come back, make me heavy, make me feel buried, be a part of my consciousness again, keep me from focusing, keep me from work, from diligence, keep me from filling out my goals, my plans, my dreams. Where are you?* Inevitably I would discover a spot on the other side with the clear sounds of digging and realize what it was up to, so I would start to pound on the fence there, and throw dirt over to fill the hole. Finally the day came when I decided to get a little bolder in my patrol. I stood up on the fence and started walking back and forth. As long as the sun was out, I thought I had the upper hand. The passage had long since been completed, and this was all just a game of nerves. Standing on the fence was my answer to its digging a hole. But then something terrible happens. While I'm standing there, a ball hits me and knocks me down, but the ball had been thrown from my side of the fence, and I fell into my neighbor's area. For some reason I found myself trapped there. I couldn't climb the fence. In time, at a distance, I came to realize that I had tied myself even more to the desired thing, not removed myself from it, that I had in fact been blocking the passage, and now it was too late. The only power I had left was to dig, and while digging I realized that the game was over, that in trying to protect what I had, I'd failed to advance, and the downfall came within me.

"Reduced to a burrowing animal, I had once ruled an empire. I'd put fear into everybody around me. I needed my newspaper and my coffee at the same time every morning in bed. My whole house was organized around keeping me happy, but I began to have a difficult time. I got sick. One morning I didn't understand why anyone needs a newspaper. I spilled my coffee in bed and mistook my housekeeper for my mother. I thought everyone was crazy, but they were just worried because if you looked behind me out the window, you would see I owned a huge estate with my own golf course, and beyond that fields and mountains. It was all mine. And it was my right to prop myself up with interests, idiosyncrasies, and bad habits. I had a staff and kept them organized, and on their feet by the intensity in which I demanded everything be just the way I wanted it. And they responded attentively to every petty thing. But suddenly their whole world is in question. I am suddenly human. I've lost my mind. It's all due to old age, they say. He's just naturally relaxing out of life. Everyone loses balance, the right sense of the things, and who can be expected to juggle as they let go? So I let the ball drop. There was only ever one. That was my expertise, what made me different, that I could mesmerize them with the one thing, which was all I had, and when I dropped it, they couldn't believe what they were seeing. It was like they'd all been duped or something. It was like they had cared for me too much, that if they'd known my powers were so weak, they would never have worked for me. And so one by one they left me, not believing for a moment that they were the ones who were weak. They picked up after me, but nobody dared touch the ball I dropped. Not a single one of them had really ever seen such a thing before. None had ever held one. It just sat there, waiting for someone, someone like a son, someone with a like mind, who knew what it was and what to do with it, but such a person would already have to have known what it was to be trapped like I was. But would anyone like that ever come along? The old man's world had tilted, but kept his door open, hoping.

"Then a man came to visit a medicine man who was about to drop the ball. He was in bed, his face was strangely painted like a cage. Inside the cage was an animal holding onto the bars, looking out. The man asked the medicine man about it, but he would not answer. The man went to his tent to sleep, and when he woke, he found there was a cage around his head with a small animal in it. He ran from the tent calling for the medicine man. People in the village were very sad and told him that the medicine man had died. That night was very dark. The only light was from a fire. At the burial ceremony, the medicine man was brought out with a clean face. The animal in the cage on the visitor's face began to bite his cheeks. Some people in the village told the man that he must feed the animal in the cage or it will begin to eat away at him. They began to prepare the medicine man for his passage through the fire, and as they lifted him, his arm fell, and a ball rolled out of his hand. They gave it to the visitor and told him that the animal would eat better if he kept the ball on his person. The body of the medicine man was then placed on the fire and cremated. The heat from the fire was very intense. The visitor tried to step back, but the people pushed him forward. The animal in the cage was very agitated by the head, running around and scratching the face of the visitor. Somewhere during the ceremony, the visitor fainted, and did not wake up until the next morning, when he discovered that the cage was gone. He felt very relieved and wanted to depart from the village immediately. As he was leaving, the people reminded him not to forget to feed the animal that had been burned into his spirit from the experience.

"When the visitor was home again, he did not feel well at his old job. Nothing about shuffling around paperwork for the company had any meaning for him. It made his head hurt. So he left the job and began to do things that did give a feeling of well-being, which came from helping people directly. It was a learning experience with some failures, but gradually his skills improved with experience. There were times he wanted to give up, but again, he only felt good when he was trying to be helpful. Most of what he did to help came in the form of intelligent counseling. Not everyone appreciated it, but over the years, people came to view him as a kind of healer.

"Then one very dark night, he was getting ready for bed, washing his face in the bathroom, when suddenly the lights went out. It only happened for a second, but in those few seconds he could have sworn he saw what looked like a cage painted on his face, the same as the medicine man had. He could see the full orb of the moon shining through the window, so he turned out the light in order to let it be the only light shining on his face, and discovered that it was true. With the light on, he could only faintly make out the outlines of the medicine man's cage on his face, but they were just very slight scars he'd really never noticed, made by the scratching of an animal. It was such a close match, that if he had wanted to paint his face like the medicine man, he would merely have to follow the lines. That is when he noticed that the ball he had carried for so many years, the one that had fallen from the hand of the medicine man, was on the floor at his feet. He felt for the necklace and indeed, it had fallen off. Once he attached it again, he turned out the bathroom light, which fell into total darkness. He looked out the bathroom window, searching for the full moon he had seen earlier, but checking his calendar, it was the time of the new moon, and he felt something new, a fullness, a sense that he understood the meaning of his life for the first time. It was like he had been running around in a cage all his life, but for the first time, he had been fed and was about to make a mark on the face of the earth."

Henry didn't so much pause here again as I found myself tuning him out, not because I wanted to but because something had been stimulated in me, or perhaps it would make more sense to say that I was for a moment rendered completely self-conscious, almost as a residual effect of the heat outside, something like that, the way I felt when I was walking up the hill toward the trailer. But it was different, something more like a distancing, perhaps with a touch of panic attack thrown in. I found myself looking around the room again. The nurse was sitting in a chair close to the air conditioner with her back turned to us, leafing through some pop-culture magazine. She had totally tuned out everything Henry had said or was saying. The sun still blazed outside the window. The humidity pressed in. Don was fidgeting. Once you make a silent pact to pick a moment to leave, it's difficult to concentrate, but I wasn't looking to get out at that moment. There seemed to be something to try to understand in what I would have to call Henry's sane babbling. It almost felt like my ears had closed instinctively from an overload of images, or that I had dragged myself dazed out of a moonlit pool of insensible clarity and was gasping for a normal breath of something ordinary, but even the bananas in the still life were starting to exude an energy of some kind, to melt from the canvas even though they were not depictions in paint but very real objects. I thought maybe my eyes were starting to fail me. I was beginning to feel like I might faint, and I started to listen to Henry again, which was like getting a glass of cold water in the face because he was talking about shit and pissing versus science.

"The first thing that scientists do is they take away the moral meaning and just try to look at the facts," he said. "But in the end they come up with this sense of the world as shitting man. We're all animals, and the universe has a beginning and an ending. Fact reduces us, relieves us of all the stuff that makes us who we are spiritually, leaves us in the lurch for any other facts that might be uncovered, drags us down, trying to remove faith while they pursue the so-called truth. But they miss the whole point, the bigger picture, the ball of wax that doesn't start with a bee. They miss what's in me. I'm just a shitting, pissing man, who you have come to see. But how many more chances will you have to be an onlooker? How many more times before it's you?"

And it dawned on me that here was this shitting and pissing man, a thing all covered with sores, but surrounded by an aura of cogency, a field into which one didn't dare dip a finger but around which one wanted to sit, to be an onlooker, having the same need for truth in a cold universe as for air conditioning on a hot and humid day. But I'd lost the connection he had made. Was he talking about the same animal in the cage? Was that his transition? I asked Don about it later, but he admitted he had stopped listening long before then.

I stood up and said that we should probably be going. Henry did not seem at all pleased, and as he shook my hand, he said, "There isn't anything in my work that I'd want you to carry with you more than what just came out of me." I had a strange feeling that Henry was looking for someone to pass the ball to, and I think it was me.

As we walked toward the dark hallway, the tilt in the floor seemed even more pronounced than before. I felt off balance in the extreme. One of my shoes scuffed the rubber mat and made a strange noise. It made me think of the voices in the temple. I thought we were walking away from a gushing fountain, and that constant image of a ball riding on top of it. We would leave, and it would gush, but did we hear it all in our short stay, get the gist of what a fountain is and what it does, or would we miss a rumbling and ejection of a key? I've walked away from many an ocean sunset after having my fill, but here, it was like I was lit by it all, but I felt like I would miss something, even if walking away from it, on fire, I was taking away the essence of what it was.

When we opened the door, the first thing I saw was the moon, the sun still bright in the sky, and it surprised me. As I said, Don had gotten annoyed and tuned Henry out long before I'd reached my limit. Going home, he talked about the upcoming semester. I kept thinking about the nurse reading the magazine. I could understand it, but I knew these were things someone would listen to if they had ears, and I realized Don was not as intuitive as I once thought.

Back at school over the next several months, I got the same feeling from everyone. How did I ever choose such dull surroundings and people? I ended up leaving my post, and I've started writing. It just wasn't the right place for me. I also came to respect Henry as not having lost it, just that nobody really listened to him. I honestly didn't read any of his other books after meeting him. It was like the short drink from the fountain of his inner life was all I needed, like I had melted into the meaning, or rather it had burned into me.

And now months have passed. It's gotten cold, and the leaves are blowing across the street, old growth shrivelling up to provide a basis for new life. Henry died today. I just read about it. Strange that it would happen when the leaves were blowing. Henry was a flower in that chair, richly arrayed in his thorns and sores. It was never about the books for him, but the living sense of thought. That's what he wanted to pass along, to plant the seed of the witch doctor. I have no control anymore. The vines from the chair are lines on my face, and I intend to go out like leaves blowing around one's feet in front of the passage, not desiring a thing. The eye, the earth, the caged head, the moon; it all makes sense, everything except the fact that based on the picture in the paper, it was his wife in the room.

Susie Inchon

I met Susie during years of frustration over my parents indiscretions that were badly kept secrets around the house. Susie was from a perfect family. When I had dinner with them, I felt a worminess inside, like my vile insides would explode onto the table in disgusting filth. Why were they able to hold together without pills, alcohol and therapy, all of which were the crutches of my parents?

When I first met her, she had a boyfriend, and I followed her one night as she walked with him in a light snowfall. She was playful like a lamb, bouncing against him, and I wanted it to be me. I found out later that he was not her boyfriend anymore and wasn't during that walk, so I wondered why she was still so familiar with him.

In brief, she was filled with a heavenly music that I could hear, and it made me want so much for her to notice me, but at the same time as her music filled me with the same joy, watching her, a hand came from nowhere and took control of the music in me, turning it way down. I had so much anger at that time, it both intrigued and bothered me that anyone could be so happy.

As my family was falling further apart, I got to know Susie a little better. She was very religious. I congratulated her for this openly, but a part of me felt that it was now between me and God. In my heart I questioned her beliefs. How could anyone be so happy was the first issue, but after that came my life, where it follows that one needs God, and even sees Him better through the pain. Looking back, I was worse than Hamlet in so many ways, and I remember having conversations with Susie about God. I wanted to learn about Him from her at the same time I wanted to take Him away from her so that she'd look into my eyes. Maybe it was that I wanted someone to worship me for a change. Nothing I could do pleased anyone in my family, and it was obvious I was being cut loose, and Susie was the thing that I most wanted to grab hold of for support. There was something in her I thought might save me.

We did grow close and dated for several years, for which time of service to mankind I think she deserved papers signifying completion of a plumber's apprentice for how she helped unclog my pipes. I mean that in a spiritual sense, and at the same time it pains me to remember how much internal sewage I must have spewed her with during those times, all of which she handled like an angel. She could not totally relate to any of it, but she empathized without restraint, allowing me to tell her nearly everything that was in me. I say "nearly" everything, and it was not revealing that last little bit that caused her to leave me. It was only that I respected her happiness, the life she came from, that I didn't want to totally reveal everything in me. I honestly thought *that* would cause her to leave me, that her knowing it would be the end, not that holding back would do it. And it really wasn't that big of a deal. It was just personal information that I learned does have a way of backfiring in one's face. I know now that others don't need to know everything about you, but thinking they do, feeling guilty for holding back, has its consequences, too.

So it was due to my never really being totally comfortable with her that led to our demise, but along the way, we had some very interesting discussions about religion, and being with her tipped the balance in me toward God and to reconciling myself to experiences in my Hamlet days, to forgiving my parents and even myself.

I'm glossing over many things, but that is the nature of life. I sit here and remember those days when I was so healthy, when God is an idea you know is important but not immediately essential with the huge swath of time before me. So many years passed between us that she became not just a mere face in memory, but of what I now consider late childhood, and there was something I wanted to say to her about that. I wanted her to know that I was sorry for putting her through some things. So I called her one day, and we talked. She was married with children, and she seemed quite happy, but when the subject came up, she told me she wasn't religious anymore.

Since we spoke, I cannot help but feel that the experience she had with me is the cause of her loss of faith. While she was infusing me the faith I craved, I was giving her faith an acid bath in my unhappiness, and we had equal impact on one another.

This is what I remember wanting to do when I followed her that night. I wanted to say, "Put God away and love me," but I wanted it to come from her weakness, not from really determining her path. But in those days, my wants were huge. I remember the issues of faith swirling in my head. Why this, and why that? "I need you to get down from that high horse and into my arms. I need someone to listen to the gospel of me, my life and my problems." That was the maxim of my will, but I learned to bide my time and wear a smile until the right moment, and then I swooped in.

I've come to realize that we have impact in chapters, not in incidents, and we change over the course of a chapter, not in a single moment. There is no doubt that Susie and I tested every angle of how we fit together, thinking we had discovered that there was no way to fit at the time, when what was actually happening is that we were slowly taking what we needed from one another, and applying that to our lives. Susie got the strength from me to look at everything her parents had neatly organized with critical eyes for the first time in her life, and I found the peace of faith that I needed after a tumultuous last chapter at home. In those first years of being on our own, by being together, we each grew stronger, more rounded as people. From one perspective, she grew stronger, and I grew weaker. From another, the opposite could be said. But in just wholly spiritual terms, we each grew up. I already had a heavy dose of the world and needed some love. She had so much love but knew nothing of the world. She got that from me. In the end, there are no simple souls, easily judged or measured by belief or non-belief. Everyone becomes the same mixture through a sum total of intertwinings with others, or if you think of it as asteroids bumping into one another, we all get knocked down to about the same size.

A Seagull in the Snow

Charlie moved to Iowa in 1945 after the war and started a family. By 1960 he was taking his eldest son James deep sea fishing in New England when he'd visit his folks there. After Charlie's parents died in the 1980s, so did the fishing, but James never forgot the ocean swells, the cod and how the gulls followed the boat back to port. By the time he started a family in the 1990s, there were no more New England connections. He taught his son Mark to fish on Iowa lakes and the Mississippi River, but the gulls had become a problem there by 1995. They had infested various playing fields and parking lots, and from a distance, it almost looked like paper blowing around trucks driving up the landfill slopes. When they dumped their load, the gulls dropped into the feast below. There was always more than one nearby when James and Mark were fishing, waiting for a handout. Sometimes there were hundreds of them. James also remembered visiting his grandparents who wintered in Florida. They loved feeding fish they caught to herons and egrets waiting nearby. But the gulls were different. They would sneak up and steal food if given an opportunity, but James was taught to throw fish, not rocks. As a little boy, Mark liked chasing them more than fishing along the Mississippi River. James insisted that the birds not be hurt, but Mark didn't listen, and one day when they were particularly annoying, he killed one with a rock, which led to a fine by a passing game warden.

James was embarrassed and apologetic, but somewhat flabbergasted that gulls were protected. "Not a game bird, not ever in season," the game warden joked sardonically. James argued there were just so many of them, that the state should do something to control their numbers. The game warden replied that until the landfill was capped off, they were going to be a problem, but there was already a new landfill opening up, so everyone just had to get used to them. James took Mark home and promised someday he'd take him fishing where there were no seagulls. But that never happened. They went out on Lake Michigan one time, and when the gulls followed the boat back to shore, James tried to make Mark see how beautiful it was. But Mark was too busy throwing things, laughing as they went after the junk he was tossing, fighting over nothing. James told his son the stories of fishing in the ocean, and how the gulls were a wonderful sight, but Mark just looked at his father quizzically, and said, "I thought you always hated them, Dad."

But that wasn't so. James remembered the gulls were an integral part of his visits to New England. Without the birds, the images of the shore were incomplete somehow. Even the sound needed to be there to put a clear stamp on it. But in Iowa, he learned to hate them. He drove through the parking lot rookeries at high speeds, not to hit them, but just to break them up. In the rear view mirror, he would see them float down to the blacktop, unruffled by it all.

In New England, they were part of the scenery. In Iowa, they were garbage birds. Certainly they fed on scraps on the east coast, but they didn't belong in the midwest. Maybe neither did landfills, but the population had also exploded since James was a boy. Maybe that had something to do with it.

Mark had grown up fast, just as James supposed he had, but James' life seemed stretched out in the outdoors, marked in increments by interesting vacations. Life had changed. Mark had spent most of his time inside playing video games, being driven to school and given money without having to do chores. In the blink of an eye, he was about to finish high school, and there had been no trips to New England, and James regretted not having shared the sights and sounds of his childhood with his son, or realizing along the way that it was a mistake not to bring him up the way he was raised.

Then one night the snow really started coming down. The next morning it was a couple of feet deep, and Mark was nowhere to be found. James couldn't get the snowblower started, and he started shoveling. His back wasn't great, nor was he in good shape, and as he huffed and puffed doing little damage to the snow on the driveway, he was cursing his son for not being home. Obviously he'd stayed out the whole night without permission. No good bastard!

About an hour later, Mark drove up, rolled down the window and said, "Like old *flockin'* times, eh Dad?" James ignored him at first, then heard seagulls. He looked up and saw thousands of them. He remembered their fishing trip, the fact the the landfill had been capped, and something else. His anger dissapated, and he welcomed his son, told him to heat up some cocoa for the two of them, and later they could finish the shoveling together. Mark asked about the snowblower and said he knew what was wrong and would fix it. As Mark was going in, he said, "Isn't it amazing to see all those gulls in the air at the same time? Unbelievable!" As James was putting the shovel in the garage, his mind went back to the night he stayed out and came home to find his father shoveling. Of course, Charlie growled and made a big scene how James was no good, then lit up a cigarette and stormed into the house leaving James to take over.

Home from college on break, James had gone to a friend's party the previous evening where he met a girl everyone said was *easy*. James tried to get her attention without success. She told him to go away several times, and she finally spit in his face in front of everybody. James acted like it didn't matter and persisted. She insulted him, a little at first, then really gave it to him, all of which he laughed off. And he kept following her around despite the looks of his friend that said, "She's not worth it. Don't do this to yourself."

As the party was breaking up, the girl finally shoved James away and knocked him down. He hit his head hard on the floor and got sick. So he stayed all night and slept on the couch, which was ill-advised because he'd gotten a slight concussion. In the morning, his friend had trouble waking him, and James had a splitting headache, but looking at the snow, he knew his father would be looking for him, so he got his coat and drove home as fast as he could.

As he drove home, he had a feeling he was trying to understand, something from the night before, about these people at the party. It struck him how he seemed lost amongst them, but they were more lost than he was. He was sorry for hassling the girl, but as he remembered her, she was the most scared of the bunch. His friend had told him how easy she was, that she'd even had a couple of abortions, and somehow through the haze, he saw how young all their faces were, how confused they were, all of them just out of high school, and he was the only one of the group going to college. The girl had even said he was just home for vacation and would never call her. It struck James that he also was afraid, even desperate to feel close even for one night, not knowing what would happen in a few years. But he had it much better than some of these others. They partied all the time and were all lost for what to do in their lives. He was sorry for how he'd treated the girl, for doing the very things to her that he hated seeing others do to people. He hadn't realized it was in him to act like that, and he wished he could take it all back.

When he got home and saw his dad shoveling the driveway, he saw a familiar scowl and knew he was going to catch hell. He parked the car and took over the shoveling right there, having had no breakfast, and still feeling a bit dizzy from the fall the night before. But his father would think he was making excuses, so he didn't complain. There was a set of facts in place that governed interactions between them, and that was the way it went. Even when he passed out in the snow, his father was not the one to find him. A neighbor across the street saw him. There was nothing seriously wrong, but it made him angrier at his father though he never did talk about it. It didn't help that Charlie referred to the neighbor as "nosy."

Just before James fainted, he happened to see a lone seagull flying by. It was the first time he'd ever seen one outside New England. He wonderedow how it got to Iowa. Looking at all the snow in the driveway, without hope of a meal, or conversation about what happened with the girl, he suddenly felt hatred for the gull. "Go back where you came from. You don't belong here." Then he passed out. Over the years, the population exploded, and he only liked them in memories, particularly when he was coming back on the boat, when he felt close to his father, and they followed them home. He was still lost in thought when Mark brought out the cocoa. Girls. Gulls. He felt it was all one long cycle with a message in it somewhere.

Life in the Palms

Somehow I found my way to a branch in the virtual top of an imaginary tree that someone in the distance finds appealing as she looks out the window of her apartment building, or rather, into her computer screen. My shield reflects light into her room as she brushes her hair at night. She throws sandwiches to me, and I sing her praises. When she needs anything, I open an umbrella and wait for the wind to carry me to the store for her. I do lots of shopping. I also fix things, and on rare occasion she lets me climb higher and through her window to fix a broken pipe or hinge on a door.

Behind this facade, I live in the city by myself. There are very few trees in my neighborhood. I have a clerical job at Government Center. I guess you could call me a file clerk. I don't want to talk about it. I've been doing it now for twenty years. I know that I have no life, and I also know it is too late for me to really do anything about this woman on the other side of the world. She has a kid, and I don't want kids. My sister had kids and used to bring them over to my apartment. By the time they left, there was a trail of broken things, leaving me exhausted. So, no kids, not to mention I'm already 63. I told her that I'm 45 because she said she was 42. I thought that was a good match. I could tell from the start that she wanted something to happen between us, but I started up the knight in the tree image pretty quickly, and it's become our passage through rough times together, and I know that I provide her with some necessary emotional support as well.

It often happens that my internet service fails because the phone lines are not very reliable in my neighborhood. I live in fairly rough surroundings, but I stay indoors and keep to myself. But when I don't show up to talk with her, she gets mad and abuses me. She was married once before, and I get the feeling that she is not an easy person to get along with, but I roll with the punches and make references to the many men on the ground below trying to get her attention. I tell her how the building superintendent is after me for usurping his ability to get in to see her. He warns me sternly never to touch specific pipes or fixtures in her apartment again, which gives me a clue which things he has tampered with, knowing that one day they will break, leading to her calling him.

When I tell her things like this, she begins to laugh again and forget her troubles. She has a rough job as well with a mean manager, and the heat is off most of the time in her building, so there is nothing to keep her warm. Sometimes we drift into conversations of how I might climb up to keep her warm, and it can be very poetic, but she quickly wakes from those dreams and warns me that I must stay in the tree and treat her as a princess.

Of course, I do this willingly. It is all a game. But I do wonder sometimes why she is unwilling to allow herself to feel anything romantic of any kind. It strikes me as odd in a way. I'm not sure why except that I can detect in her a kind of willingness, like she is sitting at the edge of a waterfall with a barrel, wondering if she should get in the barrel and roll herself into the water and go over the falls.

She has told me on several occasions that she is concerned that if we reveal ourselves too much to one another that we will lose the magical connection of a knight and his lady. I can see her point. After all, I've already told her so many lies, what could happen except to burst the balloon? But on the other hand, something in me drifts from the fiction. In the middle of using my shield to send moonlight to her room in a storm, which of course makes no sense, I often wish I had a computer with a camera to see what she looks like, and she's obviously come to appreciate certain qualities about me that I sometimes just want to tell the truth, that I'm an old man living in Boston, and see what happens.

But I know what would happen. Much of her willingness to continue the deception hinges on her wish to find a husband, so I know

Life in the Palms

this cannot last forever. We reach a point where that question hangs in the air, that we might take the next step, which would be to tell one another something more than our first names, but there would be so much to do. It's impossible.

Everything she writes, I have to translate before I can respond, so I have to translate my thoughts into her language. We have discovered that misunderstandings of any kind exacerbate any kind of disagreement. Translation also slows down communication so much that one cannot really have a healthy argument. The translator only gives the gist of what one is trying to say, and arguments with a woman demand a finely tuned sense of semantics. In the end, the only thing that works and that we have to fall back on is the silly metaphor of knight and princess in the tower.

Silly as it may seem, and yes, I always considered it silly from the start, over the several years now that we have been communicating regularly, the image has become not only very complex and vivid, but it is also somehow comforting. I don't know why, but even though it repels me as rather hackneyed, we have turned it into a poetic database. All I have to do is mention the navy, and she knows what I mean. At the very beginning of our conversations, there were many problems with the internet on both sides. Once or twice she disappeared for several weeks because of service problems of one kind or another. Anyway, she lives not far from a river, so I invented a navy outpost where sailors are stationed and always ready to assist her when I am not available. Of course, every sailor has a secret crush on her, but they put that aside for the greater interest of helping her. So if either one of us won't be available for any reason, a simple reference to the navy makes perfect sense.

So we have this simple, yet rich imaginary world that we've come to realize is necessary for us to effectively communicate, given our distance from one another, our language barrier and our personality differences. I fear the day will come too soon that she will close the window, that I will look up and see the face of her lover in the room with her. I could not stand in her way. I could not be that person. All I can say is that I will keep the account open in case she ever were to really need me again, the navy being an imaginary thing.

The Long Beat of the Metronome

We've talked about an end coming eventually. I might have said there will come a time when I might fall out of the tree. She would say something like the umbrella will catch on my belt and carry me down gently. I might answer that the crowd of unhappy suitors would take advantage and kick me apart, and she would reply that a basket of sandwiches reserved for me would deter them long enough for her to climb down and rescue me. I might answer that my unconsciousness might be very deep indeed and require some kind of resuscitation. She would promise to give me all the mouth to mouth that I need, and I would say that hearing such things was making me feel unstable and likely to fall out of the tree. Then she would say I was the most amazing person on light (an error of the translator that I have come to prefer over most amazing person in the world), and I would say the light from my heart ignites the shield and is there for her even on the darkest nights.

This is sheer nonsense but welcome in both our lives. Hardly a moment passes as I collect and deliver folders on the fourth through sixth floors without thinking there's a living presence in the void that appreciates my humor, ridiculous as it is when reduced to a mere imaginary figure, clad in armor sitting on a palm with a navy backing him up, serving a hard-working middle-aged woman with a child who lives on the tenth floor in a sea of high-rises. Somewhere in the fabric of the mind, I believe there is a wire that at some point sends out signals for help. This wire was in my father and grandfathers before me, but until the invention of the short wave radio, nobody ever recognized it. In the entire history of short wave, there were far fewer incidents of connections through modulations and demodulations of this inner signal than in only the first few years of the internet. If it were not for the internet, I might not have learned the significance myself of this need to connect with other people.

Strange that other people are so abusive of it, who have partners already, who not only meet people in cyber space but in real life, leading some to unexpected discovery. I've come to think of the signal in my mind as coming from a wire that carries very low voltage, something like the one that operates a doorbell. It really doesn't take much, at least at my age, to satisfy my need for companionship.

But it isn't like a dog or a television can supply the same energy. Even if this wire handles a signal that is low key, not demanding too much energy, and nothing that would give anyone a shock, what it brings from the other end is like water to quench a deep thirst. That thirst is what turns the wire on to a signal for help. That need for another is what has made people turn on their computers and aim them into the valley of voices hoping to find a kindred spirit.

I admit, in order to find this one branch, I heard many kinds of voices. It was like walking down a dangerous street being accosted from every side by someone who wanted something out of me. Until I figured out that by wearing armor and a shield, I was very vulnerable. All the conversations were about reality. People wanted to know who I was and what I was doing. These are people obviously searching for someone who is interesting even though they should know that all the interesting people have lives and spend little time on the computer. It didn't make me feel good at all to be so scrutinized. It felt like I was being interviewed and evaluated on the very things that disturbed me. I hate my life. Only someone who wants to talk, who has failed in previous commitments would be interested in someone like me. I am a harmless drudge who sits in a cubicle until called into action. Yes, when that call comes, I spring from my seat and collect or distribute file folders where needed. It's a dirty job I know, but someone has to do it.

That is my world. It is as searingly real to me as if I were sitting under the sun in the desert. Am I delirious that I equally visualize myself in this tree in the moonlight next to an apartment building, not far from the river where a navy is available in case of trouble? I see myself there more clearly than in the office because I am connected to something real, someone on the other side, in real time, talking to me. To me. She doesn't know anything about me and doesn't care, only that I give her what she gives me, which is the very thing we don't get in the crowded world in which we live where people see us every day. We are outcasts from everyone except one another. Lords and ladies of Byzantium can listen to the golden bird singing what is past or passing or to come all they want, but they have nothing on how I control my own peace of mind.

Making the Turn

It is not a terrible thing to be forgotten, to take one's place in the street scene as observed from the emperor's window. Millions of souls have made passage from whatever place in time they occupied into whatever lies beyond this life. Looking at an intricate rendition of the temples and tombs of ancient Thebes, I have a sense that it may have been unwise at the time to complain or question the state religion, imbued as it is in daily life. Humanity itself from an historical perspective can at times seem to be taking a series of steps. Toward what end remains to be seen, but isn't it strange how similar some cultures were to one another at a given time, even when they had no inkling of one another, far flung around the world, but totally immersed in their own peculiar mythology?

Looking at these images of the great temples, with thousands of tiny homes peppered about, I have an improved sense of the grandeur of a culture. I can almost see it moving, be that pharaoh looking out his window at the culmination of several thousand years of workmanship, not the smattering of ruins and smashed faces we see in museums today. I admit that Egypt, while it has always been fascinating in many ways, still presented itself always with the smack of sand and mummification. Whatever appeal there is in golden orbs and hieroglyphics, the image they cast together unfolds into a scattering of what it was, into flooding caused by the High Aswan Dam and a giant nose broken by drunken French cannoneer.

All this teaches is that from the perspective of almost any present culture, there are bound to be temporal similarities because we are all in the same era taking the same step. But it also indicates that from a future perspective, much of what we are in everyday spirit will be undiscovered and replaced. People will impose on themselves a sense that they are walking where we were a thousand years earlier, and then go back to what they were doing. When we are seen from that perspective, no better or worse than ancient cultures that fascinate us today, we might wish that we had been careful to store some kind of essence so that we might at least pass on the soul of what we are, but in so many ways, our very essence is to shade our colorings into gray areas and hide behind the facade of our great society. We too will leave pyramids but no clear record of ourselves. Even with all we have in archives, it will pass as a blend of madness and fantasy. We will be seen as running for our lives at the same time as we entertain ourselves in order to forget that fact ourselves, eating popcorn and watching fictions into oblivion. Our great concourses and parades of important historical figures that project our significance to ourselves are no more than soft walls that give an army an ideological obstruction to plow through or lovers a romantic shadow under which to mingle together.

    I say all that to help me to answer a question, which is when and how one makes a turn into that great past. When do we consign ourselves to a specific position in the event, which is passage en masse out of here, where both the position we hold and the parade itself will be forgotten, and the only thing left will be an artist's rendering of what it might have looked like back in the day to have stood by and watched the sun set and speak the long forgotten language that filled our minds and formed our queries?

    It's not something where we might easily close our eyes. This isn't really organized that we do this as a society. As we leave this world, we go out more conscious of who and what we are as individuals, not as part of any age, even if we're covered with so many aspects of it that we could be dated to the decade by our appearance in the coffin when it is raised from the ground, the stone that marked the grave long since removed.

    The reason I wish to know the answer is because of a day I spent with my father, and a dream I had about my grandfather. These two things play in to my having made a necessary assessment of where I stand as I move toward the afterlife. Everything I do and have done has been geared to the music and the flavor of the age in which I live, but now, all at once, it is as if a signal has been given, calling me to make the turn, where even if the march is long from here to the temple, for the rest of my life I will be on that walk, thinking each day that I am proceeding toward that end, not just because we all die, but as part of a ritual that is not tied to any one culture but to all cultures. In short, it is the one universal procession that is not just the foundation of every culture but the source of all its mythology. Just as a river ran alongside Egypt, the river I'm talking about runs through mankind. I'm talking about the water of life, which is also spirit, and the fact that there comes a point where we don't just get a taste of it like some form of communion, but a dunking, more like a drowning than a baptism, and this comes in the shape of an immersion into ourselves and history, some of it familial. We almost die in a dream, and wake to know the course we must follow. We head off in the intuitively recognized direction, and we call the process, "Making the Turn."

Now my father called me with some bad news, and I went right over to his house. The doctor told him he only had a year to live, and I said we'd savor every moment and slow time down. So I took him out to breakfast, and I drove very casually. I kept track of my every movement, and I told him to do the same. Together we would take so much in that time couldn't help but stand back and wait for us to finish taking it all in, at which point it would resume. So we took our sweet time doing every little thing. We became living microscopes and looked at everything carefully. Even taking the paper off a straw became an action of a thousand tiny movements. Even the first tear in the top of the paper cut through so many fibers. Each one had to be accounted for. We let every bite of food rest on our tongues to test the temperature and texture, then slowly chewed it twenty times at least before finally swallowing. Only an hour into the day, we realized it was working.

So we went fishing together, and there are lots of details in tying hooks that can slow time very effectively. And before we had our lines in the water, my father started talking about his life. He'd been a soldier, a good one, and later served in a company with the same high regard for authority. Being just some Joe in a company, he came to understand the importance of being a company man, but now, standing on the brink of the abyss, he questioned where he was going. Since his retirement, it almost felt like he had been abandoned. While actively engaged in one service or another, he felt anchored and productive. For years he'd been floating and not enjoying it. He complained that the years of retirement are painted up like they are some kind of clear goal rather than a pasture into which one is led. He sat grimly with his line in the water. "No more fish to catch for me," he said. I said that we had slowed down time so much that it would take the fish a while to show themselves. "I want it to speed up," he said. "What can we do to get this over with?" That was more than twenty years ago.

In some ways it seems like all I did was scratch that day into memory by watching everything so carefully. My father led a robust, active life with many friends, but when he died, there was only family, and when I called his closest friends, they expressed their condolences and went on with their days. All of them are dead now, too, and I am suddenly aware that I am quickly closing in on the age he was when he died.

That is where this dream comes in. First, a little background would be helpful. My grandfather was a powerful man in the community when my father proposed to his daughter. He never liked my father. He made that clear. I inherited all my grandfather's papers, and while his story is very interesting, he is completely embedded in his era, a man of his times. But unlike my father, he never questioned belonging to his era. I have pictures of him in his army uniform from World War 1. I never saw anyone look more comfortable in his skin. He kept careful records of the associations to which he belonged, and he rose in the ranks to the top of every one of them. When he died, they all paid homage to him. There was a great funeral for him that I attended as a teen. Letters came from around the world offering condolences to my grandmother. Only when it was all over did his corruption and time in prison come to light, but it did not matter since he had managed to keep his public record spotless. Nobody seemed to want to entertain the thought that he was in any way a criminal. He was the family connection to some kind of fame. Even if he didn't help his sons in any way, even if he cheated on his wife, when his name came up in conversation, it was his celebrity and accomplishments that people discussed because some of it rubbed off on them.

Now there were many years while I was growing up that there was a great rift in the family due to my grandfather. I recall my mother not speaking to him for many years over one petty insult or another. I was named after him, and so I was alert to him in ways that others were not. On one visit before the feuding began, when I was only five or so, he took me to the zoo, held my hand and was very kind to me. But years later, when we were visiting for the first time in years, a visit that was intended to end the feud, he snubbed me, and I turned on him in my heart. That same week he died, and he became so much larger than life even then, first because of the funeral, and second because I never got to speak with him and give him the chance nobody else would give him. He died and put me in the same boat with everyone else.

That was forty-five years ago, and just a few nights ago I had a dream that I lived in a place that was filled with water, but all photographs depicted life in a desert. I remember looking at a photo album of places I knew to be taken when I was sailing on lakes or fishing in rivers, but in the pictures I was exploring the arid lake and river bottom dunes. In this dream, my grandfather had come back to life thanks to something unexplained that I had done to save him. But this did not please everyone. My father was there as well. He complained that something should be done to put him back in the grave. It was as if I was making a choice between the two of them. My father said he didn't want him having any influence over anyone, that he had his chance and shouldn't be getting another. As I walked by him to take my grandfather to the doctor for an examination, my father snubbed me.

Everywhere we went, we were surrounded by very deep water. In some places, you could look through windows and see that there had been a city underwater, that the city in which we were living

Making the Turn

had come out of the water over time, most likely as the waters were rising, but if the water was ever to recede, it appeared that many of the submerged places were habitable. There were numerous stairways ready for such an event.

At the doctor's office, my grandfather started a conversation with a man who, like my grandfather, had lived his whole life in New England culture. They shared the same accent and mispronounced a few words in the same way. I remembered the sense of New England insulation when I visited in my childhood. I felt I wanted to belong, but I could never be a member because I knew too much of the outside culture, and so I would always be looking in, never out.

The doctor said my grandfather was in excellent health, and when we stepped outside the office, he stood by a railing overlooking the water and did an awkward jump for joy that threw him over the rail into the water.

I watched him and fully expected him to swim over and grab a post, but he did not. I froze and watched him sink, thinking each second that he would do something to swim upward, but he did nothing at all. I could also hear his thoughts. He was more intrigued by the irony of being about to drown so quickly after being brought back to life than thinking of doing anything to save himself. He actually found humor in it.

I did not, and I finally jumped in to save him, swimming down after him, and soon felt that I wouldn't be able to hold my breath for very long though I still had a long way to go to catch him. He had already been in the water a while and had a head start, so I feared I was already too late. When I reached him, he was still amused by the fact he was about to die again, and he did nothing to help me. I grabbed hold of him and started to push him up, but he was not buoyant, and his overcoat seemed to drape over me, complicating matters by blocking my vision. I used the stairways of the submerged city at times to push off to a higher level, and push off from a rail on that level to a window ledge on the next one, trying desperately to get him to the surface, sure that he couldn't hold his breath any longer, and feeling myself that I couldn't make it either.

I finally got him to the surface, but I couldn't push him out, and

I had to leave him momentarily, face down in the water, for he had turned around to survey the depths, remarking in his thoughts that he recognized this part of the city, that it was above sea level when he was alive. Many of the places had been his haunts, and he was still enjoying himself, now even more, and I was afraid he would sink again like a rock if I let him go.

So I took a corner of his coat and got up far enough to call someone to help. I went back in the water underneath him and gave one final push, and we were able to get him out of the water, and then I came up, exhausted, not knowing if he'd made it. He was lying there on the concrete looking like a corpse on a slab, and I watched and waited for him to show some kind of sign that he was alive, and finally it came. He took a breath, and I breathed a sigh of relief that I had saved him. I woke to the remembrance of the horrible way he had died forty-five years earlier, kidnapped from his home, put in a sack, murdered and thrown in the reservoir, after which there never was any serious investigation. The night he died he kept looking through the curtains like he was expecting someone. Apparently, feeling safe, he took out the garbage where his killers were waiting.

There are many things too dark and too deep on which people do not like to dwell. It sounds cliché. If I were to recommend detachment from all that one knows, who would listen? I thought about my dream. For a time it seemed the best interpretation was that I was digging him up, or saving him from the reservoir. I'd always wanted to conduct my own investigation into his death, but by the time I had reached the point where I might do such a thing, everyone who knew anything salient was dead as well. But I wasn't digging him up and laying him out as much as joining him. His fall into the water drew me in, and it was all I could do to get out from underneath him, and even after doing so, he was still alive, perhaps still dangerous in some way, I thought. But the surroundings, the fact that when I saved him, we were basically occupying the same space as his era, surrounded by the same structures as they appeared when he was alive. His own world was merely taking him back where he belonged. Perhaps I was just an interloper with unresolved emotion over a dead body in a reservoir who happened to be my grandfather. I have mulled over these questions now for several days, all the while filled with a strong sense of what I witnessed, of it having been real. This was one nightmare that filled more than my mind. It crept along my skin when I thought about it.

I've reached the point where I think I understand what the dream was about, but I have a hard time putting it into words without the image of Thebes as I described it earlier. I can do the same with any era really. They're all the same. They hold people. They are containers of people. People do not leave them. Someone will say, "I am French." Someday he will die and be buried at the foot of a castle in Perigaux along the Dordogne, and on the grave will be a picture of him from which you will be able to place him in time by the style of glasses he is wearing. He will have most likely been Catholic, for generally speaking that is the religion of the nation. And if you look up, you will see the eglise is not far from the castle.

It doesn't matter who you are or where you are in the world. You are tied to that sector in time and place, and for all intents and purposes, you are as forward looking and introspective as a pineapple. You cannot cut loose. You cannot simply say, "I am going to be something else. I choose to be a Chinaman of the Ming Dynasty." Your time and place are no different than an ancient setting. You live in the present moment of the past, only your belief in its importance gives it any more life than a Roman villa being excavated somewhere off the Appian Way. You are on a ship, possibly better described as a sealed tin can with a wrapper on it that says, "Ingredients: five thousand Christians from the village of Marmarita in Syria from the 1980s."

All of these possible cans sit on shelves. They both are in themselves what we call history, and they contain what we call history as well. At some point we must realize that even if nothing can be done about adding more cans to new shelves year after year, decade after decade, that this is all we are doing. It is possible to organize the cans in so many ways. They can be assembled into steps to show how man has progressed, or they can be heaped on top of one another to show battle scenes, but we are not dealing with people in this instances, not with individual souls, but with villages, cities or even nations from particular periods. All that is unavoidable, certainly, but finally we come to you, to me, to being a living soul at a given time and place. It isn't easy to merely adapt to imagining that being in a can on a shelf is all that we are. In fact, it is because we imagine something more that something more is not just possible but necessary. Every culture teaches one the importance of belonging, of learning both the secular and religious rituals, many adding penalties for non-compliance. But in the end we all comply. We absorb the influence like the mysterious chemical bath that made the petrified forest out of prehistoric trees that had fallen, and we both live and lay there after we die with all the earmarks of where and when we lived and died.

    The thing we seem to miss is a universal factor running through every culture of any given time, which exists only as it runs through the individual. It is not present in assemblies nor in group shots of any kind. You cannot see it on faces at a family reunion or in the eyes painted in true likeness on a sarcophagus. You can only find it in yourself because you are a living thing. You can trace it through every other face or society on the planet if you wish, from time immemorial until now, but its only relevant factor is in your grasping that it is in you, and that to any degree that you would feel it essential to follow what it tells you to do and not the ephemeral dictates of your culture, then you do so and make the turn, which is exactly what it is, a turn, because you must step out of a true yoke, one that may be tied to you over several generations, as my father and grandfather are linked to me. When my grandfather fell into the water talking to himself, if I had waited long enough, the rope would have pulled my mother and father in before dragging me in. In reality, my grandfather occupies a place beneath the surface, still concretized in the newspapers of the day, easily recognized in the typefaces chosen for menu selections and the styling of jalopies. I woke up to the fact that my father realized when he stood on the brink of the abyss and questioned where he was going that he needed to make a turn, that following along in every ritual, finishing every grade in school, marrying, having kids, holding down a job, serving his country, not necessarily in that order, left something to

Making the Turn

be desired although he could not say exactly what it was. He could watch the war movies and be inspired to think that he had been a part of the Allies' victory. He gave me his army uniform and scrapbooks, which are full of pictures and letters all supportive of the fact he belonged totally to an era. Every page is a line that draws a face, adding features until you can finally almost feel what it was like to live at that time. It is again like Thebes where when you see the artist's depiction of what the place looked like with all the temples restored as they looked when it was in its heyday, you might almost visualize being a part of it, in your youth, relishing in its power and vitality, except that its glory was fleeting, and the civilization fell more than two thousand years ago.

Knowing the ephemeral nature of all things, there is only one thing onto which we can latch our true yearning to take the correct path, which is the life force within ourselves. There is very little one can do to wake anyone up to this fact. I have avoided it myself at all costs, burying my head in all the petty political affiliations passed down by my family down to the last detail, and I have been inculcating them into my children for as long as I can remember. I know there is some truth to the fact that I must do this, that we all must do this, in order that our culture may survive in the living press of angry mobs shoulder to shoulder, ready to unleash years of hate and frustration upon one another at the slightest provocation due to various rituals being different for having evolved separately over centuries. There may be no way to escape it, and there is certainly no way to escape becoming a niblet in the can of corn once you have grown up on the stalk in the field on the farm in the town in the county in the state in the country defending itself from all manner of foreign influence or invasion. But once in a while, someone is awakened to the need to make the turn, to walk the other way for what is inside, to not believe what may be a false religion and not go along with politics or rituals of daily life just because they have been followed by one's forefathers. I am getting old, and I'm not trying to lead anyone to follow me down this road. I have seen the sorrow on my father's face, felt my grandfather's murder and drowning in the reservoir and decided to make the turn for myself. That is all

I'm interested in, knowing that I have managed to separate myself from the bonds of time and place and reflect properly on anything pertaining to the subject. What is the correct way to think about God, for example. Rather than fall into step, not just shoulder to shoulder but surrounded by shoulders at close quarters leading me to the altar or into battle, my intent is to consider all the questions and discover whether there is a proper portal through which I must aim my soul. Some are content to sing praises, believing that beyond what facts may be wrong, faith in any god or gods, however described, creates a complete soul to be looked upon with kindness by the heavens, which need to be recognized, commanding only that there be some kind of belief system for any culture to find its human side. Others insist there are interesting distinctions that arise organically as a culture develops its natural feeling and interest in the infinite into a religion. Tell that to the human sacrifices. No, I will not allow myself to be carried by anyone as to how I should think or why I should think it. Nor am I saying that I am preparing my mind like an antenna to receive a signal that I am on the right track. It is more analogous to sitting on a rock by the ocean, not pondering, but playing chess and having the upper hand. Who does not have the upper hand over the ocean? Sometimes I sense in its great expanse a readiness to flash over into a life force itself, one that has a greater appreciation for something that lives outside of it over anything it contains. And that goes for the rest of the universe as well. Whatever is out there must have formed into the vault and sanctuary it is so that within the free song of the free man are the echoes of eternity. Only in a wordless space of the mind beyond comprehension but inwardly sensed to be present can one be distinct from one's place, and this means one must tune one's heart to that vibration both to receive and broadcast. I have reached a point of no backing off from making the turn. Even if I get nowhere from here, and receive no indication that I have successfully changed my course, I know I've made the turn into all I am by my new hat. It's the same hat my father and grandfather wore as old men when they went fishing, a hat that I was always too embarrassed to wear until now.

Fresh Start

Michael Stone was a little bit deluded and often saw things that weren't there. This was not common knowledge, and he did not tell anyone about certain experiences he had, knowing that people would think he was odd and not believe him. One day while he was at work looking out the window, the weather took a turn for the worse. The sky had been brooding all morning, and there had been forecasts for storms, but it was only when he slammed down the phone and swore against the heavens that they opened and let loose a furious deluge. There was a special kind of violence in it, as if the ocean were lifted up, and forty days and nights would fall in just that afternoon. Michael glared through the window. He cursed her and muttered, "That's it for her." God, how he'd loved her! Now, he wanted to kill her. But it was over.

He was staring through his face mirrored in the window. He had her by the neck, but it was the rain that was gagging her. If she could only read his mind. How he loved her! But wasn't that what drove her away? Lightning flashed, and thunder roared, bringing him back to the storm outside. Suddenly, he remembered he'd left his windows open at home. "Oh no! God no!" he shouted.

Michael ran out of the office so hastily he'd forgotten his umbrella. The wind would have destroyed it anyway, and against such a downpour it wouldn't have been any use. Before he was halfway up the street, he was drenched. The train had air-conditioning, and he shivered for the forty-minute ride.

The power of the storm did not diminish. It was torrential in the towns all along the way. The train had to slow down twice to pass through small rivers formed by minor flooding. The sky was a strange shade of brown. It looked like a funnel-cloud factory, and the treetops were touching their toes. As Michael hopped off the train and ran to his motorcycle, he saw it had fallen over in a puddle. He cursed. Lightning struck nearby.

After he'd picked it off the ground, no matter how hard he tried, he couldn't kick-start the bike. He finally gave up. He kicked it in disgust, letting it fall into the puddle again. He lived more than a mile from the station, and the storm was getting worse. The winds blew harder, and hail started to fall. He trudged along the road hitchhiking, but no one would stop to help a soaking, beaten man. He swore revenge at every car that passed.

It was dark, but it was only noon. There were at least fifteen vehicles in ditches, but he jogged by the stranded motorists. When he finally reached the top of the hill, he recoiled in horror. It looked like the river had overflowed and flooded the gully. But the river was still a half mile away. He wondered how the water had risen so high. Then he saw the sewers were actually gushing water.

The flooding hadn't damaged the upper floors of his house, but the water was knee-deep in the basement. He waded around, lifting precious possessions for a last look at them. He stored much of what he owned down there, and it looked like a total loss.

He went from door to door asking to borrow a pump, but no one would help him. He swore revenge, and he returned to begin bailing. Listening to a transistor radio, he heard that the city had shut off the storm sewers that drain into the river as soon as it was close to overflowing its banks. This saved the relatively few houses along the river. Residents there had lobbied successfully after a particularly bad flood, and the storm sewer shut-off was the compromise reached. The result was that thousands of houses a mile from the river experienced flooding. He swore revenge.

As he was bailing, he was picking out whatever items were floating around him. His marvelous collection of books was turning to pulp before his eyes. He started to cry. Wasn't there anything he could do? Was there nothing that could help him?

As he blinked through the tears, he saw a page of text waving on the surface. Picking it out by a corner, he was surprised to see it was blank. He thought he must be seeing things and wiped the tears away. Still, no ink was running off the paper. Yet a moment before, it was covered with text. What had happened to it? He looked at the water, and instead of a cloud of ink, he saw the actual text floating where it had been, only without the paper. Amazed, he started reading it to see what sort of text it was. He stood still, fearing any movement would dissolve it. It bobbed in the ring-waves pulsing from his legs, but remained intact.

You want to make a fresh start, but you're ordinary and don't make things happen. Stop talking, and start giving to find renewal.

"Hogwash!" he shouted as he finished reading, and in anger, he kicked through the floating text to scramble it forever. Even as his foot was halfway through it with unstoppable force, he knew he was in trouble. He realized when it was already too late that he was kicking water straight into the electrical transformer. He remembered noticing earlier that the water level was dangerously close to it.

As he completed the kick, he could already feel the certainty of electrocution. His eyes were wide open as he watched the gush of water proceed and follow his leg to the power source. As the wave hit, he cursed, and there was a loud crackle followed by a bolt of electricity. It knocked him unconscious, but he was fortunate to fall head first into a box of old newspapers that kept his head above water. But he proceeded to have a dream that he was still awake.

So when Michael kicked through the text, something amazing occurred. The letters weren't alphabet pasta waiting to be rearranged. It was already a miracle that they were floating without the page. Instead of scattering the text, Michael's foot only caught it like a net. It wrapped itself around his foot and stayed there when the water hit the transformer. When the electricity struck him, it hit the text, which protected his foot from injury. At the same time, the electrical jolt fused the text to Michael's foot. The text also merged with the electricity such that what did get through became a permanent part of his heart, fusing there with all of his anger and desire for revenge.

The result was a new Michael Stone who suddenly believed he'd been entrusted with a gift of changing others. He thought just as he was changed, his foot must have the power to change people, and still dazed from the electrical transformation, he daydreamed.

First, he imagined calling Linda, the woman who had caused him such grief earlier in the day. Although he apologized, she quickly started where she'd left off, accusing him of not understanding her need to explore life on her own terms. When he heard that, Michael drop-kicked the phone, sending a jolt through to her end of the line. The spark changed her. She didn't know quite how, but she suddenly felt love as never before. She was overwhelmed by the love Michael had made her feel, in her and all around her. They experienced incredible rapport, and as he hung up the phone, he saw through the window that the sky had cleared.

He then imagined paying a visit to his neighbors who had refused to help him earlier. He asked them if they needed his help. To the last, they all told him to go away. They didn't need his garbage on top of the junk the flood had made of everything they once held dear in their lives. Seeing their hostility and hardness, Michael started kicking them one by one. In a group, they resisted until he'd chased them all down. Afterwards, a change was perceivable in every one of them. When Michael went away, they were helping one another, working as a team.

He then conceived what would ensue in the next several months. Michael envisioned himself accomplishing much in giving the world the swift kick it needed, but because there were other forces working hard to stir things up and set people against one another, it would seem at first that little was really changing. He would, however, quickly become famous in small circles. Those who had been touched would spread the word. Their claim that they'd been healed in the blow, purged and made whole, would make most believe he was a dangerous, arrogant charlatan whose kick only revealed the fact that many people enjoy bowing to abuse.

Michael dreamed of a typical day in his new line of work. He knew that the world reacts uniformly to all those who come with the gift of love, so it wasn't going to be easy. It doesn't matter by what means the gift is applied, whether it is a hand, a foot or the

Fresh Start

entire shape of a man. People pay tribute to love until it comes asking them for commitment, whereupon it's too much work. But he would bring them fullness by emptying out the emptiness.

Enemies would argue it couldn't be done. He would explain that just as the creation of water requires a mixture of hydrogen and oxygen, without the spark and explosion, the combination is just so much gas. What his miraculous gift of love would help them achieve could not be otherwise reached. But change is always feared, especially instant alteration, even when it's natural and promises relief. So the world would say it wasn't necessary. It would bend over backwards ignoring what it needed most. Like a doughnut denying there's a hole, the world would say the sun's in orbit, and the center is most full.

Michael dreamed this posture would only make his work easier. He wouldn't care what was thought of him or what they thought he was doing. Let the world come bowing to him backwards, he thought. It would only single out those who needed him and where they needed it most.

As for how he would deal with others, he dreamed he wouldn't just go around kicking people. He would freely discuss matters that were undeniable in any heart that could hear them. He would exchange and collaborate with anyone. His patience would wear thin, however, with those who rejected it as hogwash. If they held up a blank page and kicked through his message delivered on still waters, he would become a dynamic electrical outlet, empowering their backwash and transforming them with a good jolt.

He dreamed that without him as a catalyst, they could never understand the steps nor take them. But when he would give them new location, their eyes would open. They would be thankful for moving them from the basements of their lives into the upper stories. After all, cellars were never intended to be living quarters.

As for the kind of lifestyle he would lead, Michael dreamed he would be a nomad who would ride around with Linda on a quirky motorcycle that would start whenever and wherever he kicked it.

And he dreamed that when he was assassinated, one of his converts would eulogize him beautifully. He imagined it would be long and flowery with a forceful ending. *If he makes no impression on you now*, the eulogist would rhapsodize, *think of him when you're young and able to say, without blinking, that the eyes of reality are not too terrible to stare into without faith. If he still has no effect, think of him as you enter the age when everything is being slowly stripped from you; when the present is emptied of all the business, people and things that used to fill it for you. If that only fortifies your barricade against him, remember Michael when you're face down in a flood of tears; when bubbles are the only tangible evidence that you're still breathing. And if you're still cursing when he arrives just in time to knock down the barrier and administer the only thing the blank page of your life ever really required, you'll see indelible for the first time what was always swirling inside, and you'll be thankful it is not the credo you etched into your empty life when you couldn't see what you were writing on the wall.*

When Michael recovered from his daze, he wasn't sure whether any of all that nonsense about kicking through the floating text had really happened. He realized that not just kicking the text, but even seeing it in the first place must have been part of the dream. All he really knew for sure was he'd gotten a pretty good jolt. There were plenty of blank sheets of paper in the detritus floating around him in the receding water. If the jolt had really been electricity, he could have been killed and was lucky to be alive. How had he survived? Could an electrical jolt cause such a strange dream?

Surely, it was all a dream, yet he wasn't ready to kick through it and dismiss it all as hogwash. Something told him that wouldn't be a good idea. He considered how a whole life is said to flash before the eyes. Why not a whole dream of a lifetime? As absurd as it seemed, some of his vision was more compelling than what he took for real. He could feel he'd regained his senses. It wasn't difficult to distinguish reality from the madness in his brain. Still, something remained, and something had changed. He knew he had no magic to change anyone, but he'd miraculously escaped being killed; and in merely surviving, he'd received a great gift, a rare opportunity to make a fresh start.

He thought of telling someone about it, but there was nobody close at the moment. He didn't really know his any of his neighbors very well, but he felt he needed to go out and see how the water had affected other lives. Outside, there were many people who lived in the same apartment complex dealing with the loss of personal possessions. He offered a hand in carrying drenched items to the curb. Someone asked about his basement, and he said the water was pretty high and had hit the electrical when he was in the water, and he felt lucky to be alive. After helping others for the rest of the afternoon, someone asked if he had any means to get the water out and offered to let him use a portable pump as well as to help him set it up. By dusk, there was a hose coming out of his window-well, blowing dirty water out of his basement, which would take a few hours, so he was finally able to take a breather.

He sat down on the front steps of his apartment feeling pain in every muscle in his body. He remembered that morning. It seemed like days had gone by since he got up and went to work expecting it to be an average day. But every day, there was someone in the news experiencing some kind of tragedy. The journalists covering the flood wouldn't even bother with Michael and his neighbors. There would be a general statement about bad weather in a specific county, and they would be somewhere in the count of people without electricity, rounded off to the nearest hundred. How many of those were in his shoes, he wondered. How many of them had seen the strange things that electricity can do? Not having it was news, but what about having it hit you and do strange things to your mind?

He wouldn't want any such thing to happen to anybody, but it was because of what else had happened that he wasn't feeling sorry for himself. He felt lucky, perhaps even chosen, not in any way that he could brag about. He knew it was a product of his mind, but it was so clear to him. He could even still see the text, and he thought he should write it down. He stood up to go in for a pencil, and it was all he could do to get the muscles in his legs to work. He pulled himself up with the handrail by the stairs, took one step and tripped over something. He looked down. The sole of his shoe had come unglued, and he'd stumbled as it flapped down and caught on the stair. In his mad rush home and wild effort to save property in the basement, he'd ruined a relatively new and expensive pair of shoes.

He sat down, too tired to do anything.

The next morning, he walked outside feeling cleansed somehow. There was something in the air, and he took a deep breath to soak it all in. He considered putting the shoes at the top of garbage heap but took them to the city. He was glad to hear the shoemaker say he could fix them, but he gave Michael a funny look and said his face was dirty. He went straight to the men's room for a look in the mirror. It was a faded, illegible ink-smudge of text from the newspapers where he fell, most likely front-page bad news.

Some Kind of Song

A man woke up one day and realized that life is all about song, that the human spirit is no more than a tuning fork that must be pitched into the sea of experiences that sets it ringing out that music. He realizes that all his fears and doubts are the periods of silence between the moments his spirit exults and that in those silences, sometimes days, he's actually waiting for the mood to strike him to sing, like someone sitting at the piano expecting at any moment a new melody to come to mind. He also realizes that the silences are getting longer, such that he cannot sense what the rhythm is. Looking back at his childhood, there was a fast song, a dance. In middle age, he guessed if it was anything, it was a dirge.

So he decides it's time for the faucet not to drip sporadically, but rather to flow, and that his whole existence, day by day in time, should flow like notes on a staff. He reasons that a negative mood must be banished with song, something like, "This is a song of the fact I still have some doubts and fears at times," or "This is a song of weaknesses/sometimes I feel so empty, lonely and tired." Whatever doubt or fear that intrudes, the original thought that life should be one long song will generate a song to combat that sadness, and if he can keep doing it, his faith (though it came late in life) will have increased to the point that he will not need to remind himself that life is all about song. He will know it throughout his whole being.

So he went about thinking that as long as he would keep this plan of his in mind, he would feel he has purpose even when he isn't particularly immersed in life as society would expect him to be. "The purpose of my life is to arrange my spirit so that it does sing, and my senses to keep my spirit singing." He saw it as a subtle point, that the issue was in present tense, as his consciousness moves along with the actual passage of real time, that the song is written as it happens, which infuses one with the ability to avoid the pitfalls of silence and depression. A song of days composed in the flow of life might even steamroll over the negative forces of the mind, breaking them down into a manageable size that is even incorporated into the song so that there's little difference between a worried state and the state of mind that changes it, alchemizes it into a sound, an instrumentation, played out against the silence of the universe, no longer a part of personal silence, and heard within, restoring a sense of tempo to life so that one is not lost in the silences but in some kind of control over them, conducting them like instruments, calling them as rests into the composition like water between stepping stones across the full length of the abyss.

A friend took issue with this argument when the point of view was expressed to her. Her first reaction was that it was ridiculously shallow, even beneath contempt since people do not live as if days were discs that might be collected and strewn about later in symmetrical shapes. Not only did she question the rationality but the sanity of the plan. She also had immediate examples to shoot holes in the theory, anomalies that would shed light on the preposterous notion. How could he, for example, believe that his life is one big song when his wife divorced him for drinking and cheating? How can there be music where a son needs help but receives none from his father? How does he explain away in song the fact that a petty grudge has kept him from speaking to his mother for a year? "Isn't it up to you," she asks, "to settle all these matters in order for there to be any song?"

He pondered for a moment, then replied, "Without song, it's little wonder there are wrecks behind me. You'd have life be perfect before you'd say I could sing, or when I am trying to sing, you remind me of unhappiness in the hope to interrupt the joy. My life before my singing started surely was unhappy, and there are wrecks on the shores where I set out to sail rough seas, but I set up to settle the rough sea and open the dark skies, not to settle scores. And it's true there's pain to think of them now, but what has that to do with being what I'm made by God originally to be? We must find the truth along the way of experience, even after stumbling, sinking, nearly drowning. It isn't something we have to maintain all along. Somewhere along the way, we lose it. Even when we seem to have it all and could be called happy, are we really dependent on those things? It would seem so, since when they are lost, we are empty. If we sing only because we have certain things, we just blind ourselves to the fact that sooner or later it all is stripped away. If we had a song of life, life would dismantle the song. No, the song is this that pours from my soul now. It is an affirmation of presence, of being, and it is commanded from a great source, however few do join the choir for recognizing the conductor is pointing the baton at them. It hurts when someone we love leaves us. People die. We're born into a race of relatives and ancestors, all are dead or die in the end. It's explained to us that we'll die no matter what we do. Still, we're told to continue to love life. We should listen, but we don't. When something bad happens, we behave as if it's all about us."

"It's a bunch of crap to me," she answered, "and I don't hear music out of you anymore than I could hear clucking from an ostrich whose head is buried in the ground. You've deluded yourself, lulled yourself into thinking the landscape is made up of hard and cold facts, when actually it's something you can change. The spirit is the wind and water that erodes the sharp edge of reality. You are saying you can turn your back on it, take no responsibility and are not just exonerated but whole. Your song is the lack of conviction."

"Hearing music out of me is not the issue," he replied. "You'd criticize the oboe that it should sound like the flute. Comparisons of any kind, or judgments from the outside, have no bearing on what is essentially intrinsic. Anyone can have a grandfather's clock, but where is grandfather's heart when the ticking has stopped? The music is the consciousness that made him the person that he was. That was his true life, his to give a certain tempo to, his to arrange, compose, play out, or if he merely struggled and gasped and grumbled and went to his grave perceived a bitter fellow, still, that was it for him despite what anyone had said or has to say about it. But within a certain spirit, no, I say as a given spirit, the time is now, the duty clear. The simple message from on high is to sing, to simply sing, not sputter, not despair, nor wonder where the music will come from or when it will play for you, but feel its presence and let it out."

She interrupted him. "And I suppose your wife, son and mother all are out there somewhere, dancing and singing with what you've done to them?" she asked. "You make me sick with your self-righteous sophistry. This is no answer. It's a dodge. What matters is not what you feel. You can feel what you do and still be wrong. No, I'm convinced I see you clearly, and how I see you is to me the key to it all. You're stagnant, empty. You're most like a car with its horn stuck on, blaring a single note. Some would say it's 'the same old song,' but there's no music to anyone's ears. In fact, all anyone can do is wonder what it takes to unstick you and hope you'll return from the land of the numb."

"Let that be your last word on the subject," he said, "and here is mine: you are faced with this, that when you did not exist, there was a void, but beyond the limit of your span of life, what is there? All that you can know is wrapped by the husk of what you are, and when that fails, where are you? You cannot touch anything except that the husk tells you how it feels, and that prevents you from saying you know truly what you have touched. Whatever has made so angry that you attack me, all that fury and frustration fills your sky, not mine. No matter how much you insist I obey the results of your math, it is not universal law, and nothing of the spirit of what you say is crossing the spaces. I cannot absorb it, let alone remember or even understand it. You are not telling me a better way to live, just trying to destroy what I am saying. I am not deaf but different; not dumb but enlightened. Between the day we are born and the day that we die, there is this, and if it were a patch of stinging bees, few would find the strength between shouts of pain to either urge others to sing or say it was all just some kind of song. We both know life, but only in terms of our base. What is universal about it? Is the blue in the sky I see the same blue for you?"

He continued. "In different points along experience, which in no way can it be said must inevitably match, spirits will always be out of tempo with one another, but if in tune within themselves, they may be in harmony. You knew me when I was in winter, and now that buds and leaves have appeared, you presume it is growth against my nature, not as anything natural in its season. As I stand here, my heart's root tapping the well of eternity, I speak of vibrations resonating along that line that I might feel and speak the flow. You speak of one cut loose, not yet connected, still wintering in silence. I pray for warmer weather, timely rains and effectual sunlight for you. Nothing we can do can make our sunken ships or rotting hulls of the past float again. My wife, son and mother will never return whatever I may do. I cannot make them yield to or fathom my song, but they left me before I started to sing like this. As I live and breathe, I celebrate what I am. God assigns experience and somewhat shrouds whatever comes next, conducting our symphony of life in mystery and wonder. When I cease to breathe, the essence and the style particular to me are lost to the world as far as interaction here goes, but only I felt and lived those aspects all along. The world has only lost a piece of what reacts to its touch, just as you will lose my reaction to you, but you will carry along whatever it is of me you've always felt, whatever it is that you remember, your reaction to me, your sense of my style, of what I was, based on your way of looking at things. I can live with that. I cannot adjust my essence when you say it disturbs you because I am not seeking to influence. I can only steer clear so as to not affect you. And as I do, I thank you for this chance to…"

She interrupted him again. "This is no song. It's a nightmare of schmaltz," she objected. I don't see sun, buds, rain, and growth, just worms in your bad poetry. As if that makes it mystical. It's more masochism if you ask me. You're like one of those self appointed, vegetable-soup-eating, magazine-selling, incense-burning freaks that talk of eternal oneness and live in a commune reliant on donations, sleeping with all the women and playing flutes and bongos up and down the street every day asking for spare change. Does that mean you need a spare tire? Got a flat in life? Stopped moving? Go for the big makeover you keep in the trunk for such an emergency. What they used to call a cop-out or a nervous breakdown. You've got this thing that gets you from here to there, spans the gap, yanks it together like it wasn't there so you don't have to feel the pain. You call it the truth and postulate that everyone is bleeding to death without it because you've found the big band-aid. You're a loser who can't make it the right way like everyone else so you invent a new way that suits you, only you say it transcends everything else, so it's only a matter of time before you have a following for your one-man cult. There are plenty of rats to follow you playing your pipe, only watch out where you're taking them, and don't forget they're only children. But before you go saving us all from some kind of plague we're all causing, maybe you should think about how much better the ground might be if your blood were mixed with it, how much stronger the grass and flowers would be in a soil fertilized with your mashed-up body. Now that would do some good because all you're doing is standing here on one foot and the other trampling down what really lives in harmony with the universe and stands for something. Anything you put over that ugliness inside you is mere makeup to conceal what is at bottom the basest sort of evil and hypocrisy. You can't rise above your nature by calling yourself a singer in harmony with heavenly vibrations." And she knocked him down with a solid punch put squarely into his nose. "Oh, I hear a song now," she added. "A swan song. No, the ugly duckling, and that was my last word, the last beat of any song out of you I'm going to hear!"

    The punch sent him reeling, but he stood up quickly and looked at her with a stern focus, took out a handkerchief and daubed his nose while speaking. "You know, you've made me realize something that may explain our misunderstanding. You don't need to dissuade me from the philosophy that puts me chanting and tossing flower petals in exchange for nickels and dimes. That isn't what this is about at all. Part of the trouble may be my fault. Some notions are difficult to alertly grasp and be attuned to at all times. I guess I had a kind of revelation that I've explained perhaps rather poorly, and though you certainly did not need to go so far out of line with such a violent, drastic reply, at least now I see clearly what changed me. You see, once I passed a certain age, where most of my hopes were dashed and disappointment had become the expected norm, I lived in a bitter mode, as if depression were meant to be the adult stage of the human being. I had no goals, I saw no reason to work hard at anything. I loved nothing and lost all those who loved me. I hit bottom at some point, still young, but something told me this was not what it was supposed to be. I started my work again, sometimes feeling that the experience would be of great value, that everything that happened was just paying my dues, and a greater maturity would be the result if I didn't quit. But when I examined the lives and works of those who ultimately produced great things, it wasn't the suffering or experience that differentiated them, but the exultation. From work to work over time, one would have to say that without long periods of no productivity between them that great things just poured out. And so metaphorically I thought of song, that their works marched out in a sort of rhythm and tempo if you speed up many years into a few minutes, and based on the spirit and vision of those great things one could only surmise that these individuals had reached a point of access within themselves, found a key to a higher plateau, found a way to compose thoughtfully and skillfully beyond any mood or fear that dominates and constrains many minds. Free of such hindrances, on track within themselves, I saw them as people of good music, of personal song. And that's the point that caused our misunderstanding. Instead of realizing that, thanks in part to my talking around it, you saw me in another guise, as some kind of feeble escapist. Maybe I'm not very discerning, but I certainly do not deserve such contempt that would lead to a punch in the face; rather I require like any human being some degree of understanding by others, maybe even by those who might disagree with me, for in its highest form, there's value to finding what kind of truth one lives just in case we might derive something for ourselves, some clue to living better. Who knows?

"But even given all this, if now I've clarified the issue, your violence still bears some scrutiny here, because for centuries, people like you have been persecuting others, not just with words out of disagreement, but with violence and control. Christ spoke of love and was crucified for it, and he still changed the world. And some would answer that the meek have inherited the earth in cubic yards dumped over their bodies to conceal the atrocities. I wonder if you strike out because you perceive weakness, that you sense you won't be resisted, that you believe in a promise that the other cheek will be turned; in short, that you can get away with it. Can a peaceful position really do so much to bring the blood to a boil unless it were truly threatening though? I believe you're closer to thinking I am right than you ever had thought or had a prayer to convince me of your argument, and just so you know that I'm not far from being the same man you accuse me pretending not to be, I admit I am livid, but in a controlled sort of way. When I evaluate this whole conversation, regarding both positions carefully, I see completely why you think I am shallow. You have made your point. I have screwed up. I am acting like I've figured out the truth and have chosen a simplistic cliché for a metaphor. But I would like you to consider that life is some kind of song even if we don't know what it is. People talk about 'the harmony of the spheres' and the wonders of nature. From the beauty of mathematics and the elements, we can't just say the mind is amazing for discovering these things. Even looking at our own bodies, how can we have become so numb to the simple wonders that we would believe we came from some primordial ooze that was struck by lightning? Did the ooze sense a spectrum and know it needed to evolve some kind of eyes? Did it sense vibrations and evolve ears? Everything that we are has an inherent complexity that we constantly forget. We seem to find argument a convenient way to mask the reality and the terror. Maybe that is why we fight, but did you ever consider that the way we've been going back and forth is a kind of dance? Maybe it isn't so much making music as much as we're trying to hum music we think we have heard, that we know there's something out there, and we know it pertains to us. We don't have words for it, but we try to put it into words anyway, and those who are intuitive will hear the music there, in the distance, and lean closer because that is what they are anxious to hear."

"Interesting," she said. "I'm sorry I hit you." After a brief silence, they walked away together continuing their discussion, and there was lightness in the rhythm of their steps, an indication that if this was music, some kind of song, the next movement had begun.

Dudot

Ol' Man River

John Doot, a man who for reasons to be explained came to be known as "Dudot," had experienced a personal tragedy that he could not reconcile, and so he was on his way to see Ol' Man River when he happened to be intercepted by a neighbor. The man had not seen Dudot in quite some time, since before ice started to flow in Ol' Man River's veins, but this chance meeting was a great inconvenience for Dudot. He did not say, "Excuse me, but I've something important to attend to," because he was not like that on the outside, but under the surface he was. He tolerated the man's general questions about how he'd been and acted as if he was not unhappy to see the other as well. But wasn't that the story of his life? Here he was in another shallow conversation about the facts of his life while the truth of his life was radiating unspoken.

All of his life there were always intrusions. Whenever there was something he needed to do, there was always something else asking for his time. He would just be about to launch himself into a major undertaking when the undertaker would get into the act: someone would die and throw the whole plan off. To some extent even meals were an intrusion, and so when he was concentrating he'd eat when he felt like it, and that brought on his having to endure everyone's telling him how that was not good for him, how he should take better care of himself, until he wanted to choke them, not at the time, but over thirty or forty years of the same thing, unrelenting as small influences persisted for their share of his attention. He just waited to choke it all off, put it in its place and be done with it, but as the conversation with the neighbor attested, he was conditioned to respond with civility because under the surface of every human being, the fields of wheat like to lay one way as they preferred to be rubbed, and anyone who didn't maintain good manners as part of the social contract would be up a creek, have to explain it, apologize for having "lifted the painted veil called life" in order not to have an exponential increase of perturbing intrusions, many of them conjured up by one's own mind. Dudot had learned that he also had to deal with the enervating influence of his own justifications for his actions, that standing firm after an outburst wore him down more than just avoiding it altogether, and so he was sick of it both ways, daring not to complain for the consequences, though silently bearing it all took its toll on him as well.

And so he chatted with his neighbor, more took the questions and gave short answers knowing that it would pass and that it was better not to reveal what he really felt or explain that he had a bone to pick with a river spirit. How would his neighbor even react if Dudot said he had to hurry as Ol' Man River was expecting him? Actually, Ol' Man River wasn't expecting him, or perhaps it is better to say that the river spirit wasn't giving it a thought either way as it conducted itself in its own business, occupied with its own affairs, which was precisely the bone that Dudot wanted to pick, the one that stuck in his craw, more enveloped him like an encumbering exoskeleton, perhaps a bit like the brown pall on the snow that hangs on in Spring along the roads, or like the mood one has after being cooped up all winter, having all that chill and ugliness to deal with before the weather gets warm again. And Dudot couldn't actually put it into words, in the sense of expecting a response anyway. The burden he felt was almost without thought, as an abandonment of thought, an acceptance of all things but a sheer fatigue of it as well, a joyless response that this is it and it sucks without any emotion for having grown numb to it; yet with a negative charge that is drawn unconsciously to a way of dealing with it. And in these cases it always comes down to seeking out a spirit of some kind, a source of quiet, meandering power; something generally unacknowledged and yet suddenly empowered in instances where one is separated from a sense of belonging or fitting into the feast of life. For Dudot, Ol' Man River was suddenly imbued with qualities or whatever it was that he was at odds against, and he was going down to see the spirit and bumping into a neighbor seemed to both intensify and defuse the need. Dudot grew weary and lost his immediate sense of why he was going to see Ol' Man River, but not consciously so. He just wouldn't spell out what it was he was on his way to do for his neighbor, filling in for the truth, preferring to say he was running an errand. Focusing on something he might have been doing, and then the neighbor's wanting to go with him made it real, and Dudot wound up at home later with a loaf of bread and some milk for his empty shelves, having gone familiar routes like an old river himself without knowing why he was doing it all, only that thanks to his neighbor it needed to get done in order to get to tomorrow. The meeting with Ol' Man River could wait. Dudot would have his say, and the river would damn well listen, though that was one of the issues, that it was on its own course and rarely had Dudot come to such a keen sense of it at all, to turn it from a mere body of water into something with spirit, not in just an imaginary sense, but having substance that he could go out to it, stand next to it and know that it was alive, and listening and depending on what he would say, might have a reply. And Dudot was usually of a mind to back away from such thinking, not allowing himself to think such thoughts and have his feet respond, nor letting his imagination get the better of him. But it wasn't talking he wanted, just to have it out, to wrestle with Ol' Man River, strangle him, whatever the power, regardless of his puny force and how many Dudots lay piled on the shore of the centuries from having fought while fed up. There is still a legacy to be told of the fed up, an epic poem for a blind Homer to tell, not sweep them all under the carpet and say somehow so many just plain lost it rather than to acknowledge that many of their harsh judges would one day go that way themselves, such that there needs to be an acknowledgement of a point at which all this reckoning takes place to a certain abandonment regardless of the cost, perhaps hoping at some point that the world will take note of it and stop feeding young people with ideals that can't ever be validated, and tell them the truth instead of calling him Ol' Man River and singing songs that all allude to mysterious power, to nail it down for what it is, put one's finger on it for good to provide a clearer picture, the brain in relation to reality, what we'll become or which way we will go on a pie chart, some to disease, others to other infirmities and then others over the deep end, into the heart of the Ol' Man himself.

And Dudot decided the chance meeting with his neighbor had been planned by the Ol' Man as a counter attack, and Dudot's sense had faded, so he would bide his time. There was still time, and so he went into the shower, into his think tank and let the purified, sanitized, lifeless waters taken from the Ol' Man spill over him, not cold and muddy and hopeless, but warm and clear, helping him to think, to clear his mind, and he filled his mouth with water and spit at the empty shampoo bottle, tainting the water with his saliva and getting a few drops in. Dudot thought of it as a kind of holy water. The accumulation of days, all of it on target, yet tainted like the Ol' Man but with Dudot's life fluid. And he thought of baptism, which for him came at his birth and was to have imbued him with the Holy Spirit. Had it? Or if it hadn't, would he be at the bottom of the Ol' Man by now? Dudot thought of how he'd always thought of remains as bones and dust, but it was really fluid and spirit, that what we come into the world with is not bones but all our fluid, and we best meet with liquids and spirit in our own spirit, and so it's a constant exchange, an ongoing spiritual cleansing. His mind was spinning. He couldn't keep track of it. What was Ol' Man River again? What are people really trying to say with such an oversimplification? What are they really hiding? And he turned off the water, dried off and went to sleep, the evils of the day having been sufficient to the hours at hand.

Vain Empires

Dudot woke wondering what the plan was, not just his for the day, but God's for the universe. How long was either going to leave the ruins in disarray? Since Satan had soiled the earth, how much longer would we have to wait for the absolutely perfect of all beings to clean up the place? And as for the further mess that Dudot had made of his own life, out of the gift that God had given him, what was the plan to fix it when he could barely extricate how and when all the things wrong had mixed themselves together and how would he expect God to help him fix it, which everyone said was the answer when God had let the whole plan go to pot all these centuries? Was he going to listen to Dudot's prayer and perform magic?

So out of the box that morning, Dudot didn't have much of a plan to do anything. He didn't have a job to go to. He had seen to that. He didn't have a wife to greet him. He'd seen to that, too. And no kids to drive to school. Now whose fault was that!? And he pounded his fist into the counter.

In the old days, Dudot always had a plan, but something wasn't worth doing unless he really felt it. Creative ideas, really interesting ones, would come to him, and he'd know, just know they would work. But then he'd bounce it off someone, and they'd just yawn, tell him it was impossible and not to get too hyped up over something, that it was just his nature to dream but it wasn't going to come true. This was not a fairy tale world, they'd say, and these were supposedly the people he could trust, whose love and support he could count on, but they were the vanguard of deflating his hopes, the first to arrive to dash his hopes and suggest he face reality. These were the ones before whom he was supposed to be able to exult and tell his secrets, but they had no faith and were not built like him. They didn't see what was inside him, and so they just went on expecting whatever it was to die down like all the other wild plans he'd come up with.

But more than half the reason the plans ever died was due to them. They'd say, "Do it if you really want, don't let me discourage you," but it still would detract, somehow deflate it, like in its unborn form one is somehow not able to project it perfectly and more liable to see flaws when they're only suggestions. Still they became preoccupations because of his lack of confidence, and seeing as how he never did these things and how he got all excited, they just kept pressing him to join the human race, get on with his life and not expect so much out of it. He was one of them, and the tacit inference was that since none of them had this drive, how could he? They were all ordinary, unassuming people, none of whom had any real success or even an inkling of what he was talking about, nor what internal organ might be present that was generating such whims and whether or not there was any real reason behind putting any kind of value on there being such an organ present. They all thought he'd grow out of it, but Dudot was no more likely to do that than a garden to lose its weeds without their input. That thanks to them there were all these weeds, and it was up to them to uproot them, not one by one but all at once including the garden, meaning a complete system reboot, a clearance of all the air, and everyone be damned, and feeling that, he felt refreshed and vindicated.

Now Dudot stood at the sink after 30 years of being unduly influenced by people whose lives amounted to nothing, who didn't believe in anything, who didn't care if they ever amounted to anything and accepted the strange personal fate of total anonymity. He felt his life force should be preserved somehow, and he feared dying, at least without a fight. Rather than turn to just give up he should go down swinging, to save somebody in a fire, make it mean something, or at least he'd always felt that way when he'd believed in life and in himself though that had all been eroded slowly by degrees with no one to blame but himself.

And on this day without a plan he felt largely in a shell of anger, as being in the belly of the beast, as if there were something God was telling him to do that he wouldn't and then he felt the anger centered in himself like a ball, that he was the beast, able to do whatever he pleased and all be damned, that this was the empowering force, the crystal drive of the ship he was flying, and on this he could shift gears somehow, look at it and derive power. He called it intuitive seclusion, and he wasn't sure if it was a good or bad thing, only that he didn't care anymore which meant he'd let a lot of baggage go. And in this state of mind he felt so focused that he didn't need a plan or anyone to advise him if it be worth attempting, nor was he going to sit and hatch vain empires either. The first thing to do was make some coffee.

The point of this to Dudot was about the state necessary to perform and the difficulty of nurturing it as one is surrounded by those who have no inkling of it that one needs not only to isolate and discover it in oneself but also to protect it, guide it, develop and perfect it, all in the face of mounting odds and diminishing capacity to believe without some degree of performance or proof. Dudot had missed his chance, now very mad, as when he made a shirt sleeve ironing board when his mother would not iron his shirt on a Sunday morning. He accepted it because it was a response to his life at the time, but twenty or thirty years later realized there were issues in his house at the time, and he blamed his mother for ultimately breaking up the family, and the sleeve ironing board was a symptom then of the full-blown heartache that would follow.

Hatching vain empires was the thinking without the action or attempting, in Dudot's sense, where the attempting was highly discouraged and the results uneven as preparation and practice always are, for there were none to see or appreciate his gifts in the confusion of getting ready for church, which was the symbolic state of his family, scurrying around, fighting, getting nowhere, least of all closer to God and half the time not even making it out the door, or on many occasions, not even getting out of bed to try, the pile of dirty clothes too high to even bother trying to fish a shirt out that didn't reek and iron its sleeves.

The Long Beat of the Metronome

It was a sorry state of affairs to look back on in light of that apparatus, thrown together in shop class. Even in the end though, when the youth is gone, and middle age is gone, and all the creating is over, the call is to enjoy the time, the dog, the walk, the sky and not feel a need that all eyes are on you or minds thinking of you, the whole point of expression is to get it out as you see the truth, and the world be damned because its current manifestation is always almost half dead and almost too juvenile, the rest too distant or preoccupied to notice. So it is all very near what you think because no one else really cares anyway. So it's all vain empires. No one will come to your table at an empty convention hall in the symbolic sense though in your mind the room is crowded, and you wish you had the attention being lavished on others, which in fact is mere disinterested chance. All artists who worry what the world thinks of them are disappointed.

Dudot Dreaming

Dudot had a dream that he was marching for the benefit of poor people through poor neighborhoods where people had shuttered their windows because they perceived it was all a bunch of wealthy people trying to get more money from them, and the weather was bitterly cold, and though Dudot was dressed for it, many weren't, and they began to lose the capacity to walk. They were freezing, and no one was doing anything to help them, neither the poor in their tenements barely able to afford heat to keep themselves warm, nor the marchers who were in an "every-man-for-himself mode," all except Dudot, who stood gazing at the people crawling in misery, a mother and her two children close to unconsciousness, and so he decided to do something about it. So he broke into the nearest apartment and looked around. The poor people who lived there had barricaded the portal to the kitchen and were hiding somewhere behind an old chair, but the living room was wide and warm enough to sustain life, so he went back out to collect the people who were dying, only they were gone.

For some reason he was on a balcony now looking down on people, and saw a beautiful woman to his left and the freezing mother and her two children to his right. He asked the woman with the children if they were all right, and she said yes. And so he started telling the beautiful woman all that he had seen and the fact that no one would help, but he couldn't stand it so he was offering assistance, and he started to show much emotion, and he could tell she was moved, and Dudot found the groove to keep the song going, and he kept depicting it with more detail and color knowing she was enrapt and himself beginning to feel more interested in her, that he was connecting, and he saw in her the beauty and felt the chemistry, so he was filled in all his limbs and his loins with a sense of longing for her. And then he saw his wife on the street watching him on the balcony, and the chemistry converted instantly to foreboding, a palpable sense that he was going to be discovered and stopped, and his wife was watching his facial contortions and emotions and she would know there was something unusual going on, and then she came over as he feared and sat next to him on the balcony and held his hand, and while he was forced to acknowledge her he had to gradually disconnect from the beauty who was already alert, he thought, to this but being what she might have felt it could be, but both so close to those old feelings there would be no hurt, all they could say was *oh well* and move on, and then his wife made a cynical comment about the poor not really needing them and that they didn't need the poor, and the beauty and Dudot were both a bit aghast, and it broke the spell, and he was embarrassed that he had to stay with his wife, that now walking with this new woman would be like thin ice, once promising but no promises now, the potential burned off, and though nothing had happened he was already in trouble with his jealous wife, and when he woke he was mad at his wife who was gone anyway, but it was that sense that she'd come at a bad time, the right time for her though, and he was mad to wake to knowing he was divorced and not having that to work for him, to ignore her influences when he had a chance with the beauty, but in the dream it was also telltale as to the reasons for their divorce, to the issues they had that were never resolved, and he looked around his apartment, and it reminded him of the tenement he'd broken into in the dream, the march, his walk through life to get something from himself for himself, an effort not only ignored but with extra barriers, walls of resistance to keep himself out, and he wondered if he had ventured behind the chair in the dream what he might have found, certainly not beauty or his wife, for they were both dispersed behind him now.

The Last Days of Pompeii

Dudot didn't feel like doing anything that morning so he went and turned on the TV and lay down on the couch. He clicked the set off when there was nothing to watch. It was a chilly morning and he scrunched up to keep warm and thought about some of his problems weighing in, stepping off the scale flabby and impossible to push off once they started taking their turns sitting on him. The recent eruptions in his life were still causing lots of smoke and fire, lava and ash, and he felt like he was getting buried alive and wondered why he bothered to live, and then he started thinking about the people of Pompeii and their last moments. They were all covered up for centuries by the hot ash, until the village was excavated and plaster of paris poured into holes that were found. The plaster hardened in the body-shaped caves revealing people where they fell in the positions they adopted, mothers holding their children, dogs lying next to their masters, on the ground in the same position Dudot was in on the couch. He stretched out his legs.

When he was in high school, Dudot had done an art project that the art teacher didn't like. She assumed she knew what it was and told him to start over. He debated her, saying it was his work. She said a dead fetus is not the subject matter for art! He replied it was not a fetus but a man still encased, undiscovered in Pompeii, given just enough ash to show he was still covered, and he knocked on it to show that it was still hollow, that the man had not been plastered yet, that this was the true remains, truer than the plaster and showed him as well as the plaster could which took his place, and he said if a modern man were entombed that way they would do more to salvage him than find a hole and pour in the plaster, that his remains were in there, and there should be no statute of limitations on remains, and he more than science was respecting the dead, not trying to disgust by showing off a dead fetus, though a fetus was hollow too in a way, never having lived at all to be filled with what life has to offer, all its joys and experiences; and the fetal position of his own work was deliberately chosen because people assume that position when they are afraid. It's a natural thing, like wanting to return to the womb, and for these people in Pompeii. They did return to the womb, Mother Earth, and their experiences were not lost on the world, and they were not hollow cores to be filled, but real people turned to dust, and the earth around them was their precious context.

The teacher was more interested after Dudot's "lecture," and she asked how he had made it, and he said he'd taken a balloon shaped like a baby and put papier maché around it, then when it dried he popped the balloon and pulled it out. Then he covered it with brown clay to maintain the look of the earth. Then she did something that surprised him. She said he took a baby and aborted it, a hollow thing filled with air and made it look like an adult, and that the process was tied to the end result, and that he would be graded down for not having considered the steps as a spiritual part of the creation.

But she stole the idea, and a year later, a similar work of hers appeared in a magazine, and she later left the school to work in a college. Thinking about this made Dudot mad. He realized he'd pulled his legs up in the fetal position again. He got up for more coffee. He wondered what ever became of the teacher. Perhaps she stole ideas of college students and took a job at some higher level where she could steal ideas, sooner or later she'd come crashing down, her ruses revealed like a papier maché exterior and the baby balloon still deflated inside, never pulled out to live again with whatever patch would need to be applied. Everyone was wounded, deflated, patched and put back. What was she hiding? He wondered what spiritual process she used in her work that could also justify the blatant theft of ideas from people who were naturally more creative than she was. He decided to track her down if he could and tell her off, but when he got the number of the high school to see where she'd gone from there, a flood of unpleasant memories of that era started rolling down on him like rocks from Vesuvius. He didn't want to start that again. He sat down and let the rocks pile up. They would find him like Rodin's "The Thinker" if they poured the plaster in someday, thinner, and not nude, but something about the way Rodin sculpted left a roughness like the plaster, faces sometimes lacked definitions, as if as the filler wore away from within, that the care on one's face from experience might be symbolized by removing the details of the face, that life gives us wrinkles, but old sculptures grow smoother, and after a while we are all walking ghosts, impressions of people we once were, lost in the ash of daily life slowly, inexorably burying us, but softened by time and erosion, making for interesting genealogical subjects with merely birth, marriage and death dates, interesting as long as they are ancestors. Dudot didn't want to be a fetus or a thinker, but he did want to be an ancestor, and it explained why he was somehow not sorry for the part of him that came to be called Dudot, which was a name that nobody knew except him, and also explained much of his sadness.

Dudot had another idea for a work of art he called the Minstrel Cycle that would be a series of musical vignettes designed to show the history of the political baloney, reverse racism and suffering of the black people all at once, and at the ending of the cycle it would be revealed that it was all a kind of giant cramp that would go away, a mood like menstrual cramps shared by whites as well, and so the moral of the story is that a quarrel on the grand scale can last hundreds of years, but it's still a bunch of baloney, just as not having a black president in 150 years might indicate that some things are entrenched and die hard. Dudot also wanted it to be a comedy but he wasn't ever going to do it because the politically-correct climate wouldn't stand for it nor understand it. Five hundred years earlier the Catholic Church burned a man at the stake for translating the Bible, then dug up another who did the same thing and burned his body at the stake after he was dead. Dudot didn't feel much warmth for the ways of the world nor any particular reason why he should go with the flow and obey its various canons or unwritten directions or stated and known general threats under the umbrella of tradition, facts of life or "friendly advice." Dudot wasn't sure how to pick it apart, only that it was all obvious except no one seemed to want to change or do anything about it.

Dudot also used to have a theory that we were all just babies curled up inside with layers of experience and a camouflage of growth and physical changes, acquisition of language, that masked the fact that down deep we were still the original self, but over time we'd become distant from that, lost touch with it, and let the other layers take over, letting them decide what we will become, eliminating what we essentially were until that original self is completely gone, and dies. And this goes on until we reach the age when we realize the world goes on as it does because we are unable to fight the external facts together and do not reach a period of ability to change the world but a time of realizing we cannot change it. And so we are really more like those people of Pompeii as the internal area of our soul dies and becomes hollow, and we are identified only by the shell that has taken shape around it, until something of spirit pours in and fills it up again to acquaint us with what the original likeness was supposed to be, which is generally stimulated in what we find during our last days. It was something like his art project that held life sacred even to the ashes and dust that flesh is heir to. We realize the awful truth of it all, which somehow revitalizes the ashes for the first time into conscious being, expanding us with all the layers of experience to explain to the dead souls a truth we were only just beginning to understand, all falling on deaf ears, turning us into outcasts, impotent prophets until a similar set of circumstances revitalizes their inner core like a living plaster freeing their spirit to move again within them, and then we have company.

At least this was the theory. Until then Dudot had only experienced a hardening of sorts, a deadening over time, nothing to test the theory yet, only he wouldn't know that until it happened, can't do it consciously anyway, have to wait for it to happen, when one knows it is happening, like waking up in the morning and not wanting to go back to sleep.

The Catch-Phrase Memoirs

One day Dudot sat down to write in his journal, and he found he didn't have a pen. But all these thoughts kept going around in his head. He tried to save them, keep track of them, and the ideas had an order. There were about five of them at the start, and he reduced them to catch phrases to remind himself what they were. Then he went over them every few minutes just to make sure he still had them. He also tried to see how much he would remember of each one, add water to expand them so to speak, to be sure that he remembered all the finer points as well, and these had numbers too. Dudot almost got angry when his active mind (while satisfied he had the whole thing memorized) would suddenly give him a new thought to write down, and the list got longer and increasingly difficult to remember. It was sapping an awful lot of his mental energy, so he put a moratorium on idea collecting, especially when it finally dawned on him how they were doing disappearing acts, as when number three in his memory was somehow impossible to remember one time through the list. So for fear of losing them, he tried to assign other things to them, like animals or objects to tie them together with pictures, and when he got home and actually got a pen to sit down and write, he was feverish in making sure the list was complete, but they still didn't come easily. He had some of the catch phrases, some of the objects and one missing completely, and he was angry and frustrated that these ideas should be lost. And then he sat and had dinner, watched some TV and went to bed. When he got an idea then, he was too tired to write it down, and put it into a catch phrase to remember the next morning.

The Long Beat of the Metronome

When he woke up, he couldn't think of it, and there had been a dream, a piece of it still in memory when he opened his eyes, but then it disappeared, and he didn't have a clue of something that had just been right in front of his eyes. He knew it was important to find a way, the time to write out all his ideas, so as not to forget the potential riches in each one of them, but he just put the sheet of paper in the journal for safekeeping with all the other strips of paper. At times he would get up in the middle of the night and jot down part of a dream. In the morning, he would try to no avail to remember it, but reading the note, it would all come back. The journal was a huge collection of catch phrases like that, things that would mean nothing to anyone. Even to Dudot, some were confusing, ambiguous, difficult to understand, lost forever. But others triggered a whole world of thoughts, and after looking them over and feeling them burst in his mind with recollection and understanding, he would close the book with satisfaction, promising himself he would work on it later, and then go on to something else with the fullness of someone who had just finished writing a great book of literature.

The Intruders

There were many intruders in Dudot's mind, people from his past who had crossed him who would cross his mind when he was happy just to bring him down. So many incidents and characters from his life bubbled in the stream of his mind that he couldn't help thinking of them from time to time. But they always seemed to walk out of the water by themselves when he was lost in his own thoughts, taking a quiet time out. When he was miserable they made him feel worse. If he felt a sense of contentment, they made him feel sad. He somehow linked them to his meditation moments and started fighting with them to purge them from his mind. He'd sit down and ring a bell for them to come, was conscious that they were always near, and for a time found himself remembering incidents in detail that he hated thinking about, but it wasn't just the thinking about them, it was the battling, trying to fend them off, defeat their insidious purpose when they were only scenes from the past, on an internal speaker he would shout *Get out of here* and fill his mind with another thought, even just repeat words over and over to shut them out and leave him alone. But they were always there the next time.

In contrast to their repeatedly harassing him every chance they could in his thoughts, these people were so totally cut out of his life that he never heard from them nor was ever likely to again. These were folks that Dudot had banished from his real life, refused to deal with because of certain transgressions. There were so many that the landscape of his social life was generally barren, and Dudot was so angry with their specters that had they accidentally appeared near him, they would certainly trigger the words that were fresh in his mind. He wouldn't pretend or behave in any way to suggest he was healed when he wasn't, so he was determined to avoid them at all costs. In fact, he made such promises to himself of how he would ignore people he was already ignoring, people who never called him who he couldn't get out of his mind as if he'd just had an unpleasant conversation with them. Remote as they were, they were the intruders, not one or two out of a crowd but generally every one he'd ever known. He was mad at the whole lot of them, and wherever Dudot went he always looked at everyone as a potential intruder, finding fault in bald heads and jackets, brief conversations, smells, anything random and unimportant, judging everyone as not being worth his trouble, though he somehow was forgiving at first with women and looked them over pretty carefully, wanting down deep to have them look back. But when they didn't, he determined them to be shallow and disingenuous, not intuitive like him, and figured they would get what they deserved and wind up in an unhappy marriage with someone less interesting than him. The scowl he had on his face most of the time was enough to keep everyone at a distance, but if you asked Dudot, he would have said he was always in a good mood and that it was their problem, not his.

Central Intelligence

Dudot dreamed that he had prepared a lengthy top-secret report covered with various connections. He needed to turn it in that morning. Then a neighbor boy pointed out an old woman getting out of her car near the CIA headquarters as the person he was looking for. She was the grandmother of the person he was to give his report to anyway, and she confirmed something like that, and so he gave it to her. Later he asked his boss who said he hadn't seen the report or the old woman. Dudot didn't press to know whether she was or was not a grandmother because he didn't want it to appear that the paper may have fallen into enemy hands. He remembered that he still had a version of it on his computer, but it was an early draft, and he had made many corrections since then. He didn't want to start the process over, so he began to look everywhere for the woman first. When he couldn't find her, he started a massive search for the paper itself.

He went down every corridor and into every office of the agency, no one seemed to mind that he was looking over the files on desks or drawers. He was treated with the respect of having complete clearance, but everything he found was unrelated. It all seemed unrelated to anything. The information everywhere was out of date, stale and uninteresting. Nobody was working on anything current or had an inkling of what his lost report was or where it might be. Then he walked into a meeting where a beautiful woman was describing it before a gathering of technicians. Even to Dudot as he listened to his research, it sounded like a waste of everyone's time, and he was embarrassed at both his lack of expertise and the fact that he would be assigned a project that seemed so unimportant. But he pressed on with his search even though the report had found its way into the system, and though he didn't find it, he continued to learn much about the various individuals in each office and how they stacked all their papers and manila folders, each with it own system. As he woke, Dudot realized that the entire agency was all one giant archive of dead dry goods, and the report that grandma had snatched was just part of it. He'd seen proof of that. And while he seemed connected to the most vital part of the organization, that of gathering fresh, sensitive information, critical to the operation not just of the agency but to the nation, he saw that in practice that he was someone who went from office to office, pouring over yesterday's news, more like a janitor than an intelligence officer, someone who had complete freedom to go through the garbage, and whose own contributions sounded stale, crumpled and dried out like they had just come out of the same recycling bin.

The Ride of Your Life

Dudot wasn't seeing life as a great journey but as being trapped in the doldrums, a waiting game, and he wasn't willing to pray for fair winds or any wind at all for that matter because the parallel broke down there. There was nothing analogous to wind that would ride him out of the rut. It was more complicated than that. Those aforementioned intruders stood a bit like gargoyles on his own mental fortifications, as if they had climbed his walls and posted themselves there, and were not looking out upon the landscape but into the castle at him. It was a great trap, the jaws wired shut, and he had more room to wander in the confines of his mind than in life, but his restrictions in life contributed to the darkness of the enclosure.

He seemed to think at one point that the solution was to cast all beliefs aside and work hard for several years to have the money to do what he wanted, but most people did that and never broke it off, never enjoyed their lives, and somehow learned to accept that state as life, working for their children, sacrificing themselves and finding a kind of peace in that rather than to realize they learned to live like this as part of a culture and were merely perpetuating a system. But he also knew that breaking away from it was extremely difficult, that it was financially and logistically difficult, not to mention the social pressures against it, and there was no way that people would all at once decide to do the same thing at the same time and change the world, so there would never be any real kind of unexpected revolution of people suddenly following their dreams.

On top of this, his own way of living was not something he would easily define or defend. He just did it his way, and let experiences knock him down a peg in the expectation that things would never change for him, but he also did things the way everyone else did them. He understood he was part of a larger group, that there were thousands of people like him, but there were also thousands of every other kind of group, including homeless people. It seemed no matter what he thought of doing, however original he thought it was, there were already lines formed to do it, people who had gone and done it ahead of him; so his motto was *Why Bother*, but it conflicted with what was also present in his heart. The baby boom was partially to blame. There were just so many people his age and only so many positions available in any given occupation. Still, he somehow had an innate sense that good things were meant to happen to him, which he knew would only occur by his doing his own work, which meant stepping off the beaten path in his spare time, if he ever found any spare time, but he still hadn't plotted out a course, and his defeatist mental attitude did not blend at all with this inner sense of purpose and destiny.

He was also aware that there were certain ways of thinking that would hang on the mind for years at a time, conditioning the soul like growing pains and during which time there were changes taking place that were as yet undelineated psychologically but still normal, so he didn't count his waging war within himself and against the world as anything but normal, though he didn't see any way out of it either. For his ship just seemed to float in the still waters of the world, raging around him, that he didn't accept and couldn't understand except that he couldn't make much of a difference, so the answer might lie deeper, somewhere perhaps in the doldrums themselves, in just sitting the way he was, and it would come to him in time, make sense not as a glitch in the ride but as some kind of mental high point with the slow development of a discovery emerging for accumulation of earth over time, that his soul was some kind of artifact he had yet to discover. But when he did, it would explain his whole inner culture in religious and social terms giving him the lucidity of an entire civilization, and he believed there was such a great order hidden within himself, something out of the combined experiences of his ancestors maybe, but what he couldn't really understand was why he was never in the mood for digging, just tired, bored, and depressed, and why he was always in the image of a boat on the water where there was no digging to be done, no diving suit and no one to pump air to him if he were to submerge. He felt like he was holding his breath waiting for something to come, and at the same time believed if he only let the breath go, there might be the wind he was waiting for to lift him out of his rut.

But he didn't want to just settle for anything except a lasting enlightenment. Too many things faded away, and if he needed an example of something that wouldn't, it was his current state, and so he had a model and fully expected it would transmit into lasting, revelation, but he didn't know how, only that it was unlikely to be a series of steps, or he would already know about it, though it might be about the presence of necessary elements including what he was living. It might only take a breath to lift him, but certainly only breathing was not living. The spirit needs more than mere life to live, but at times it swirls in eddies where even the sense of swirling is lost, where there is so much sitting still that even death seems preferable, to stop altogether because it is painful to know one has stopped completely, and one has to ride at times where to ride is to live, and to not ride is to die. But the tragic events that had happened to Dudot seemed like the biggest roller coaster had taken and thrown him for a loop, that he'd been dropped from the ride and hit bottom but was still falling.

On a lark, he went to the bank and cleared out his savings. "The ride of my life indeed!" he muttered to himself. "If I handle this right, it should be enough to pay for whatever there is left of it, and my life, whatever it is from here on out, will be the ride."

The Sense Creeping In

Dudot didn't like the way that making sense of the world was so difficult. It seemed to him that there were two camps, the one that said the world made perfect sense, which was broken into hundreds of factions, and the one that said it made no sense which also had factions but nowhere near as many. What Dudot found was that he only had his own wits to go by, and even there he found himself generally split between the two camps. On the one side, he could feel it make some kind of sense, but the missing elements and the fact that the reason for the world might never be made plain made him question whether the meaning man ascribed to it was just to fill the huge gap in his knowledge. But that was largely about groups, and Dudot thought most people assessed the world from a group standpoint and didn't work from a personal point of view because it is too difficult to communicate let alone universalize. Still, that is where Dudot felt it was necessary to start, almost from a Des Cartesian standpoint, to find whatever basis for believing something makes sense, "I think, therefore I am," was done by shutting everything else out. So Dudot focused only on himself and refused entry for any other ideas, except those that came from him, and he found he became a single entity, but a kind of jungle man, in a short time, sure of himself but able to deny everything else in the universe for all intents and purposes though all of these things seemed to follow him as kinds of strange spirits out of which one might make masks and hold religious ceremonies around a fire.

It started with strange dreams that he couldn't shake. Why he was concocting them he didn't know, but it was as if he were in a grass hut, and it was easy for these things, shadows in his mind, to make noises, rustle the grass, peek in windows, convey a sense that they were present, and initiate also a feeling, disturbance, discomfort, that made him want to tie it to the outside, that something was trying to creep in, speak to him, but it was only teasing, if an outside sense, a living presence, then something that wouldn't come clean, whose testimony was on his life to a degree. The dreams reminded him of issues that he had. But all he could say was that he had a capacity to drive toward order and understanding within himself against all that was amorphous. And in society where the personal is generally shut out, so has whatever is spiritual or ambiguous been exorcised and simplified so that people are comfortable there and not driven to find themselves through dreams. Thus the group over centuries has taken away all the bushes and shadows, razed the sphinxes with their riddles and swept the boogie man out from under the collective bed. First came the refusal to address the question of nightmares in the individual, and then came the inability due to unfamiliarity and disbelief. Now the world doesn't consider it as mentally healthy to explore the unconscious; rather, it treats a sense of them as a problem fitting in with the rest of those who have gone under the knife to have an unnecessary organ removed. Dudot saw that a certain area of intuition is treated as a psychological issue, the result of which is to operate and deprive a person of an essential nutrient, which is a kind of starvation over an amputation, but either analogy makes the same point.

Dudot felt he benefited from his metaphysical excursions even while they frightened him because he would see the façade that stands between man and the truth, the wall that is built around the cemetery and encourages the inborn drive to fight whenever war needs to be fought, to get it done, then add another stone to the wall in memory of the dead whether it has your name on it or not.

Dudot felt it was the whole world's lack of individual pursuit of getting to the root causes that made for the social nightmares, the failure of the façade, the provision of sense that didn't make sense. The patches that didn't seal, left people patched but not cured though among the patches some miracles and wonders might exist.

He remembered something someone told him that Martin Luther supposedly said, that truth was the most intolerable thing in the world. He thought about that. If by truth he meant ultimate reality, the fact that we all must die, then yes, that is an intolerable fact from which everyone buries his head in the sand. It's impossible to face the fact for too long, just as looking at the sun can cause blindness. But Dudot thought there were too many ways of avoiding the fact, that looking at it on occasion is a healthy consideration, but modern society is all about youth, and proffers a replacement reality, which diverts one's attention from one's own state and implants a vision of a kind of constant life in others, and the only remnants of reality in that state of mind are desire and sadness, not any real focus on the truth. But the world's answer to that is there is no point to it, no reason to dwell on negative thoughts of the eventual end of life because the belief is that this is all there is, that science has done all the thinking for us, and our job is to just enjoy life and to get through the night as best as possible, shaking off the bad dreams if they should come without asking too many questions, for that would only lead to trouble as there are no answers. Everyone has nightmares, and they don't mean anything. Dudot just liked going back into the jungle of his mind and exploring, but nobody really understood why he bothered or what good could come of it.

Dudot felt there were dreams the whole world was having, woods we all shared, and that we were all really huddled in a hut, trying to calm each other down to deal with reality, not convince one another that there was nothing outside rustling the grass or peeking in windows, but describe and understand what we are in order to evolve beyond being prone to suspicion and superstition, to grow into being strong without removing intuitive capacities according to a new social contract supplied by Madison Avenue and the pharmaceutical companies. When there is not at least a trust of what we are by nature, then sooner or later everyone signs off on theories of junk science, takes the pill that gets them to get through the night.

Dudot thought man is just like the animals except that with the higher level of consciousness, and awareness, something has been let loose in us, unleashing so much terror that the cute bunnies no longer entertain as it floods in and washes them away. But we can somehow manage it, push it off like the cover of a pool or skin of the pudding and let it bunch up on the side, not permeate us into tribes and drum beats without wondering why we behave as we do. The world for Dudot had become an incredible pressure cooker with all the bolts on the inside, that anything he touched was likely to explode from any direction, and yet there were so many who set themselves above such a fray, who pushed his buttons and brought him to the brink of explosion, but he was so small that there was nothing they could feel from it, and they were also immune to larger pressures it seemed, as long as they persisted to subscribe largely to what the world was promoting at the time, politically, in its own natural environment, which was the city, not the jungle anymore.

Dudot thought of death as a final relaxing, that living was just a continual tightening up over time, a constant collecting things to fill all the empty spaces. Such collecting was the game of life, and it didn't matter except to the individual collector what was important, the emphasis placed on random things without any special properties of their own except price and availability, and then in the relaxing end at death, a loss of the glue that kept things together and disposal of the items as the controlling influx is gone, and no particular sense by anyone left that anything important is being broken up and sold off because it wasn't anything that particularly interested them nor is there retention of the person who made it his business to acquire all of it. But in life there was draw and direction, a reason to get up in the morning, but once the soul is gone, the objects float randomly again because the whirlpool they were caught in has stopped spinning, and Dudot wondered the same thing about thoughts in general, that there was nothing all that interesting about mere thinking, just that like a kaleidoscope there were all kinds of ideas floating around, and somehow any mind would create a pattern, yield a symmetry, a collection to press on other minds, a mold to stamp a mental impression that was either favorable or not; or in pop-artistic fashion, to prepare designer feelings and cause the senses to flourish like grass in the spring, to hear birds that weren't there and then try to develop a school of thought about it.

Dudot thought that if by night he thought of something while falling asleep and the next morning couldn't remember what it was that the pattern was lost by whatever current had taken its place, washing it away, and all that he had left of it was a sense of loss that it was there, a desire to get it back, but nothing more important than that, and half the fight to retrieve it was about being perfect and whole, not human, forgetful, limited, and also the need to ascribe a certain wholeness to the project of thinking, that everything has it place, and the lost thoughts all together form a dark space that would have been largely light regardless of whatever else was in the picture, or, when all the lost thoughts were back in place, that we would still be only human with higher self-esteem.

But to Dudot they were links in a broken chain like a batch of donuts boiling in the grease where each had come loose one at a time, similar in shape as all thoughts are, but none more important or more edifying than any other, just broken away from one another, and not very important because this world doesn't pay like that for donuts, more for personality, presence, putting anything on a t-shirt to put bread on the table even if it's about murder, depicting Bundy and Gacy as kings in music videos, serving to fill pockets and coffers, not worrying about kids' minds, and in succeeding somehow prove that people have the mind and spirit of a rabbit, easy prey and pickings, mindless by nature and doing exactly what they always do, willing to mix it all up, all of history, and make no bones about any of it, no attempt to prioritize or discern the truth, do anything immoral, just make a beeline for making a new high-water mark, above which begins a new stench in the air, where poets singing man's praises make no sense and have no place anymore.

The poets meanwhile project their own spirit into the heart of every person, but Dudot saw the modern world as one giant rabbit and all the truth as just a hair or a flea unable to influence where the rabbit hops or munches, for that is all it does though the great wind around the rabbit rustles its fur, the rabbit looks up and heads for the bushes to hide where there is nothing from which to hide, but it is in the rabbit's nature to know evil's out, a pertinent fact in its heart, and to walk into every trap it sets for itself as it were.

A Rare Occasion of Happiness

Dudot sat one morning and felt all kinds of thoughts crossing his mind, all of them not so much fleeting as hard to keep in focus since newer ones were quickly knocking them out of having much of a moment in mind. So it was a breezy day of thinking. Winds were gusting. So much was going through his mind, such unexpected things. It was a rare event of mind, something he didn't know quite what to do with or control, but when it was gone, it was also something he missed, even wished to experience again. But Dudot kept thinking at the time that he wished it would all settle down because he could not seem to keep track of any of it.

One unpleasant thought was of days not going by but death coming closer, born when one is, but there is a distant spot at the exact distance of steps as days one lives, and if you listen closely you can hear, even feel the footsteps like the panic of something coming up behind, of being run down, and this sense of doom before him and behind him made Dudot feel a kind of heaviness in his chest.

Another unpleasant thought was of the way that God appeared to the ancients so that robes and rock and thousands of years of confusion and continued struggle are thrown into the balance yet still upending modern efforts to control and abate it, as if the robes and the rocks still have greater force in barren stillness, more authority in being totally foreign than all that is comfortable, loud and familiar, whether it be bells, domes, pipe organs or banners. He was tired of God being depicted in any sense as a human creation, and it was more that some religions are made more by what man thinks God is than what can be felt as spiritual force in words spoken by God, and as such, these writings appear dated, and the words are no longer useful except to keep people in the dark ages.

Another thought that struck him was how such thoughts were just passing so easily through his mind. He thought of novels that purported to use what is called "stream of consciousness," art that so many critics and classrooms were made to stand at attention to, where in the end it was just a stream of words from the mind of the writer as he sees the character, not consciousness, not Dudot's anyway; and consciousness itself, he found, was not at all a stream, for in it there are wafting veils, curtains blowing gently in an open window, and sudden changes in altitude causing a sense of imbalance as a plane settling in the sky. And then there is the quality of space, of three dimensions, that cannot be captured in prose, and Dudot thought the lavish and grandiose praise for abstruse approximations was laughable, as if the result of artistic exploration had achieved its own consciousness by the use of run-on sentences, lack of punctuation and italics. From all his reading, Dudot felt the need to not willingly suspend his disbelief when it came to literary criticism. He chose to make up his own mind on what constituted a look at the mind, and he was content to look into his own mind rather than a book to experience the thrill of knowing how a mind operates, how one day there isn't a cloud in the sky, and the same evening there is lightning and thunder, and on another day, like this one, even as thoughts might seem to be either pouring in or pouring out, they were just happening, and in such a way as to have a life of their own, and unlike the state of his thoughts on a slow day when he usually felt depressed, the nature of these thoughts bubbling out of nowhere made him feel joyful and alive.

As he watched his mind, he could not get an exact grasp of it, and there was no single metaphor, no capturing it on paper, for it was rounder and more personally grand, so much so that he had a sense of hopelessness of it all being soon lost somewhere during the day, or that sleep that night would undo the connection, and that the sadness he knew all too well was just around the corner, hiding somewhere in the back of his mind waiting to return or be scattered into globules like mercury needing only the gravity of a morning funk to repool. Recent events in his life had been heavy on his soul, and he was reacting to thoughts that were his own but without a usual sense of depression, and he was grateful that the mind on its own can choose its own form for itself and remind one that there are surprises and even a kind of balance to moods in the long run. Even if he could not isolate, preserve or share it, enjoying the strange elated stream of his consciousness was something he wanted to continue, to dwell on what it afforded him of fire, of a living sense like poetry that cannot be written or extruded into words to evoke a sense of it, for the quality he was experiencing was not particularly worthy of poetry. It was not an especially significant emotion. The quality was in his breathing too, in being alive, and it was not so fleeting a part of his consciousness that morning such that every time he had it for a second, a second later it was gone. It was real and long-lasting. Some called it an "unbearable lightness of being," but that was a poor approximation. It was more something related to being somewhat bored despite being surrounded by the ultimate reality, and whether created by miracles or an accident explainable by science, boredom was not the right emotion because surely one should be amazed, except that after 40 years, anything gets old. A moment later he realized it was perhaps worthy of poetry, of being awash in midlife's amniotic fluid, perhaps not on the way of being reborn, but in all respects, it was about being alive.

He was also thinking of how some thoughts acted as a gentle guiding hand for the emotional aircraft of thought buffeted about, helping to stabilize the mind and generate for itself an abounding resonance, resulting in an intuitive and natural affirmation of life. Some poetry and some movies did this for him on occasion, made him believe he was part of the human race and imbued him with a sense of purpose, but the effects of these tended to wear off quite quickly. There were also certain memories, as simple as the wind blowing in the window when he was driving. Something from long before might suddenly clear in his mind like it was just happening, and all the spirits of those in the remembrance, whether they were dead or alive, were all at once intact and intensified along with all that was known about them since the remembered experience itself.

Another thought that occurred to him was about how he did all he could to cultivate a greater possibility that his mind would be allowed the proper setting to experience itself, but he had no real control over it or anything else. He could not in any way replicate the occasional good night of sleep by simply going to bed at a specific time. Some days just had better symmetry, like a snowflake one would try to preserve, treat with extra care in a kaleidoscope so as not to shake it. And he had even less control over what was outside him. As one who couldn't seem to affect any changes or improvements, he caught himself sometimes admiring the lives of others caught in extremes, lives that could not extract themselves from circumstances beyond their control, lives lived to the hilt, lives of people with little time to factor in the meaning of dreams. At times this seemed to Dudot to be the more mature pattern, an example of what his life should be, one where dreams were not examined for truth, crumbs of enlightenment along the way to help one find his life. Some never learned to read them and waved them away like cobwebs in the morning. Wasn't that more mature?

Dudot was slipping a little into negative thinking and surveying his life again for the moment. He was convinced he had made some serious errors in judging what choices to make. He had rendered himself more useless than he imagined he would, found himself generally unwilling to move his body or mind when there might be alternatives that would present themselves, all due to a general desire not to be thwarted or hindered from thinking though in general he did not succeed very well in accomplishing what he hoped. He stagnated generally and was unambitious for the most part. It was as if he loved opera but was a part of the play, the guy lying around on stage, contributing nothing but enjoying it immensely. Then he thought of it the other way around, that he actually hated opera, but he was a part of the play anyway, but a good thing it was not 1915 anymore, and he wasn't in Europe for the war, not to say that there wouldn't be a worse war before the fat lady sang for him.

Dudot felt there were overall sensations that would be captured, that it was his duty to isolate them by living them over and over, fill his mind with ideas, kidnap experience if he had to, not holding it for ransom but keeping it for himself; that out of holding it, something must come, even if only from familiarity, that he would become the expert of his own circumstances and inner life and find in it also some universal aspect, an overall sensation others would apply to themselves as what they were looking for in a book or movie, anywhere they moved at others' commands, that he would in a way be living for them, doing the research for them, and through him they would find more meaning from the small visitations they had with the same phenomena, that they got in and out of a car to avoid the storm, windows closed all the time, while he went through it and got drenched and knew what it felt like for them. But he didn't actually go out in the storms, he only played the ones he got stuck in over and over in memory, becoming expert and a Christ figure in past moments, not in real time. In fact, time was his enemy, passing around him with ever increasing demands like some kind of landlord about to make an eviction if he didn't come up with the right cash in acquiescence or attitude. Christ was watching him, too, after all.

Dudot was on trial due to a sense the world was out to get him, that it didn't like his kind or point of view, that it suspected him and would have its judgment day and hang him out to dry, so it wasn't just time, it was everyone. They were all geared to live and respect dead individuals, romanticize their hurt in different ages and languages, cultures and dress, but did not think themselves partners to some current crime against Mozart, open minded as they were but like people in a pool waving for everyone to get in with them and mostly keeping track of who wouldn't swim, marking them like biologists to study their movements and their behavior. But making certain creatures only feel marked hurts them too, in some cases marks them for death as certain birds won't return to their nests if they sense it's been touched, and man is just such a creature who in self-consciousness loses an element of being able to totally let go and dance all the years of study into applause at the simplicity and effortlessness of the thing. It is not so easy to be "one's self."

Dudot was aiming to be master of himself and live the light as he saw it, but the forest canopy of seed sown with him had long since grown past him and was shutting out the light, taking all the seats in the theatre where standing room below isn't seen as getting a chance for a drink nor is meant to because all the light is up above the treetops, for you if you can climb up, but only if you can let go.

And Dudot was to blame for letting his consciousness and the study of it roll around like a whirlpool with no outlet, like a roll of toilet paper being turned the wrong direction won't give up a flap for you to pull, and so he closed himself off, became his own counsel, using his own will, his point of view, and limits of the world to justify his stern silence even though he felt he had everything to give, yet resented the world for not respecting him, and so his consciousness was a pot on the stove, on the wrong burner, not involved as the burner was off, but the fire was close enough to feel the warmth from the pots boiling on the other burners. He knew what steam was like, and he was part of the picture, part of the kitchen, but he was not sure exactly what he was, whether he was an ingredient, something left over, an abandoned meal or something to be mixed in another time. He huddled close to the other pots yet felt he was all alone. He was not totally cold but was colder than most, mostly medium, but well done and anything but rare. He knew he would not last forever and was not doing much to keep warm, unaware of his own purposes, but in a molecular war there was movement and evaporation, and lots of stuff at the bottom that he didn't want stirred up as he explored and mapped it out. It was his right to know himself and sneer at all the convenient ways of thinking because he was a living testimony, an example of it, whatever it was, of not going bad even if he was rotten because as long as he kept moving, the flies couldn't sting and lay eggs in him. No poster serves to explain anything to the world, and much of the message of history was made to fall on deaf ears for lack of anything better to say. Dudot wanted to do the world one better but needed something to douse, not light a fire under him, and if messages and maggots did not get through, what could he really hope to say or do to change anything? No, he was in a kind of flow, as this day of thinking reminded him, which would still be a flow even when the swirling eddies and dams were there to catch him and lock him again in stagnant backwaters the next day. He was happy even with the unpleasant thought of that.

Selfty Struction

So much of Dudot's daydream time lapsed into a kind of passage through time as if stunned, not thinking, not even passing but more like being frozen, and it was more a state of mind than anything else, and ground he couldn't plant on. It wasn't fertile soil. He couldn't turn it over and find anything beneath the surface, nor force himself to find things in his mind worth his attention. It was like the day after a blustery day where everything has settled but there is nothing interesting in what is blowing around, only in when it was actually moving a day earlier, memories and senses still lifted and swirling. Perhaps Dudot wasn't so much lazy as expectant, needing something, anything, to occupy his mind. But he'd work himself quietly into a corner, drained of thought because he didn't provide himself with the necessary input to inspire reactions and thinking. He chose rather to drain himself and wonder where the profound sense of emptiness came from, why he could feel so bland about everything, disinterested in the risks and dangers of the world and not contributing a daily dose of effort to fortify the foundation against the eventualities and inevitable consequences of time, fortune and living. He could waste whole blocks of time waiting for a blockage to remove itself without so much as getting up to take a walk or turning on a radio. He went through motions his body commanded, getting up to use the bathroom, eat and finally to sleep and hope that the next day had something more for him though he knew it was his fault it was empty, and in the emptiness was fear and himself, and he feared the emptiness because he saw it was essentially the way he was, not at his best, but in some way parallel to it, and that scared him. Whatever life and experience had taken away, whatever drinking or drugs had done to him, this view was a clear image, and it was a useless, empty, not even brooding soul, not reacting to anything, as if over all the cities in the world one would choose the most sterile place to sit and do nothing, having no friends or communications, and call that life. He knew somehow it was like the stomach where it is empty and eventually it starts feeding on itself, taking body tissue from the only place that can process it and processing that even though it might kill all other processing out of its need to get through that moment of starvation. He thought that the mind also had its own analogous acid and ways of eating away the place where thinking is possible so as to possibly prevent further thinking, all for taking a given mood so far that it was capable of doing damage. That was food for thought.

Dudot remembered when he was a boy how much he hated mowing the lawn under the heat of the midday sun though he had no way out of it. His father would just make him do it, not let him put it off until evening when the sun went down and play baseball all afternoon under the same hot sun instead. He remembered his terrible anger at the crickets because they kept him awake at night right outside the window in the bushes, and when he mowed along the fence, he would uncover their nests and stop to kick and kill them however far from the window they were. He remembered his father once brought the gasoline can to the back yard and found Dudot in a frenzy, stomping on the crickets, and his father told him it was a case of "Selfty Struction," that Dudot had set himself like a golf ball on a tee and driven himself into this field where he was just a part of nature, and was growing up, was under construction, and eventually would experience destruction, dissolve and rejoin the earth, and he had a choice of what he wanted to experience off the tee, whether it was constructive or destructive, so for the purposes of instruction his father just referred to it as "Struction." Dudot thought about that, about having control over returning to the dust, of rejoining the soil, and he finished mowing the lawn without killing any more crickets, and that night he listened to them instead of hating them, and he challenged them to keep him awake, and thought of their songs as a funeral song for their dead, and he felt sorry for them and fell asleep.

Dudot knew that having so much anger could be self destructive and was present even when it seemed it was neutralized, that doing nothing and not thinking could just as easily be another manifestation of anger, that denying it was not to be rid of it, nor did it make it less effective, that it was not like shutting off the electricity, and as all systems were still running, that there would be a bill at the end of the month, a big one with all the anger he was hiding inside. But if it wasn't so much self-destructive behavior, but more "Selfty-Structive" in the way his father had explained it, then he could actually see it as contributing to a certain kind of mental health, or natural state of mind, not necessarily an unhealthy one, but the only one through which he would force himself to the next level of seeing things no one else would, that he was in control of his flight and the effect of stress on his system, that there was a kind of release along the way since he was conscious of what he was experiencing, that his life was again about dealing with issues as he had when he fought the crickets, and he could just as easily conquer them in the same way and reduce the tension by choosing not to dissolve into them, not enter their nests and fight visions and nightmares of what had driven him to the brink of Ol' Man River, and made him give up. So he gathered himself up instead, and mowed the images, not out of a hatred or in keeping with being in a self-perturbing state. Instead he just saw it as cutting back the growth of these vines that had overtaken him, providing safe haven for crickets of all kinds to gather outside his window when he closed his eyes and keep him awake, tossing and turning all night. Another man would have waited for the mind to think of something even though it meant playing chicken, running up against one's fears until the mind couldn't stand it any longer, as though it really were an adversary, something outside him against which he should do battle rather than something that comes from within, which he knew it was, and that's what made him different off the tee. He could see it that way thanks to his father and help himself out of this kind of depression.

So he took the road of "construction," realizing that his mind was not his mind when it was sitting still and empty but on loan to his inner adversaries, anything that taunted him, dared him to blink, to wonder why he was being treated that way (by himself) with such scorn. He laughed that only a day earlier it seemed his birthday with all the thoughts showering on him, gifts out of nowhere. And not long before that he was only by chance sidetracked from throwing himself into the stream of unconsciousness.

   He could not define these states as a process, one to another, or assign them to ingestion of nutrients, as a sense of well-being after a good spaghetti or a good night's sleep or the day after a migraine headache, which had its own kind of poetic logic, the muscle of the brain smoking intelligence after the juices have been seared in. He could say there was no logical pattern to it, only that he needed some kind of consistency in the ups and downs, even the plateaus, and he had learned it would all come and go, that all he could do was ride the waves whether the water was cold or hot or the sky cloudy or not. But though the crash of a plane is utterly unpredictable once the pieces start to fly, experts can usually discern the reasons why the plane crashed, so Dudot knew it was faulty logic to study only his crash and not why it happened, but looking back he couldn't see the controls, only the fireball, the heat. He didn't want to look back. He wasn't ready to interview himself. He didn't have any plans to go back to the river that he was aware of, and he thought of these days as a crash site in another sense, of rest and recovery. He was in shock and as a result felt dull most of the time and didn't fight it, and he removed himself from himself not as best as he could, but out of necessity, and placed all the issues on a sense of himself as another self, and he looked at his mind as a motor in itself, capable of internal combustion and processing of its own generation, such that he was an observer more than a passenger and let his mind go off and leave him in the dust, where what was left watched himself leave himself and stood there looking out into the distance, still a part of it as if in radio contact, able to listen in but not contribute, watching himself being left in the dust, and watching himself watching himself where his mind had just left him, knowing and not knowing what he was thinking.

Selfty Struction

Sometimes it all seemed just like a daylight dream, and at the same time, most nights he didn't dream, and yet there seemed to be a full night of programming for how we woke up, but he couldn't remember anything. The days varied. His mind was either active or it wasn't, but he was always pushing anyway, demanding of "it" to stay busy, asking "it" where it was, telling "it" to come out wherever it was and be for him the best thing for him, which in previous states may have been on the heels of a terrible headache after drinking too much. It didn't matter. He knew his mind was there but wouldn't come. But in all the externality of demanding what was essentially him as if it were another thing, he was creating of himself a general attitude that was totally adversarial within himself, acting as if everything about him were some other entity under its own power, so he only had this voice of authority and the anger to explode off the tee to test his conditions, ultimatums, sentiments of having been violated and from there plot constructive course corrections, though all he got was silence because there was no one else there, which gradually increased the tension in this attitude to an attack within himself on himself though he understood that is was the mind feeding on itself, choosing destruction, and he was the lion's mouth chewing on his thoughts, his own paw, the result of which could be weeks of limping around unable to react at all to the real prey, real situations, real people, all of which would come his way as the world swirled around him, offering a chance to give his mind something else on which to feed, which would work if there hadn't been the crash that would have proved fatal if he hadn't been accidentally diverted from the river. And what if his father hadn't told him about "Sefty Struction?"

So he sat licking his wounds, exposed in every way yet insulated somehow. It was all part of a process though he could not define it as such, evolving too slowly to detect any change or results, and he didn't recognize any logic or end to the madness, nothing as a step in his recovery. It was all a dead end. He was going around in circles, but something kept and was keeping him from going over the deep end, and if it wasn't the mind, what was it? Maybe it was the crickets at night. Their chirping helped put him to sleep.

Genetic Lynx

Dudot's mother was detached, probably at birth, and in healing grew an attachment like a tree regrows its branch. With a stub instead of the natural overhang on which other life can thrive, she healed over and grew inward through the dark years of the depression, her childhood, and by the time she was married with children, she already felt she'd had to give up everything for others and never had anything for herself. But it was the severed limb talking as if there were still feeling in what had been cut off, but imagined feeling projected for what might have been, bitter that it was lost and planning its retrieval like a search for the Holy Grail, not sure exactly what it looks like but pretty sure it will be obvious when it's finally found, so she set off within herself keeping track of every little thing her husband did wrong and resenting time with the children, not raising them lovingly like a mother but begrudgingly, constantly betraying them and her husband for not supporting her by which she got the green lights to proceed outwardly to do as she pleased and carte blanche to continue proceedings against them, blaming them, as it were, for all that happened to her before she knew any of them more for preventing her, innocently or not, from achieving goals that only started becoming clear to her after she made lifetime choices that she grew more and more willing to put aside regardless of the cost or how it hurt those who loved her; and there was the rub, for in her mind it was all about not being loved, that inward sense trapping her feelings, limiting them to herself so there was no real extension to others, not even her children, and so she was crippled, and continued to be so, and with Dudot this was passed on, and his wounds too were shaped by her and healed over as hers were, in the same kind of residually painful form. But as alike as they were, bound by the same experience, each blamed the other, she the children, he the mother, and as much as both vented their anger on one another, each was insecure in giving feelings away to others, having low self esteem. He did not trust women generally, and he wasn't sure himself if it was a similarity due to experience or something generic she'd passed on, but either way he hated her for it. As much as he did not trust them, he pursued them, and in the same way, she did not trust men, but had relations with many.

His father was so preoccupied with his work that he had no time to spend with his son, and though he was generally kind, gave nothing of any dimension within which Dudot could ever remember feeling secure. But he remembered when he did, sometimes his parents would go away for a week and his grandparents would visit to watch over the children. The smell of cooking would fill the house and a warmth like a cloud he would pass through, and he could do no wrong, the wall was deep with them, and when they were there, he knew what it felt like to be loved and didn't care when his parents would come back. It also gave him a sense of what it had been like for his father growing up, and it explained why his father didn't pay close attention to his family, for he was raised with all the focus on him, made into a self-sustaining, independent and responsible worker, keenly perceptive of every nuance of the business world, which took him to the executive level, and yet somehow the parental spoiling made him oblivious to the needs and feelings of a son who needed his father.

All of this filled Dudot's head one morning. He caught himself repeatedly with clenched fists, which he would relax only to find them tightened up again. His genetic links descended into the past too many generations to count, and yet he could count only several, back to his great grandparents. Why was there no greater effort to collect the information going forward? Why did nobody have more insight to offer him on his ancestry other than that his grandparents came over on a boat as children? He wondered how it all gets so easily lost. But why was he looking to know the names of people a few hundred years further back? He had plenty with just his immediate family, all he could handle in fact. It had been like being stalked by a wild cat in the jungle, this dealing with his father and mother. Yes, it was a lynx, something between a pet and a wild animal, something supposedly domesticated by breeding but having the natural tendency to dominate, even to lash out unexpectedly. Dudot wondered why thousands of years of history had not produced a calmer society. Instead, all he saw was a series of dots made up of genetic information all separated but connected like a constellation into the form of a wild cat that is your hearth, your refuge, your only hope. Dudot's mother often warned him that he'd be thrown out of the house at eighteen, kicked out of the nest to fly on his own whether he liked it or not because that's what had happened to her, and so this was a family tradition, he supposed, one he wanted to end right there though it would take years before he would have any opportunity to shelter his young. He would look out his bedroom window into the night and imagine the day when he had a family and how he would never dare to threaten casting one of his own out, and he would listen to songs on his transistor radio under the pillow in order to go to sleep.

Then one day his mother's sister died and she swept Dudot out of his bed into her arms out of a dream and put him into the car for the long drive to her parents' home. When he woke up, they were on the highway on the plains, and he was told nothing about the reason for the trip. There were two funerals that passed going the other way, headlights on in broad daylight, and his mother warned him not to say a word about these sightings to his grandmother. Dudot asked what they were and was told they were funerals, but he didn't understand, and then they told him about death. It was the first moment he realized that his own time was limited, that he was going to die. His father said, "You'll live a long time, don't worry," but the words were hollow in the new reality, which was devastating, compounded by the eventual realization that while he was not considered fit to understand the passing of an aunt, he was made to realize his own mortality. In that moment he evolved from a free bird into a Dodo kicked from the nest before a hungry wildcat.

Preparing for Voyage

Dudot thought his plain conscious mind by itself was a dreary platform with lots of assorted objects on it, and the more he thought about what went through it, the more things were removed from the platform, leaving him with little but a dreary mood that alone he was so very small and helpless. He tried playing piano and recorded an original composition, and when he played it back some time later, it didn't do for him what good music does, and he wondered what has to be infused into the music for it to have that amazing quality of looking into everyone and touching them in some way. If at bottom he was nothing but a dreary singularity, it was likely that this was true of everyone, so what must he put on the platform of his thoughts to make both him and everyone else excited? What was the missing element? Was it something he must do, or were the necessary objects all hard-coded, unremovable, fixed pieces of furniture that made him who he was? Perhaps they were mechanical, best used in movement and invisible in action like humming bird wings and concealed when not in use. And he wondered what essential aspects must be added to his dreary platform that would enable him to be slightly higher than the dreary low. How could he rise above his current state in understanding or spiritual grasp, and how would he beckon that out of wherever it was hiding and make it a part of his daily life and enrich himself? Were spiritual types or enthusiastic people just beaming with energy to compensate for what was actually an essential dreariness, determined to pass the time in a positive state of mind despite the overwhelming presence of the negatives just to fight it? Why had he given in then and acquired the banal sense of his normality. Even about the mean, it was his own consciousness, and who devises the mean, and who can state what spiritual states are valid, or what ideas flush out the cobwebs from the mind conscious and sick of its own limitations?

Dudot could remember all the times he had been happy, only to have someone ask him why and make him conscious of it. That was like a slow leak in a beach ball where he never quite went flat, but the play was taken out of him, and he resented people for questioning what they perceived in him as if it were an awkward display when to him it was joy. Why were they not happy that he was elated instead of giving him grief? When Dudot thought of hitting bottom, he always figured it was a very painful low that frightens one into action away from the pain, up and out at any cost, but to him it was all numb and empty and he wanted something to fill him but it had to be real, not anything artificial and temporary. He wanted it to be something on which he would depend, to keep him from going over the deep end.

Dudot wondered why he had started thinking about spiritual things when he was the least alive. Perhaps his own spirit was so low he needed an infusion of that, something that had to come from within, but he was all tapped out on self-starting. For what purpose though? Only to have it, to counteract a natural state of depression that comes from keen awareness, so it would essentially allow him to forget, to not be so aware, where happiness is more desirable but still a lie. Joy was artificial, wasn't it, something cast and lost in the air, washed on people who were immune if they didn't know and appreciate him? Why bother at all? You can't dance in front of strangers without being thought of as weird. What he wanted was a total infusion of something real that would not have to come from him but be there always in him, never to drain out, ever to afford him strength, but he witnessed how so many weak people seemed to need to try to find that outside themselves, where could he look outside himself, what answers would he get if he called? He didn't know what to say, and didn't have the energy to shout but if it mastered his need it would have to be a scream, a very dull scream.

There were incidents that Dudot remembered from certain times in his life, and especially the older ones from his boyhood days had congealed into a core group, a few from each year, routine examples of a link to a time but no whole recollection. He wondered how these had come to be the ones he recalled out of thousands of days and felt it was largely due to repeated accessing, they came to be remembered because he remembered them more than the others,

But he also knew that the years before his recollection had been more fluid, that the times recalled were markers, not mere incidents, and every year as he pushed through life, less aware of the days passing by him, not seeming to gather anything new, the old memories seemed too to be falling away too. He couldn't distinguish whether something had taken place three or four years earlier, and was beginning to have trouble remembering the old days. He would spot check his mind and gloss over related blocks of time, reassured the full text was present by the recollection of a title, but he was actually trimming them down because he wasn't examining them closely enough, only reaffirming a few highlights and assuring their permanence but enlarging them to block access to many others. Second grade became just the face of a teacher and a few incidents. After a few years of this, that was all it was. And he wondered by the end of his life what few memories would be the ones he would recall of all that he had in his life, whether there was something significant about those other than they were just standing in the front row of his mind, having raised their hands when he called out, stepping forward for promotion into significant types when in fact they were no less ordinary than thousands he could no longer recall.

Dudot had worked himself into a corner and he knew it, thought he'd be his own coroner for how dead his mind was becoming, as if thinking in itself is not something that happens, anymore than growth is possible alone without light, moisture and nutrients, that in the physical world all chemicals are used and combined, nothing is lost, so if the brain needs a complex vitamin, it will find it if it's out there and make it if it has to. But in the mental world there is no Periodic Table of the Elements, no listing of what's out there, not even considering what is vital to the spirit, and that seems to be the bone of contention in all of humanity, of what is necessary for a full spirit, and in what order it should come or be administered. And Dudot only had a sense from his own experience that deliberately denying the mind a dose of everything shows just how thirsty an organ it is and how it too sends signals to the body like the stomach and the lungs that its essentials are needed and needed immediately, a kind of choking or hunger in the mind from the low seat of depression. In the lungs the face turns red, in the stomach you can begin to see the ribs, and in the spirit there are signals too on the face, in the actions and the attitude, that something is missing, that it must be gotten now, but there are no supply stores for the immediate injection with a cost per dose, no easy way to evaluate the current condition to make an easy determination of exactly what's needed, broken down into spirit groups so the plan to repair regimen is quickly felt, there's no fun that can be injected or distraction that can be forced down one's throat or love that can be poured on to soothe, no answers to deliver one from depression for lack of them, or if they are there, they do not have the immediate impact like a cleared obstruction in the throat letting the air through or water through a needle in the arm or spoonful of bland food to starvation, the spirit has its needs but the needs do not have an outward counterpart that can be administered. It becomes an inward matter, and while attempts are made to *Ouji* it in seance or control it remotely, there is no hands-on treatment guaranteed to do the trick, no panacea when one hits bottom or is on the way down, for the mind sees and hears it all, knows it all is designed to do just that, and while the stomach and the lungs are just muscles and react positively to the infusion of the right substance, the mind has a mind of its own and sets up barriers against first aid, refusing any and all entreaties, locking everything out, holding just to its rightful place next to the wall where it's handcuffed in the dungeon, having tried every way out while it was locking itself in. It doesn't need any help.

And Dudot seemed to see every argument against his situation as a mere prop in an already, blown-up mine to seal others from getting in, not lead anyone out. Most of the arguments for a healthy mind had gone down in the explosion, so how could they serve him

Preparing for Voyage

now to put out the fire when they served as fuel for it in the first place? Dudot had been all propped up from the beginning, through school, work, marriage. All of the correct all-American values had been properly measured out and instituted, dropped into place, tested and retested, then sealed and given the seal of approval, and his approval rating had always run high. He had always been liked by many, so many though that there had always been some who didn't like him, and he wondered about that, and as clean as he was he lived in a time where there were enough counter-culture alternatives to test that he dipped into those as well and equivocated, began to question what was the right structure, more in terms of the whole world as a batch, not thinking of himself personally, but he considered all that just a fine retooling of the die, determining his own beliefs for a lifetime and stand for something once and for all.

But it took a really big blow to demolish an entire system and leave so much wreckage that he didn't even want anyone paring over it to stupidly suggest where he ought to start to try to begin to fix it. In the aftermath of the explosion he branded himself with his new name, *Dudot*, as if it had the significance of a baptism or first communion, and he shut out everything else to head off in a new direction, but instead he only started drifting like dust around his mind and settled into the wreckage with an absolute letting go of all that he once had counted important, the force within himself, stopped working. It was the day Dudot stood still, when all spiritual mechanization was stopped, and the starvation and breath holding of his heart began. But now he realized he'd worked himself into a corner. There were headaches, terrible ones, and a whiteness coming over him, a pale, sparkling aura he couldn't explain, and an almost lifelessness behind the eyes. But something left within him asked the simple question whether he wanted to die, and he said no, and it replied, *Well then clean up this mess*.

But even then he only did what he needed to, subsisting not improving, maintaining the level above bottom like laying on a raft so that his arm could dangle in the stagnant waters and touch the bottom, stirring up the muck. The idea of cleaning up the mess sounded to him, even if it came from inside him, as a hypothetical imperative, his choice, not categorical, and if he were ignoring Kantian ethics now, that was his choice, and he saw it as ironic that it was outside the scope of anyone's knowledge, that there are no things in themselves except the mind and all is choice, except that it was imperative to choose morality, and he didn't want completely not to choose, to completely believe himself to be closed off from everything, for that seemed to be a choice for death, for a living death in a way, but all else, even most of that which came from within, mirrored and paralleled all that he'd ever learned, bore a semblance with man-made malarkey, which is what he called it, and he couldn't put his finger on much that hadn't been made by man, and that was what he was waiting for, something from outside, and it wasn't acceptable if only for him and something that he would make out to be from outside, for that too would be man-made in interpretation. It would have to be seen and known by others as truly other-worldly, born of spirit outside of man but made to communicate to man that there was something more to life than an ultimate acceptance of all faith being a dead end, something more than making the best of being painted into a corner where we must affirm the dead end and blot out the spirit wherever necessary. It would have to really be something to move us beyond a stultifying consciousness of the total ridiculousness and impotence of the whole condition of life and make us believe it's some kind of miracle.

But he didn't ever realize he might really be waiting for something to come from outside, or that he'd worked himself into a corner, but he did believe if he stopped everything he could and sat in the corner long enough, he might at least see what was real, and he looked in the face of death and didn't like the looks of it, and starring at life didn't like having to dress up and know all the songs, equip himself in trivia as the era expected. No, he'd rather be free even if he was in chains of his own making. They were his links and walls, a prison of final discovery if prison was at the bottom of removing all the facades of freedom. He was willing to wait it out as a kind of cold war against God, if He were there. He couldn't force him out because God would be aware of all tactics too, and not respond any more than he would to the entreaties of the world to come out of the collapse and do calisthenics again and stop when the whistle was blown. The world believed in God but not in Dudot, at least not in how he was acting, because he was one of them, and it made them uncomfortable to see anyone act that way because it forced them to consider what it meant to not be well-balanced. It threw them out of kilter. But the God they believed in appeared generally unresponsive both to the times and to the individual, which was humorous because there had been no appearance reported in quite some time. It was not an era of miracles, and Dudot thought if God could be quiet to the whole world, then so could he, and if God wanted someone with whom He could engage in a dialogue, maybe he'd pick Dudot as a kindred spirit.

It was more a joke than a plan or a prayer. He was stirring up muck on the raft, his hands dangling in the water, his face contorting in the gentle waves. The bright sun in the sky was more like a light fixed to the roof of the mine where he was buried. But he was not calling for help. It didn't take long for everyone to abandon the mine while he was still in it, and now it was taking on a different shape, of a sheet of logs taking on water, not a hole in the ground doomed to be shattered at the ignition of seeping gas, but a boyhood dream, a raft on a lake. Dudot had hit bottom, but he still chose life, which filled the bottom up, took what was mined out into nothingness and made his quarry a pond, on which he placed boards strung together into a raft so that the one light in the mine became the sun. At least he wasn't stuck in a corner anymore, nor buried underground as it were, and it was a slight breeze blowing him around, not just the empty disconnections of one thought going into the next, and he could tell from the reflection of his face contorting in the ripples of water that there was something to relaxation and to dreaming which could turn coal into water, which was growing fresher to his taste every minute, and for the first time in months he actually could say he felt what is known as pleasure, and from this he knew he wasn't on the bottom anymore even if his hand was there in the muck, stirring it around. Though he didn't know how it happened, he was somehow above the bottom, even if not yet back in the world.

On the Brink

Dudot floated on this raft for a long time examining the bottom for both its growth and debris. The weeds seemed to climb up, floating in a brownish air, and occasionally he'd spot something unusual, half-buried, but accepted by the environment. The water was not deep, but it had all the same qualities of deeper waters where the bottom is still bottom and whatever grows only grows so high. He enjoyed looking at the rocks hoping to see some kind of crayfish or other things he'd caught when he was a boy. He spent so much time near water then, in creeks and rivers, turning over rocks for whatever he could catch, when it was snakes and frogs and crayfish hunting all through summer, and he would spend the whole day there laying on a raft floating no where, in circles was fine, peering through the cracks and leaving his arm dangling only so long in the water for fear of getting bit by something. Turtles were impossible to catch, peering up just long enough to see where you were, then disappearing. He'd never caught a turtle in the water, and there were snappers too, so he knew not to think it simple or without danger. In time the sun made him relax. He floated and daydreamed, just watching the bottom like a pilot flying his plane over a forest, not thinking he was lost down there, shooting flares up, drowning, living in his last bubble and only able to reach as high as a hand, his own hand dangling, almost but not quite, and that hand was what was most deeply feared as the thing to pull him in like a monster under the bed, the night light a flare of a kind, declaring in its way the place off limits to intruders and safe for sleep.

And Dudot tried to sleep but couldn't, there was something in the weed tops like former acreage in the rain forest canopy, long gone, something familiar in the skimming over like pages of the old encyclopedia one knows is missing certain entries, incomplete. There was something missing from the picture, but Dudot didn't want to go there, didn't want to find it. But there it was, a tiny hand, and not his, but part of him, connected to a body, a small girl in the weeds with a doll's face calling *Dudot, Dudot* as if to offer him the precious air to breathe, but killing him for being out of reach, for now he was trying to pull her out, grab the arm, get her on board with him, but it was to no avail, It was more a baby doll, a toy that had been there for some time, not his precious wonder lost to him, and seeing her, he breathed a sigh that took in her calls, the air he needed, and felt overwhelmed with the warmth she'd given him.

And though he sailed with just a memory of her, he wouldn't give up the raft and go sinking in the weeds where he'd lived for more than a year in her absence. He maintained the image, the floating passage and distance from it all, not just in feet, but in atmosphere, the one foreign and deadly, the other lonely but the only way he could live, keep the memory. She was lost to him, but he couldn't do much more and not be lost to himself, and so he rested on the bubbles and loved her so they would not break, the time they shared and the hope in the exchange becoming the raft, his saving grace he was able to pull himself from the shallows on, not riding them, but having to choose, distinguish one feeling from the other, love from death, to die to everything or cherish the memory of a daughter lost to him.

Dudot kept his head down, peering into the water, drifting away from that center but to what place he was going in the expanse he wasn't sure, nor sure how vast it was, as perhaps the mind cannot be helped, but to be followed like the universe around as space and consciousness are both curved, that given the right ship to go the speed of light, the whole universe can be circumnavigated in a lifetime, fifty-four years or close to that, though millions of years would have passed at the point of origin; and so, in the mind, with the right way of thinking, all the ground can be covered in a lifetime but leave the origins so far behind that a return to it will place it in a totally different light, all things changed, and in no way being the same oneself.

But Dudot was only on this voyage, and it was weeds, not stars he was passing through, and he wasn't as much looking to trace the outer boundaries to define the end of possibilities of his mind but resolve as best he could, part science, part emotion, the underlayment of his life, why he didn't care anymore and why he was a coward, even to face the question. But he'd come to that point of having to face it, like being called out to a funeral that changes plans and is gotten through with a stance that eventually starts to accept the message of the tolling bell, and sets back into life a bit more reflective, a touch more removed. But Dudot's was a place of near total removal. Somewhere in a swamp, was it? Out in a raft looking in the shallow waters at a dead baby? Was that his reality? He swung the craft around at a mere thought and headed back to her, for it was time to reach in. He feared even to touch her, hold out his hand in the cool water and have to see the changes the world makes to those who are gone, how it rots them, robs us of the view we had of their smiles, makes us realize they are leaves on a stick where even the bark wears off in time, and he feared she covered some kind of drain that would just take much more than he could stand out of him.

Yes, a drain, that his keeping her, leaving her there, was the *Ol' Manner* by which he had progressed to this point, of being one or two feet of water above the bottom, thanks to the hundreds of days that had passed and all the rains and snow that had fallen, like music, distraction, a kind of background noise that keeps the mind from feeding totally on itself, focusing not just on the issue but having something soothing like a wind blowing a bag down the street and a dog playing in the yard; and all that was the water on which he floated, sunset as chest protector, backdrop to the daily shootout with oneself and unacknowledged reason for survival, that one tends to hang on somehow by following the tempo, morning, noon, night, rain, snow, wind, that all of it somehow keeps us inclined to wait it out by degrees, diminishing but only in the long haul, that really we are more resilient than we would think, and somehow keep going. But Dudot had lost his sense of how to do that, knew that the shallows were not enough, like living in an algae-filled birdbath, and there being a kind, of scarecrow that keeps it from being what it's supposed to be, floating around and keeping birds out, and the birds are there to pull him out, save him, but he was having none of that and seemed to prefer the potential of being nipped away from beneath by whatever ailed him.

And so he moved back to her tiny shape in the water and looked at her, really just as lovely, more like a doll in this view, and having been at the bottom so long, and not having moved much in his own circles, in the doldrums he was determined to just have it out with all of it, drain or not. It could be no worse in the end to walk on the bottom than float just over it. So he reached down and took her hand, and he drew her up to him, feeling no resistance, even feeling as if the moment he pulled that she rushed up as if driven, and that's when he felt the current. It almost roared up as he held her, pushing out from the bottom not as a drain but a fountain, a spring that had been blocked, and as the water rose and rose, taking him up to a shoreline, he recognized in himself, or if it were the birdbath it would have been like a blow from below to send him out onto the lawn, and he stepped out of the raft onto his old haunts, now a new place, on dry land, the bottom far behind him, not even visible from the surface but well known and utterly mapped as he scanned just having been there. Such a landscape would last. It would be a ridge in the distance, somehow "a sign and great sufficiency" like the strawberries and milk taken by the knight on his quest to beat death in a game of chess, marking the basin he knew surrounded his life, reminding him that he could not go down again without being the blockage, where the rain and snow this time would melt, and he'd be in way over his head, no way out, and by becoming the blockage, be long forgotten, and the basin of his life be a valley of death for everyone to avoid.

That was how he'd felt about himself, and he didn't like himself any more than anyone else, but he didn't like them any more than they liked him. That hadn't changed, and he knew this was only one day, but at least it was a minor miracle that he was able to hold his daughter again, even in memory, and have her be a light to him as she was in life, and have that lift him and be a saving grace as it were; and he resolved to make her be a reason for going forward, to do things for her so that she would not be forgotten, to not leave her at the bottom but hold her high as something to hold in order to keep from going down. That would be her place, not a resting place but a *raison d'etre* and eternal life for him as long as he lived.

Now, after a long and desperate lull, a kind of wallowing he could not have imagined before, Dudot was ready, determined to move forward, resolute but not loving, full of fire but not dignified, if he was going to go head to head with the ram of fate he needed strong horns to do battle, and they were growing quickly, Dudot tucked his little doll under his arm, the plug that had set him free on dry land of his life again, and set out to face whatever it was that was his enemy. He knew it wasn't himself as adversary, not that his own mind didn't drag him down. It was more like a bad influence than an enemy, something to avoid at all costs for the damage it could do, but not an enemy, a great difficulty, a trap, but not an enemy, not a friend, but easily held at bay, even something he could coax to stand at his side in the end when he had made up his mind, made up with himself. No, the enemy was *out there*. Maybe it was the system. Maybe not. But he could only do damage by summoning up all his will to move again, and stop trying to figure everything out or battle windmills until battered by them. All those weeks and months passed, and all he could say was that the bottom had a life spring to put one back where one started, amazed at the waste of time. The bottom was a drug that comes with trying to kill pain. Dudot decided to live with it and let it live, even feed it, give it everything it damn well pleased and watch what would happen then, for he would not be overwhelmed. He could grow along side it, playing chicken for which would blink first, which would burst. It was only a kind of pain, something easily altered by the gritting of teeth and damn anything that got in the way. Dudot had a few things to do. The most important was to try to have another child, and that meant making up with his wife which wasn't going to be easy. But the way he felt, it was going to be the easiest part of the whole process, Ol' Man River having been taken out of the picture.

A Drop in the Ocean

Dudot's hatred of himself when he was dipping deeper into evaporation of spirit into the morass of weeds under his Nile barge was what kept him from believing his wife's pain any different than his own. He would not let himself think that he was hurting her even more, and all he could muster was she hated him too. That it was all his fault he would allow after the fact, but up to the point he left, he blamed her for driving him away. Whatever else he had done, Dudot had turned all the ordinary, impossible-to-alter circumstances that led up to his daughter's death into things he might have seen and changed. It even occurred to him that living in a city near an airport was a bad choice, that the air she was breathing while pregnant had been a major factor, and there was again the hatred of himself for the kind of job he had, the income level, the choices he'd made along the happy-go-lucky, ignorant acceptance of the staus quo that had gotten him stuck at his level, and he never felt so stuck as when he wanted to undo it all at once, when he recognized his whole story constructed all around him such that he wanted only to deconstruct it all in an instant, to come up with the funds to right the entire judgment seat against him, pay off the powers that be, buddy up to the lords and hosts who play the sucker world for all it's worth and laugh amongst themselves at the club.

Dudot always felt deserving of belonging to another club of respect and admiration, but he'd come to realize suddenly, brutally, that it did not exist. He saw that he'd been played for a sucker too, given drugs by friends and kept down, and now he realized it all at once, and he was resolute to walk alone and see it through, that whatever was possible in clean living and rising to the top, he had gone his own way, taken the path of his chums, of least resistance, and by the birth of his daughter, he really didn't have much of a life to offer a child but believed as he always did that things would all work out, which is just what his friends all told him when his daughter was dying, that she would be alright, that everything would work out. After she died, he resolved to let go of them and everything else, become entirely insular and self-sufficient and be driven to do all he could. But that was just the first day, and it faded on awakening the next morning into despair and blaming all who said they understood, who didn't know how it felt. How could they? He hated them all for their superficial hopefulness and the sympathy cards bought at the grocery store with cheap rhymes of peace and sympathy that had the same effect a shower has on cooling the pyroclastic flow blasting out the sides of an exploding volcano.

    His wife tried to give him comfort but her hands were cold on him. She needed help more than he did, but now he was determined not to fuel the feminine flower with honey. Through courtship and marriage, the demands had always been about love, but now he just wanted to be left alone. He tolerated her for a few months and let her go back home to be with family because he knew that was what was best for her, and then his solitude began, and it was a good thing she was gone, and he didn't care at all about her not being there or what she was doing because she was like all the rest, hating him, judging his personality excesses as needing to be changed, and he was tired of making sure his nails were clipped, be certain not to ruffle feathers or make anyone uncomfortable. But now the gloves were off, and he couldn't wait to see the kind of wolf man he'd turn out to be full moon or not. Every day was a screaming scratchy hell, months going by without so much as a call from her, he figured she would file for divorce, not wonder if he were getting better. He watched TV and drank quite a bit of scotch, so it was a good thing she never called. He got lots of headaches, bad ones, and was mad when he had to decide not to drink because headaches always had the upper hand in his decisions, so when they were too much for him, drinking was out. He started feeling a little bit wobbly in the daytime too. He had anxiety attacks and wondered about his heartbeat. He was palpitating quite often, and uncertain when he was walking if he could make it the rest of the way, and so he'd often turn around, and feel better that he had, and so he figured much of it was psychological, but he didn't care to do what he needed, to undo his new bad habits that he could clearly see contributing to the problem, and in this manner the water level dropped him down to the bottom, and that's when he finally cried for his lost little girl, so tears were the first new drops of what needed to come back as an ocean to carry him first to the surface and then back to shore.

But his life had been full, all the way to the brim and overflowing with his little girl on his shoulders to give her a rest, to breathe for her, which was no effort for all the energy she gave him just by being there; and he should have known he was unprepared for what was to come if he lost her when she disappeared one night in a store while they were shopping. She was only playing hide and seek under a clothes rack, but the heart went out of him. He screamed to the manager to lock the store and not let anyone out. Just as quickly, his wife found her, and he always felt he'd made a terrible presence, of someone who might have to appear on camera and plead to a sick stranger for her safe return, going up and down the aisles as he had, shouting for her, caring nothing for what other customers thought of his panic, and it was only a foreshadowing of his walking between everyone later, caring nothing for what they thought, ignoring the entire world. But the fact was he shouldn't care for what they thought, but being independent and confident is one kind of not caring anything about anyone, and hating everyone and thinking they are the enemy is another. He was only too caught up in what they thought, too easily influenced, unsure and unable to let anything wash off him once it was said, starting to stand against the notion that other's opinions matter because he made them count so much, taking so much to heart of little things they said to him that even saying he was sensitive stung him profoundly, and he had half-written off the world before he lost her and the last half was a breeze when to stand alone was suddenly all he ever wanted, the real goal of life realized only then. It was respect he wanted, something from above though, respect from chaos that this was his share, all he was going to have to endure, but it was already too much of a piece of the pie, and he knew there was no such promise and that the premise for life was that there was more coming.

But at last he didn't care, and now he hated them all for being petty on the smallest level of connections. When in all good nature people tend only to try to say humorous things, he took it as hiding criticism, and this perturbed his wife to no end that he wouldn't live with what he asked for, dishing it out to their faces and behind their backs but unable to stop the itching of their little bites later only returned in kind, trying to be funny and direct like him.

And when they found her in the store under the coat rack, a gulp went up like a prayer of thanks and he was almost shaking as whatever intensity left him revealed how much he'd climbed by how wobbly it made him. He tried to summon words to tell her not to do it again, but tears ran freely and he just held her, and she wanted to play more, so they just took her hand and left the store, thanking everyone for their help.

But for the first time he saw this child as a threat, realized that while she'd never have existed but for him, now she was in the curious place of being a new artery in his heart, one he wouldn't control by eating right or getting exercise. She was totally out of his control, utterly meant at some point to be free and on her own, but for now she was such a part of him that he had no idea he could react so strongly, and over the next few days as they told the story he saw how common it was, how everyone's children got loose in stores, how they all knew the feeling and terror of losing sight of a child, but none so much as he had felt it, and even his wife added how he'd become almost a madman, demanding of the store manager to lock down the store and get the police into the parking lots, but all Dudot could say was the world had changed, that every day children were disappearing, and the situations must start off somewhat benign, and that unless people are willing to turn it up the necessary notches from the get-go then much can be lost all due to an unwillingness to assume that it's a worst-case scenario. Better to proceed to red alert, a controlled panic than wait.

A Drop in the Ocean

But they concluded panic didn't help in any event, and the clock is the clock, and they were looking for her within ten seconds of the last moment she was seen, children can be gone that quickly, so Dudot again was left feeling there was something wrong with him, but part of him agreed, how could he get that worked up? He was astonished at this other self he'd never seen, at whatever had gripped him. It was like something wanted to change fate, trying to reach out, grasp the neck of the universe and turn the clock back, find her, find her now! Don't let this be happening, super charging as in a centrifugal force machine to test astronauts, the forces doubling and trapping in his gut. He would almost summon part of it back at will for several days the memory was so clear, and he knew he'd have to deal with it only he wasn't sure how he would cope or rate himself in advance of a bigger scare given the experience in the store. How could he hope to handle it before it came on and watching the pyroclastic flow rush down the volcano, how could he hope to sail it? For him it was like a hurricane that isn't there to make better sailors, but the kind of test one tries to avoid as it is not there to evaluate but to overwhelm in silent, perfect power. But what he didn't think was that it was only a drill, and that a great wind could flood the village and empty the life out of him, kill all he ever loved and leave him on a heap to try to make sense out of it all. He believed through everything until her death that he would never wander into the path of any force so terrific that it would undo his sense of control. He had somehow trained himself not to look into the future far enough to realize the ultimate fate or reality and so try to make sense of it. He believed he was in a safe zone in a random universe, a slot in a roulette wheel where the ball with his number on it had never landed and never would. He knew like everyone else that the world was spinning and the ball was dropping into various slots all the time, but in his mind he was above the fray, rubbing shoulders with those who run the table with repelling magnets, not one of the pawns ducking disaster in an uncertain house of cards stacked against them in their silent terror strung to their fate, doomed to pull the pillars of their lives down on themselves.

Mary and the Fish

Somehow this little girl came to call him Dudot and stuck the name on him herself when she was still months away from her first birthday, giving the sound a special inflection when she spoke, filling it with personality. Her mother countered "Daddy," and she replied "Dudot," emphasizing the difference, saying "Mama" with nothing added, and "Dudot" every time she wanted her father. It was never encouraged, nor was it even much noticed for a time until one day he debated her saying "Dada" and getting "Dudot" every time, and so the name stuck, and in a way he rather like it and thought of her "waiting for Dudot" and singing *Camptown Races* with "Dudot" instead of Doo-dah. He even made it sound like a Japanese word, and he acted like a Sumo wrestler by that name, making everyone laugh, but it was only a small part of the day and made hardly an impression until she was sick and he became helpless again only worse than when she was lost in the store, which quadrupled when he started to think she might not get better.

When her terminal condition was confirmed he felt like he was the victim, singled out for things he'd done, and would have tried anything, even a rain dance, if he thought it would work, But he chose the paradoxical path of acting as if he believed in an essential live presence in the cosmos doing these things deliberately but one that was not watching his life or listening to him and so something that would not change a thing, a God perhaps, but one he wasn't going to pray to, not in peaceful requests anyway. He was making demands, silent one, from the inside that he knew a God would hear if He were listening. "Put it back the way it was! Don't do this to me! How can you do this to her?" were more the spirit of his anger, and he thought it was prayer, that he was doing everything in the proper format, even supplicating himself. He would tell himself that he would say a prayer, think of saying it, as if that were saying it, but wouldn't actually say the words themselves, speak to God directly because he did not even want to link up and have whatever he had done to deserve all this thrown up in his face. He didn't do this often, but rather just waved the concept off in a denial of the necessity as he headed into the last days of her life when then he was mad it was all set in stone and too late to change.

And so he watched her die, slowly change from pain, crying he couldn't stand to hear, to numbness where he wanted to hear her cry, saying "Dudot" was there with her, and she would say "Dudot" so plaintively, acknowledging him but without the strength to throw herself into it, and he knew he was losing her, but didn't know where she was going.

She breathed her last in his arms, and a novice chaplain made uncomfortable efforts to help them deal with it, the nurses encouraging his wife to keep holding her dead child, and Dudot found himself stripped of all convention and began to try to make the chaplain feel more comfortable, calm him down, once in awhile looking at his little girl and crying again, wishing that God had sent a better, more prepared emissary to help him understand, not this kid just out of whatever school probably practicing on bereaved dummies in the classroom before getting this baptism by fire, so Dudot decided it had been long enough and told them to take her away from his wife, but he never actually helped her, never grabbed her to show that love. He was incensed with anger, helpless, and he didn't touch her, not until he reached beneath the raft and pulled the plug and let all he ever held back pour under to restore him.

The sad event also put a huge crimp in his "Nothing-ever-happens-to-me-things-are-going-according-to-plan" attitude, but instead of realizing his "Things-happen-to-others" philosophy was flawed and thinking it needed improvement, he began to look at others as all having his old view and that they needed him to remind them that shit happens, and when it didn't to them he was angry that life still seemed to grant them the kind of immunity he used to have, that it perpetuated the myth for them but not him, and he felt tossed out of the club it was ridiculous to belong to given the end result of life in the long run, but he had nowhere to run from the encroaching realities and breakups of his system than back to the past, into the old ignorance that he wished more than anything to have back again. He even looked at old pictures of himself and wished it were the present again. That he didn't know what was coming then made those the days, for now what he knew he knew for good, even that there was no going back, just the longing for it.

Only a few days after they buried her, Dudot was sitting in his most comfortable lounge chair, and though he had cried earlier in the company and solace of friends and family, now he was alone, and for the first time, he let it all out, or thought that was what he was doing. He'd heard that the meaning of a death doesn't really hit one until later, and he almost had to stick a finger down the throat of his spirit to get it started, but he wasn't prepared for what followed. It was such an outpouring, like something chugging out of a volcano into the sky, that he was able somehow to separate himself from himself while it was happening. He was totally immersed in the emotion, but at the same time, there was a mental echo spawned from it that allowed him to track and examine it, and so he looked at himself from within while he was agonizing, and what he saw was that there was no relief to the crying, no end in sight, that this was an abyss before him capable of endlessly receiving his discharge of emotion, that it was cycling back to the beginning, playing a loop, and as he realized this, the terror of it all went up a notch because the abyss became the great terror before which we all fear standing before, a hole he understood was engulfing him the more he unleashed his frustration, and so there came a moment when he sent a message to himself, composed by the calmer echo watching it all unfold, that it would do him more harm than good to continue and that he would need at some point to just shut it off.

And now the plug was really pulled from his basin. He was no longer laying in a raft able to reach down and run his fingers through the weeds. Yes, he had spun downward a bit at a time over many months, but now he was in a swirl, and from there, from that terrible outpouring of grief, he finally chose to walk to the river to see the Ol' Man and had an accidental encounter with a neighbor who unknowingly deterred him, and it didn't seem long then to the imaginary ride on the raft when he pulled his dead daughter out of the hole where upon the source of the leak became the source itself of restoration, to embrace what he lost and fought against looking at, and once he stepped out of that river it wasn't long before the days stuck together as one blank sheet onto another, and he went through the motions of his life more like a ghost haunting a house, a Fleshy Ghost, as he called it, believing after a time that that's all we were anyway, just Fleshy Ghosts, here for a time, taking everything in, then all at once dispersing, where all we've gathered both physically and mentally is all at once dispersed and scattered into the great chaos, resuming its meaningless course.

Through it all, he would get up in the morning and take a shower. One day he got water in his ear that resulted in an ear infection, which took a week to heal, but he never went to a doctor. He just gritted his teeth and took it, tossing and turning with the sudden pain that shot through his head for a night or two, then deciding that something needed to go in his ears. So he took two squares of toilet paper, folding them and ripping off a piece, which he continued to fold, then press into his ear, doing the same with the other square for the other ear, a process he refined over many days until he knew exactly how to fold it, just how to press it into his ears. It took him a while to get into the habit. Some mornings he was already in the shower before he remembered he needed to protect his ears, and so he would step out, dry his hands and go through the process, and after a few weeks, he generally remembered every day to do it. And then after a month of that, of never forgetting, he recognized that he could do it all with one square, fold it and break it in half, then press each half into his ear after folding the tip like a paper airplane, then press each half into his ear. All the while, each day, when the shower was almost finished, after he had washed his hair, he'd remove the wads from his ears and combine them to shoot for the garbage can next to the toilet. He was absurdly successful at this game. It wasn't so far away that he should miss, but he was very surprised, given the law of averages, that he was able to keep a perfect record going, even when he forgot to push the garbage can against the wall to give him a backboard, even when he left his pants on the toilet and partially obscured the opening of the waste basket, which is more what it was, a small receptacle that became a game in which he took no interest until it was time to shoot.

He would wet them down when he took them from his ears, and then squeeze the water out before he shot. After a few months of this, he realized the halves were once in a while splitting after he threw them, so he began to develop a process of unravelling them, making an "X," which he then folded in a manner where it would be very unlikely that they would come apart when he made his shot.

At about the sixth month of wearing toilet-paper ear plugs, and a few months of making an "X," one morning he saw an eagle in the shape, a bird in the "X," as one part that came out of his ear had a beak and tail, and the other seemed to be perfect wings behind it. He stared at this for a moment before he made his shot, and he considered that perhaps there was some sense in which the power of the bird itself, a spiritual source that connected with its ability to fly, was being lent to this ball of paper and enabling his perfect record of hitting the waste paper basket every day when he took his shower. After that, each morning when he folded the paper to throw it, he looked to see what kind of eagle he had, and every day for some reason, there was a bird, or it didn't take much twisting or pulling on one side or another to fashion a pretty nice likeness, and he became very adept at making a bird every morning, which he would then fold in on itself, tucking one wing under the other from around the back before bending the head down and folding the tail over, after which he would wet it all down under the shower nozzle, squeeze out the excess, open the curtain, locate the basket, make a practice motion or two, then relax and shoot, and wonder how many that was in a row, for he had lost count from the beginning and only felt that it was hundreds of days into a depth of fog for whenever it had started, this mindless shooting and a perfect record. He couldn't recall when he had had the ear infection that got it started, and he didn't connect it before that to his disconnection from life due to the loss of his little girl.

But in the same way that he had perfected a process of making plugs for his ears into eagles that flew for him into the garbage can, he had also in the shower completed an essay of imagination on the meaning of life over the same hundreds of days, which simplified was that each person is a fleshy ghost unto itself that was here by itself reacting to stimulation and having experiences, which contributed to the world within the body, meaning that the ghost within the flesh was able to acquire a specific sense and understanding of the outside world even though it was unable to effect any changes in the world. He may have thought in one shower that we are temporary vestiges of our greater selves, aiming toward that, but being limited here, being a part of something bigger but being apart from it at the same time, realizing that the answers are not present even if the search is necessary, that one can destroy himself looking for a natural fact, for example why nobody makes it out of here alive, or why on a very windy day you can remember what it was like to be young, flying paper airplanes that get caught in the tree and only later wonder why the trees have the faces of the dead, peering out of places where the branches are cut off.

The thoughts went through his mind like that, and he let them go. He did nothing to preserve any sense of where his mind had been nor collect any data to review at any point so as to consider in any way that his thinking might be construed as a building process. So the only process was in the manufacture of spit wads into birds. And time was the only factor working on him, but he was not interacting in time so as to stay one step ahead of it as most people running from reality. He was letting reality overtake him. He was letting it wash over him, so if there were a process of any kind that one could say his thinking was changing, he was unaware of it. If it could be said that grief has stages, the spit wad factor would in his case require consideration, that it was the only manifestation of his internalization of his spirit and withdrawal from life, and it was invisible to everyone when he shut the curtains of the shower, just as the walk to the river and the ride on the raft. It was all to do with water somehow though, but there was no trained physician who was ever going to know any of this, or be able to make any sense of it, so Dudot's healing process was entirely metaphysical, without shape or form except that it was personal and made sense to him, which was enough even when it made no sense for he wasn't looking for anything, and if anything was looking to shut everything out so that there would be nothing that could get it, which is how he wanted it because he intended to affirm totally the truth of being a fleshy ghost, live reality as reality actually is, that when a hundred years go by, the world is generally bereft of all living spirits that inhabited the place when the hundred years started, and so the place exists entirely and is entirely perceived by a temporary society of entities that leave the place as they found it, inflicting damage on one another and creating others to be unreceptive to whatever actual truth is out there so that in the end there is only a perpetuation of the imperfection, not an acquisition of the perfection, the little that can be said to make life worthwhile.

And then in the middle of one shower, he pulled the earplugs out in the same way he had refined over months, a process that developed naturally, that he had settled on comfortably. But on this day he unrolled one plug, and it didn't bear the usual resemblance to a bird or the easily molded, amorphous shape. No, on this day, it unravelled into the shape of the kneeling virgin. Yes, it was Mary herself somehow, like someone had fashioned her out of clay into a tiny ceramic. Dudot was amazed how like her it was. He pulled out the other plug, unravelled it, and it looked like a fish, and when he made the usual "X," it made a cross, and he stopped.

He had always dismissed stories of miracles, and this experience was nothing like a statue of the virgin suddenly crying, but he was moved enough to let it dry in his bedroom on the shelf, where it lost any defintion of the religious symbolism and once again took on the look of twists of toilet paper. It made him think how the mind looks for things, makes them pop out, when it wants to connect dots and make shapes out of things that aren't there. It was at this point that he began to care less about his process of moving the basket to the wall, of hanging his clothes in precisely the same point, or of any of the steps that he had created by rote that seemed to control him now that he had been stopped to give it thought. It wasn't like he'd planned any of it, but it was certain that his going through the same motions had grown nearly neurotic, and he remembered Xeno's paradox that taking half steps to a goal and never getting there is the appearance, but the reality is that the line is easily crossed. In the same way, he remembered the joy of his daughter, the one good thing that had happened to him, which he had lost, and realized she was just the icing on the cake, that there were so many good things, and all at once he realized another paradox, which was that life seems to be all about the one, the single individual fleshy ghost coming, taking it all in, and going along until it dies, where everything is lost, and that is all. But it turns out to be more. There's a need to interconnect, a necessary exchange between souls.

He had been thinking of saving all the birds until he had a flock. He thought when he had enough that he would arrange them on a black table in various ways. He thought it would be nice to arrange them like birds in flight. But one day he saw pictures of bodies from the death camps in Germany, and the whole idea of saving the earplugs seemed suddenly ridiculous, as did the notion that he ever could have seriously considered a shape similar to Mary. He recognized that he'd become overly wrapped up in himself without the proper distance or detachment that comes from having a life. He remembered the line from Paul Valery, *Un homme seul est toujours en mauvaise compagnie.* "A man alone is always in bad company."

He worried he had taken it all too far and become weird. He recalled when he was a boy how he'd gotten overly wrapped up in the process of puberty, waiting for the first hair to appear under his arms, a time in his life he'd always seen as an anomaly. He thought it was probably time to cease the kind of mental gymnastics he'd gotten used to performing in his world where time had ceased to be a factor. Each day was a repetition of the same emptiness, but he had managed somehow to create a kind of mythology in it. Perhaps he had done it all to fight the terrible boredom, or maybe it was part of the healing process, and maybe it had served its purpose after all because he was embarrassed about all of it and wondered where the time had gone since his daughter had died and why he had not opened up to his wife and been there for her.

After that when he took a shower, he did not wet the ear plugs down, which was an essential step in his routine. He purposely varied because he no longer cared about the routine. But instead of taking a shot at the trash can, he got out of the shower and dropped the plugs in the toilet and flushed them. From the first shot until this last one was one long beat of a metronome. It spanned and contained a still-flowing awakening made up of moments divided and subdivided. But removing first all the repetition, and factoring out the splash of analogous atoms when those in his life hit the fan, resulting in an unexpected spiritual formation.

He felt he'd finally merged with the river, but he'd always been a part of it, though whatever had tossed and spit him through a spillway into a quiet pool, there were no rapids in its mysterious, meandering ways. The river was ever quiet, and he hadn't stirred up even the least part of it. But when he jumped into himself, the Ol' Man took his keys, disconnected all links to external systems and let him run until he'd etched his own banks through sands as far as the eye could see. When he crawled up on shore, the keys were waiting on a fertile plain. Tossing them in the river sent the heavens reeling in reflection, distinguishing them from the real thing hanging in perfect stillness and clarity despite constant efforts to distort it.

When he had these thoughts, he smiled, got dressed and drove to his mother-in-law's without so much as a warning, walked up the steps and made it clear he wanted to bring his wife home, his attic clear of all the webs that cluttered his mind of confused thoughts of who was angry or what anyone thought of what he was doing, all of it getting in the way of his making a decision. So here he was with a clear mind just doing it, saying what he wanted and seeing it get done, his wife's mother was glad to see her go. Before they left, they had lunch. Nobody said a word about the year that had passed.

They drove back home, but he stopped at the Ol' Man and walked with his wife, stopping about where he might have jumped in, and he kissed her, glad to be part of the temporary collective again. His wife said she was happy he was back. He replied he'd taken the first step which had brought him half way home.

But he knew he was all the way home one day when he realized the crosses were "X's," days gone by, two at time, and he had let so many go down the drain that he might have wept over it, except that tears had greased those days to fly in bundles. They were not eagles but delusions in pulp, made to be flushed away, only they just may have saved him from the beckoning river, the Ol' Man calling all Nouveaux Dudots, "new fathers" of lost children, or turning them into old men before their time if they don't go with the flow.

John Doot was well aware of the terrible abyss before which nobody can stand, of the danger it will flood at any time and disconnect one from life without softening the blow. He was just a child of the world with only so many days to live, and he wanted to use them, not waste them. But he had discovered in a great drought of spirit something that put everything back on course. He'd gone from feeling old and hating his life, but he was past being young. John had seen bottom and was glad to have kept his head above water, and all that water, the being on the raft, was the amniotic fluid of his birth out of old ways, was his baptism into a new life of acceptance for the drill in the tooth, the end to teeth, and to false teeth when the time came. He thought he had returned to the normal rhythm of his life until one day when he threw his earplugs from the shower, it struck him that he was always missing the garbage can. During the time he was alone, he never missed a shot.

He thought he was just too intense and overly focused on useless things, that his life's rhythm had stopped. But he realized he'd gotten caught in the long silent space between beats of its metronome, lost in the intricate, delicate machinery of his life, and that these were not junk moments, but an essence from which all is derived. Diluted into years, it would be a river by the time he was an old man, transform him from a son to a father, from a fish to some kind of amphibious creature comfortable under the sun on a rock or beneath one on the dark river bottom. So, with inklings of eternity through connections to the Ol' Man himself, he willingly threw himself back into the transitory thick of things.

www.ingramcontent.com/pod-product-compliance
Ingram Content Group UK Ltd.
Pitfield, Milton Keynes, MK11 3LW, UK
UKHW041416180426
11947UKWH00007B/168